KATRINA McKEE

THE SEARCH

BOOK TWO

The Search © 2026 Katrina McKee

All Rights Reserved. No part of this book may be reproduced in any form or by any electronic or mechanical means including information storage and retrieval systems, without permission in writing from the author. The only exception is by a reviewer, who may quote short excerpts in a review.

No generative artificial intelligence (AI) was used in the creation of this book. The author expressly prohibits the use of this publication as training data for AI technologies or large language models (LLMs) for generative purposes. The author reserves all rights to license uses of this work for generative AI training and the development of LLMs.

This book is a work of fiction. Names, characters, places, and incidents either are products of the author's imagination or are used fictitiously. Any resemblance to actual persons, living or dead, events, or locales is entirely coincidental.

Published by Toshiro Books

Cover by Kristine Slater

Internal design by Coven Press

www.covenpress.com.au

First printing: March 2026

Paperback ISBN 978-1-7641340-2-6

eBook ISBN 978-1-7641340-3-3

 A catalogue record for this work is available from the National Library of Australia

Distributed by Lightning Source Global

ALSO BY KATRINA MCKEE

Portal

For Kristine. Thank you for supporting me all these years, little sister.

PROLOGUE

'FATHER, I really must ask you to reconsider this endeavour,' Kingston said as he followed his father into the tunnels under the Adelaide treasury building. 'With all that has happened, it feels unwise.'

'Your problem, Edward, is that you worry too much,' George Strickland Kingston said with a tight smile of amusement. 'I will only be gone a little while.'

'Months,' Kingston said. 'Possibly even a year.'

'Which is no time for us.'

'I still fail to see how this trip to India is necessary.'

'You know my health has been troubling me.'

'All the more reason to stay.'

George stopped, turning to his son and resting a hand on his shoulder. 'I know you worry about me, but I assure you everything will be fine.'

'I have a bad feeling,' Kingston said.

'You often do. Come now.' George patted him on the shoulder and turned towards a doorway at the end of the hall. 'Redmond will be waiting for us.'

'Yes, Redmond,' Kingston said, following his father down the hall. 'Strange how his own health has been failing, just as yours has.'

George didn't answer. Instead, he pulled a brass key out of his pocket and unlocked the door. They stepped into the small room, George turning straight to the door on the left and opening it. Knowing his father was ignoring him, Kingston sighed, straightening his shirt and following him into the Melbourne homestead.

'So nice of you two to finally join me,' Redmond Barry joked as he pushed himself up from his seat at the dining room table. There was a pot of tea and scones in front of him. They probably came from his beloved. Louisa Barrow always baked them something when they visited, even though Redmond had never brought her downstairs into the homestead. He cited the bad air.

It was a cool, late winter morning in 1880, and Kingston could hear the footsteps above him in the State Library of Victoria. The library was one of Redmond's greatest accomplishments, as were the journals that lined the wall of one of the small rooms of the homestead. Redmond rarely stayed there anymore, spending more time above ground with his family. Kingston had to respect that.

'We apologise for our delay,' George said. 'Edward here has been trying to dissuade me from my future voyage.'

'Still?' Redmond looked at Kingston and chuckled. 'You've not long arrived, and already you're trying to influence your father?'

'It does not seem fair that I should arrive, and he would leave so soon,' Kingston agreed.

'We will have all the time together when I return,' George said.

Another wave of unease washed over Kingston. He wasn't sure that his father *would* return. The man looked tired. He seemed to have aged faster than he should have and his health was declining when it shouldn't be. It worried Kingston greatly.

'Don't look so forlorn,' George said, smiling at him. 'We will only be separated for a year. In the meantime, you can get to know

Adelaide better. Perhaps even travel to Ireland and see where it all began.'

'You mean where the first portal opened to this world?' Kingston said.

'Indeed,' George said. 'Although we swiftly built a new one.'

'Does that new one still function?'

'No, no,' George said. 'We moved it here. It's across the hall, in fact.'

Kingston looked back towards the doorway they had come through and across the space to the second door. He frowned. 'I still do not properly understand how the portals work.'

'Neither do we, lad,' Redmond said. 'But it's not our job to understand. It is simply our job to protect.'

Kingston nodded, turning back towards him. 'Are all the keys hidden?'

'Every one,' Redmond confirmed. 'Across here, Adelaide and other places.'

That caught Kingston's attention. 'They're not all in Melbourne and Adelaide?'

'I may have hidden a few elsewhere,' Redmond said with a cheeky smile. 'There are only so many buildings to hide them in, after all.'

'And where do they all lead?'

'All in good time,' George said.

'But that's what concerns me, Father,' Kingston said. 'You're training me to replace you once you retire, but you're leaving before the training is complete. We've barely begun.'

'There's no rush.'

'And what of you, Redmond?' Kingston asked, taking in the other gentleman. He couldn't help but notice that his health was also deteriorating. His skin was pale, and he had developed a cough. How he had aged since Kingston had come through the portal from their home planet. 'Have you even begun training your replacement?'

'They know of the journals and that the code is hidden within them,' Redmond assured him. 'I fully intend to begin teaching them how to decode the journals over the next few months.'

'Why not begin forthwith?'

'As your father said – all in good time.' Redmond chuckled, looking at George. 'Has he always been such a worrier?'

'Takes after his mother,' George said.

Kingston couldn't help but feel that time was against them. It worried Kingston that foul play was involved in the declining health of his elders. There were those out there who would try to gain access to the portals, which was why the Keeper and Protector were necessary.

'You forget, my lad, that we live longer than most,' George said. 'There is at least another century in both of us. Perhaps more.'

'But your health is failing,' Kingston reminded him. 'That is why you are taking this trip.'

'I'm overworked,' George said. 'The same can be said for Redmond here.'

'Perhaps I should go with you,' Redmond joked. 'But I dare not leave Louisa or my work.'

'Yes, you're trying that bushranger,' George said.

'I imagine it will be a short trial,' Redmond said. 'The evidence is against him. He will hang. The trial is merely a formality.'

'They should have executed him on the spot,' George said.

'There are those who support him,' Redmond said. 'But I will see that he has a fair trial.'

'Not exactly fair if you already view him as guilty,' Kingston pointed out.

'His peers will judge him,' Redmond said. He looked at Kingston. 'Interesting that his name is also Edward.'

'What are you implying?'

'Nothing, lad.'

Kingston didn't believe him, especially with the way Redmond's eyes sparkled. He was thinking something negative of Kingston. Kingston didn't know him well enough to know what he was implying. Instead, he looked at his father to see his reaction and saw only a serious expression.

'You should introduce Edward here to your grandson,' George said. 'The one who will replace you.'

'I shall,' Redmond said. 'I intend to bring him here next week. We should make a time of it.'

'Does he know?' Kingston asked.

'About the portals, yes,' Redmond said.

'About us?' Kingston clarified. 'That we are not of this world.'

Instantly, a serious expression settled on Redmond's face. 'We need not worry him about such things.'

'So he doesn't know.'

'The fewer people that know, the better,' George said. 'That is why my children do not know.'

'And why you've never introduced me to them,' Kingston said, remembering his conversation with his father when he'd first come to this planet. It had surprised him to learn about his father's three wives and several children. George had made a point of telling Kingston to say his name was merely coincidentally the same and they were not of the same lineage. It was altogether very peculiar.

'For their protection,' George said.

'And why we will quietly disappear before they become aware of our inability to age,' Redmond said.

'But you *are* ageing,' Kingston said. 'Rapidly.'

'Overwork,' George said again. 'We have done a great many things in the time we've been in this country. The building you stand in is a testament to that.'

'I am not doubting your achievements,' Kingston said. 'I am simply concerned.'

'Perhaps you should concern yourself less with worrying about us and more with finding yourself a lovely lady to have an heir,' Redmond said. 'Lineage is important.'

That was unlikely ever to happen. Kingston had zero interest in relationships of any sort. Finding out that his father had taken so many wives and children had done little to help this opinion. Back home, he was expected to marry and have a son to continue on the family name, but with his father gone, he'd avoided it. He had a sinking feeling that now he was here, his father would push the issue. Perhaps his father going away for a while would buy him some time.

'Enough chatter,' Redmond said, returning to his seat at the table. 'Come join me and have some tea. We have business to discuss.'

George gently pushed Kingston towards the table. Kingston knew he was about to get the talk about the responsibilities of the Protector. He'd have to fill in while his father was away in India, even though Kingston wasn't fully trained. Still, training had to begin somewhere. He joined Redmond at the table alongside his father, and they got to work.

CHAPTER 1

SYDNEY Madinah awoke to the sound of rain hitting the glass window of her apartment. It was another dreary Adelaide winter morning. She sighed, not wanting to get out of bed. It was only Wednesday. There was still half of the week to go. She would walk in the rain to work again. She wasn't looking forward to it.

It had been another dreamless night. She preferred them to nights of dreams filled with gunshots, torture and dead bodies. Some nights she'd wake in a cold sweat, not remembering what she'd dreamed but knowing it had been bad. She'd been having them ongoing since the whole ordeal with Marcus had ended. It was over – she reminded herself of that constantly. It was over, and he couldn't hurt them anymore.

Sydney pulled herself out of bed and started getting ready for work. She dropped bread into the toaster while she got dressed. She stifled a yawn with the back of her hand. Yesterday had been a late one. A guest had checked in just as she was about to clock out and had caused so many problems that Jake had removed them forcibly. She hoped they didn't show up to cause more trouble.

Troublesome guests were rare at the Medina Grand Hotel but

weren't non-existent. She could count on both hands the number she'd come across in the six months since she'd started working at the hotel. It took a lot to rate a guest 'troublesome' in her book. There were always hiccups, but a guest had to be bad to earn the rank.

Jake Peterson, the head of security at the hotel, had stayed later than she had. He'd hung around just in case the guest had come back. He had texted her around midnight to let her know things were calm. She hoped he'd gone home after that. At least the traffic wouldn't have been too bad for him to get home. Unlike her, Jake had a car. But then, he parked in the same parking lot as the guests, and she realised it would have been closed by the time he clocked out. She wondered how he got home.

Sydney jumped as her toast popped, pulling her from her thoughts. She shook it off and chastised herself for being so jumpy. As she buttered and spread jam on her toast she looked at the clock and was pleased to see she was early. Some mornings, she had to eat and run. This morning, she had time to enjoy her breakfast.

Sydney took the time to scroll through the news on her phone. She liked to keep up with the city's news and events, as guests were always eager to discuss them. She saw there was an art show nearby. An author was speaking at a bookstore in the Myer Centre. The city council were holding a special meeting, which was unusual, as they typically left Wednesdays clear. There were a few things on.

Once she finished breakfast, she locked everything down, grabbed her bag and headed out the door. It was only a few blocks between her apartment and the hotel. She took her umbrella and people watched as she walked to work.

Since the incident with Marcus Connolly, Sydney had become much more aware of her surroundings. It wasn't easy to trust people like she used to. She couldn't help but wonder if they had an ulterior motive when they talked to her. She hated this new part of her, but being burdened with the secret of the portals meant she had to be extra careful.

Another thing she had realised was the sheer amount of security cameras everywhere. She was half tempted to walk different ways to work to avoid settling into a regular path to prevent people from watching her. The number of cameras meant someone was always watching, no matter where she walked. It made her shiver, and not in a good way.

Reaching the hotel, she let out a sigh of relief. The hotel felt safe, a feeling she didn't even get at home. The warmth of the building enfolded her in a comforting hug. After closing her umbrella, she walked into the building properly. She was cautious not to let her umbrella drip. She didn't want to give the cleaning staff something extra to worry about.

Sydney greeted the woman behind the desk before going to her office. She put all her things away, removed her coat, and clipped on her name tag. She was still a little early, so she switched on her computer to check her email, finding one from Jake updating her that the problem guest had indeed returned. At one a.m. Which meant Jake had still been at the hotel.

Worry washed over her as she headed to the security office. Jake's shift started before hers, so she knew he'd already be there. Sure enough, she found him studying the screens with a warm cup of coffee. It was in a takeaway cup, but the logo told her it came from the hotel's cafe, which had only opened thirty minutes ago.

'Jake,' Sydney said, getting his attention.

'Oh, hey, Syd,' Jake said with a tired smile. 'You're in early.'

'Did you go home?' she asked.

'Um …' The guilty look said it all.

'Did you sleep at all?'

'Yeah,' he said, shrugging. 'I crashed on Kingston's couch. I'm sure he wouldn't mind.'

Sydney glanced up in the direction of Kingston's room. He was away and had been for over two months. He and Raymond Barry had gone to Europe to escape everything. They had wanted to leave sooner, but Raymond needed to heal after his torture, and it had taken a while for him to get clearance for time off from his work as an archivist.

'You should have called a taxi,' she said. 'You can't spend all night here when there is a problem.'

'Sure I can,' he said. 'I'm the head of security. It's my job to handle these things.'

'That's what the night shift is for.'

'So I gave them an extra pair of hands,' he said. 'Trust me, we needed it with this guy.'

'So he came back?'

'Waltzed in completely drunk. I think the pub kicked him out.'

'Did you call the police?'

'Damned straight I did.' Jake set his cup down and stretched. 'We had to sit on him until they arrived. He wanted to throw down.'

'I should have been here,' Sydney said, guilt washing over her. She knew he was a problem, yet she'd gone home.

'The night team had it covered,' Jake assured her. 'I doubt there would be much more you can do.'

'I should have known you two would be gossiping.' Rita Taylor's voice sounded from behind Sydney. Her bag was over her shoulder, and her red hair was pulled back into a tight ponytail. She was still in her coat, and she held an umbrella loosely in her grip. Like Jake, she parked in the hotel parking lot and walked to the hotel.

'We're discussing work,' Jake said, running his hands through his spiked blond hair. 'Problem guest.'

Rita's eyebrows rose. 'How much of a problem?'

'Called the cops sort.'

She narrowed her eyes. 'Are we going to get sued?'

'I doubt it.'

'We had already asked him to leave,' Sydney told her. 'Before

I clocked out. He was looking to start something then, so Jake trespassed him.'

'Was it related to …' Rita pointed down. The portals.

'No, just a dickwad,' Jake said. 'The sobering-up-in-jail kind.'

'I hope you did all the paperwork.'

Jake patted a thick folder beside him.

'I should probably finish my report as well,' Sydney said, realising she'd need to update her report with the information he had returned. The night manager would have written one up so she could add it to the file. That was the downside of problem guests. There was always a lot of paperwork to cover them in case anyone tried to sue.

'Anyway, did you want to see me?' Jake asked Rita.

'Yes, actually,' Rita said. 'Kingston and Raymond get back tomorrow. I think it would be a good idea for us to hold a meeting.'

'What, already?' Jake pulled a face. 'They haven't touched down yet. They probably haven't even taken off.'

'Maybe give them a couple of days to settle in,' Sydney agreed. 'Nothing much happened while they were gone.'

Rita set her jaw, her expression hard. Sydney knew how much she liked order and efficiency. She would want to get back in the swing of things as soon as possible. As Kingston's PR and secretary, she was the one who handled everything in his absence, and sometimes Sydney wondered if she was the one who ran the whole thing. Kingston might be Sydney's boss, but in reality, it was Rita she answered to.

'Anyway, you need to get to the front desk,' Rita said to Sydney. 'And I need to get upstairs. I have some phone calls I need to make.'

'Please tell me you're not organising a party,' Jake groaned.

'No,' Rita said. 'It's a supply matter.'

'The new towels,' Sydney guessed. They were supposed to arrive the week before but hadn't.

Rita nodded. 'The tracking number updated to "delivered" yesterday.'

Sydney frowned. 'There wasn't a delivery.'

'Exactly. Someone needs to explain.'

'I pity them,' Jake muttered.

Rita shot him a firm look, but Sydney could see her eyes twinkling. Sydney thought Rita got off on telling people off and liked a good business confrontation. It was the sort of thing Sydney avoided and was glad she wasn't the one who had to deal with it. However, she had to deal with the fact that they needed those towels.

'Let me know what you find out,' Sydney said to Rita.

'I'll tell you at lunch,' Rita said, turning and heading out.

'Goodbye to you too,' Jake called out after her.

Sydney frowned, seeing the annoyed expression on his face. Were they fighting about something? Rita was always a little harsh on Jake, but he usually sweet-talked her. He was smitten with her, so his reply was out of character for him. As was his annoyance. She was going to need to dig into that.

'I'd better go too,' she said to Jake. 'See you at lunch?'

'Same place, same time,' he told her.

Mid-morning, the police arrived to take a statement about the troublesome guest. Sydney was happy to hand over a copy of the report. Rita came down to speak to them and Jake left the security office with a copy of his report and spent almost an hour reviewing it with the police.

It seemed like a lot of excitement for a single bothersome guest. Sydney was glad it was just a run-of-the-mill situation and not something involved with the portals. Marcus' death had quieted things down on that front. She had not seen his body, mercifully, but the gunshot haunted her dreams.

Before she knew it, lunchtime rolled around. Sydney headed into the cafe and noted that Elizabeth and Dorothy's table was empty.

She paused, slightly panicking that something had happened to them. Then she remembered some bus lines weren't running during certain hours because of a worker strike. Their bus must have been impacted, meaning the two cheerful women didn't get to the market that day.

Kian MacDowell sat at his usual table, sipping his coffee with a sandwich from the cafe on a plate beside him. He had his laptop open and was typing away. Was he prying into their security system again? As the system's creator, he often monitored it. That, and the man had turned out to be the Overseer of the portals, so he was watching things on that end.

It had taken Sydney some time to wrap her head around the fact that Kian was Marcus' father. She had many questions she wanted to ask him but had never had the time. Getting an urge, she crossed the courtyard and pulled out the chair across from him, dropping into it.

'Miss Madinah,' Kian greeted. 'To what do I owe the pleasure?'

'I wanted to see how you were,' Sydney said. Her stomach grumbled in a reminder it was time for her coffee and muffin. This was more important. 'After everything.'

'It's been six months,' he reminded her.

'Do you ever get over it, though?'

'I guess not.' He sipped from his coffee. 'You do, however, come to accept things.'

'You've accepted what happened?'

He nodded. 'I regret not becoming involved sooner.'

'How did you realise it was Marcus?' she asked. 'Did you know the whole time?'

'No,' he said. 'I knew there had been incursions, but I did not know who was behind them.'

'When did you work it out?'

'When Kingston became sick,' Kian explained. 'I looked back through the security footage to see who was involved, and that's when I saw Marcus.'

'And you said nothing?'

'I wished to speak with him,' Kian said. 'Unfortunately, I didn't get the opportunity.'

'You really didn't know where he was?'

'No.' Kian sighed, leaning back in his seat. 'Marcus made it clear several decades ago that he no longer wished to contact me. I respected his wishes. I regret not tracking him.'

'Do you think he knew you were here?'

'We'll never know.'

Because Marcus had died, and all he had wanted was to go home. 'Why didn't you tell him the key to your home no longer worked?'

'He never asked.' Kian pressed a hand to his chest, Sydney knowing the key to his home planet was hanging from a chain around his neck beneath his clothing. She didn't understand why he kept it. Perhaps it was the last link to the past, and he kept it as a keepsake. 'I saw the footage of him kidnapping Kingston and followed him. That was how I could rescue Kingston and Raymond.'

'Thank you,' Sydney said. She blamed herself for letting it slip to Marcus that Kingston and Raymond were involved with each other. Marcus had used it against them. 'I'm sorry about what happened.'

'So you've said,' Kian said. 'But we cannot change the past.'

'Do you wish you could?'

'I do.' Kian smiled tightly. 'But what is done is done. We can only live with our decisions and accept them.'

'You've moved on?'

'I have.' He regarded her. 'Have you?'

Sydney wasn't sure. The nightmares that plagued her told her that she hadn't, but she would let no one know about them. Instead, she put on a brave face and went about her work as if nothing had happened.

'I understand the two of you were getting close,' Kian said.

'He wanted me to return to the planet with him,' Sydney confirmed.

'Then he liked you,' Kian said.

'Or he was using me.'

'He wouldn't have suggested taking you there if he didn't think fondly of you,' Kian said. 'To begin with he may have been using you, but you must have won him over.'

'I just wish I could have stopped him.' Sydney stared at a speck of dust on the table.

'Don't dwell on it,' Kian said. 'Dwelling on the past will trap you in a spiral of regret.'

'You say that like it's from experience.'

'You don't get to be my age without making a few poor decisions.'

Sydney wanted to ask him how old he was but bit her lip. He was at least over one hundred years old. He looked to be in his late forties or possibly early fifties. There was a little grey at the temples of his close-cropped hair and peppered in the dark hair of his well-trimmed goatee. But there was something about his eyes that clued her into the fact that he was a lot older.

'I wanted to help him,' Sydney admitted. 'I looked for the key for him. He promised to let Raymond go if I found it.'

'You understand he was never going to let Raymond go,' Kian said.

Sydney looked up at that. 'You don't think so?'

'Marcus doesn't believe in loose ends,' Kian said. 'He would have killed everyone except you.'

Sydney shuddered. She remembered Marcus standing over them with a gun, pointing it at each of them as he commanded Lucille Barry, Raymond's mother, to use the journals to break the code to the keys. Lucille would never have done it in time, which meant they would have all died. She'd spent many nights wondering who he would have killed first. Sydney had a horrible feeling that it would have been Jake. She was so thankful she would never have to find out.

Seeing movement out of the corner of her eye, she looked back and saw Jake wandering into the courtyard. He looked around for her, frowning as he saw her sitting with Kian. Sydney knew their conversation was over, so she turned back to Kian to find him already on his computer.

'Thank you for talking,' Sydney said.

Kian gave a nod but didn't look up. He was busy. Sydney slipped out of her seat and headed to the cafe counter to get her coffee and lunch, then joined Jake at a table. Soon after, Rita joined them. She didn't always join them as she was a busy woman, and it was not unheard of for Rita to work through lunch.

'So, what was that about?' Jake asked Sydney.

Sydney brushed a few wispy strands of her blonde hair back from her face. They had come loose from her ponytail and were annoying her. 'Just … talking.'

Rita looked at them and waited for an explanation.

'She was talking with Kian,' Jake explained.

'I'm still trying to wrap my head around everything,' Sydney admitted. 'I don't know how you two moved on after what happened.'

'I went home and threw up,' Jake said. 'I've seen some things as a security guard, but a dead body is new.'

'You mean one that isn't vaporised,' Rita said.

'He blew his brains out,' Jake reminded her. 'There was literal brain matter on the wall.'

Sydney felt sick, and even Rita looked a little green.

'Sorry,' Jake said. 'You probably didn't need that detail.'

'No,' Rita said.

'It surprises me that no one came looking for him,' Sydney said. 'This was the last place he was seen alive.'

'Not that you can prove,' Jake reminded her. 'I deleted everything. Made it look like a system failure.'

'I will admit I expected some form of retribution from his followers,' Rita said.

'Me too,' Sydney agreed. 'Didn't Raymond say something about a woman?'

Jake nodded. 'The one that tortured him.'

'We don't even know if she can use the portals,' Rita said. 'She's probably moved on to a new job already. I'm sure a woman with her talents has a calling.'

'It has been very quiet, though,' Jake said. 'Too quiet.'

'Maybe with Kingston and Raymond not here, the people who want the keys have been waiting for them to get back,' Sydney said.

'The thing is, now would be the perfect time to attack,' Jake said. 'Without the Keeper and Protector, the portals are wide open.'

'Except for us,' Rita said.

'Trust me, I've been keeping an eye out,' Jake said.

'Me too,' Sydney said. 'I've been paranoid about being watched.'

'You're not the one they're after,' Rita assured her.

'But Marcus came after me,' Sydney said. 'He targeted me specifically.'

'Any of us could be a target,' Jake agreed.

'Now you're both being paranoid,' Rita said. 'Let's take one day at a time. Tomorrow, Raymond and Kingston will be back. Then everything will be back to normal.'

'Doesn't Raymond still have a couple of weeks until he has to go back to work?' Sydney asked.

Jake nodded. 'I think he wants to settle back in before he does.'

'Kingston makes his own hours,' Rita said with a resigned sigh.

'That'd be nice.'

'Speaking of hours, we should eat.'

They finished their lunch, Sydney mulling over everything in her head. They talked little about what had happened the day that Marcus had died. She could count all the times on one hand. She looked back at Kian. He was sipping his coffee, eyes still on his computer screen. Whatever was on there had his complete attention, although she couldn't help but wonder if he was listening in on their conversation. It wouldn't be the first time.

Once they were done, they bid farewell to each other. Sydney returned to her office to review her emails again before she returned to the front desk. It was going to be a slow afternoon, given the bookings, so she'd have to keep busy. It wasn't hard. She completed the hotel rounds and checked in on the other staff to see if anything was needed. She did her work, which kept her mind off things. She couldn't wait for Raymond and Kingston to return. They always made things more exciting.

CHAPTER 2

'HAVE I mentioned how much I hate plane travel?'

Raymond Barry had to bite back his smile as he steered his Nissan GT-R through the traffic of Melbourne. They had touched down a few hours ago, but it had taken them a while to retrieve their bags because of an issue with the plane's unloading. He glanced at the man in the passenger seat and saw his scowl.

'You might have mentioned it a few times, yeah,' Raymond said.

'And car travel.'

'Portals are so much more efficient,' Kingston said. 'One step, and you're there.'

'Unfortunately, there isn't a portal to Italy.'

'That we know of.'

Point taken. They still hadn't uncovered all the keys, so there might be one that went to Italy. If Raymond had to hazard a guess, he'd put money on one going to the Vatican. There was also the chance they had already lost the key during the decades-long demolition of buildings.

'Would you rather plane or boat?' Raymond asked.

'Plane,' Kingston admitted. 'I get seasick.'

'Noted. No taking you on a cruise.'

'No.' Kingston shifted in his seat. 'This car needs more legroom.'

'It's not exactly designed for comfort,' Raymond admitted. 'It's more about bragging rights.'

'You know what they say about people with this sort of vehicle.'

Raymond's eyebrows shot up at the implication. 'I've never heard you complain.'

'People will wonder.'

Raymond gave him a half glare as he negotiated a hook turn. It was one downside to Melbourne. Hook turns confused even the most experienced driver if they didn't have to go through them enough. 'You never mentioned why you hate plane travel.'

'Everything,' Kingston said. 'The lines, the rushing, the confusion. The hours sitting down in a cramped space with no legroom.'

'You were the one who wanted to fly economy.'

'I immediately regretted my decision.'

'Yet you didn't upgrade.'

'I was trying to save us money.'

There was no arguing with that point. Flights could be pricey, and they had made a strict budget before they left. They both had enough money to cover everything but didn't want to splurge on unnecessary things. Every part of their trip had been planned out to the detail. Nothing had been done on a whim except for what Raymond's father, Antonio Contiello, had come up with.

Relief washed over Raymond as he pulled the car into the parking garage. He was both sad and happy about the trip being over. He'd miss spending time with his father, but Melbourne would always be home for him. He'd never been a fan of driving in the city, but his frequent trips to Geelong to see his daughter meant he required a car.

He parked the car in his assigned parking space. Kingston stretched his body out the second he was out of the car. It didn't help that Kingston was almost 6'4'. Raymond's own 6'1' was cramped in the car, so he knew it must be worse for Kingston.

They retrieved their luggage from the car's boot. Raymond's luggage had a series of small gifts he'd bought for his daughter. He couldn't wait to give them to her, but he knew it would be a little while. Raymond double-checked that the car was locked and they started the short walk to the State Library of Victoria. The home under the library had become Raymond's more permanent address since he'd broken the code to find the keys. He spent more time there and less at the apartment on La Trobe Street that he shared with his mother.

They negotiated the foot traffic and made it to the library's side door, Raymond opening it with his key card. They no doubt looked odd as they brought all their luggage into the building. There was a drizzle in the air that Raymond was glad to get out of. They followed the familiar trek down the stairs, carrying their baggage. Reaching the door to the homestead, Raymond swiped the lock, popping it open. He waited for Kingston to enter first, then followed him down.

The air was musty. The place had never had great ventilation because it was so deep underground. Something about the air told him no one had been there for some time. He frowned, hitting the light switch as they descended the staircase and into the homestead proper.

'Mother?' Raymond called out, hearing nothing in reply.

'I don't think she's here,' Kingston said.

'No,' Raymond agreed. 'I half expected her to meet us.'

Kingston set his bags down on the wooden floor. 'You think she missed you?'

'No,' Raymond said, shaking his head. 'I expected her to rip into me for not having worked on deciphering the journals for so long.'

'Ah.'

Raymond dragged his things to his bedroom, opening the door with his hip and switching on the light. His room was as he'd left it, only now with a layer of dust coating everything. No one had wiped anything down since he'd left.

'I must agree that I thought she'd be here,' Kingston said, coming up behind him. 'It is the longest the two of you have been apart.'

'She'll be working,' Raymond said, dropping to the bed. He toed off his shoes and stretched out over the duvet. Nothing compared to his own bed after time away. 'She's married to her job.'

Kingston came and joined him on the bed after removing his shoes and settling beside him. Their bodies touched. 'Your father seems to think so.'

'They always argued about it,' Raymond said, staring at the roof. 'You know, I miss him more now than my mother while we were away.'

'He is a remarkable man,' Kingston said. 'His knowledge is astounding.'

'That's what makes him good at what he does.'

'It was a privilege to sit in on one of his lectures.'

'Yeah, it was.'

They lay for a while, simply content with each other's presence. Above them, the footsteps of those in the library sounded. Someone was moving around in the catacombs. The roof was thin enough to listen to those above, but Raymond knew it was thick enough that you couldn't hear anyone talking from the homestead.

'We should let Rita know we've returned,' Kingston said.

Raymond grumbled. 'It's not like it's urgent or anything.'

'She wanted to know.'

'You realise she wants to drag you back to work. She's probably got a whole pile of files you must go through.'

'No doubt.' Kingston chuckled. 'And they'll be perfectly ordered by a matter of importance.'

'Mm.' Raymond sighed. 'Can we just stay here? Pretend we didn't fly in yet.'

'She had our flight details. She'll know it's touched down.'

Raymond grunted, rolling onto his side and regarding Kingston. 'There's no rush, though, is there?'

Kingston must have heard something in his voice as he turned towards Raymond with a knowing look in his eye. He reached out, fingers trailing over Raymond's jawline. 'What do you have in mind?'

Raymond smirked, leaning in to kiss him. Kingston chuckled before he kissed Raymond back. Raymond lifted his hand to card through Kingston's dark hair, losing his fingers in the loose curls. He kissed him deeply, savouring the time they had together. It was nice not having to hide their relationship from their friends anymore, but that didn't mean Raymond didn't enjoy their alone time. And after their long flight, he'd wanted to curl up with Kingston and just kiss him. Maybe even more.

He groaned as he heard the house phone ring. They were deep underground, so mobile reception was terrible; they still relied on a landline. Raymond had zero clue how they had installed a phone in the homestead in the first place, given that it was a hidden home. Right now, he wished it didn't exist.

It tempted Raymond to ignore it, but Kingston pulled back from him with an expectant look.

'It may be important,' Kingston pointed out.

With a heavy sigh, Raymond untangled himself from Kingston and rolled off the bed, padding with socked feet out of the bedroom and to the landline on the wall between the kitchen and dining room. He picked it up and brought it to his ear.

'Hello?'

'Hello, Ray-Ray.'

He scowled. 'What do you want, Margarita?'

'You're back then.'

'We literally just got in.' Raymond checked his watch. It would have to be mid-afternoon in Adelaide. 'Shouldn't you be working?'

'I am. Knowing Kingston's whereabouts is part of the job.'

He smirked. 'Well, I could tell you where he is, but you probably don't want to hear it.'

There was a pause, and he could imagine her glaring at the phone. 'We should all touch base.'

'There's no rush. Like I said, we literally just got in.'

'Which means you're still dressed. I'll see you in ten minutes.'

She hung up before he could answer. Raymond scoffed. He had to admire her nerve. Kingston was her boss, though sometimes it felt like the other way around. Rita kept Kingston focused. Raymond shook his head and hung up the phone, returning to the bedroom. Kingston was still on the bed with his arm under his head. He looked relaxed.

'Rita?' Kingston asked.

Raymond frowned. 'How did you know?'

'You always get an annoyed yet impressed expression after talking to her.'

'She wants to meet in ten minutes.'

'I had a feeling she might.' Kingston pushed himself off the bed, reaching for his shoes to put them back on. 'To be continued.'

Raymond would hold him to that. He grabbed his shoes, pausing momentarily after putting them on to take off and clean his glasses. They'd gotten slightly smudged while kissing Kingston, and Raymond could never stand even the slightest mark on them. He smiled as Kingston came up behind him and pressed a soft kiss to the back of his neck.

'We best not keep them waiting,' Kingston said.

'No.' Raymond put his glasses back on. 'Barrys are always punctual.'

Kingston grabbed his bags, and Raymond offered to take one, but Kingston turned him down. They walked towards the door at the far end of the dining room. Raymond opened it, allowing Kingston to step through the portal first. He felt the air shift as he followed him into Adelaide. It was less musty on this side. Adelaide had better air circulation and wasn't as deep underground as Melbourne.

Kingston carefully opened the door to the little room on the other side and checked to ensure no one was there. Raymond closed the portal door behind him, following Kingston out into the corridors of the vaults. They double-checked that the door to the portal room was locked before heading to the staircase.

Raymond again offered to take one of Kingston's bags as they negotiated the staircase. Kingston relented, handing over his carry-on bag so he could focus on the luggage case. They made their way up to Kingston's permanent residency. Following Kingston in, Raymond spotted that Rita, Jake, and Sydney were already there.

'Welcome back!' Sydney chirped.

'I didn't realise we'd have a welcoming committee,' Kingston joked.

'I've got to say your tans are impressive,' Jake said. 'You really took advantage of the Venetian beaches.'

'But of course.'

'They were way overcrowded,' Raymond said, following Kingston over to his bedroom so they could put the bags away.

'What's Italy like?' Sydney asked.

'Like Raymond said – crowded,' Kingston said as they rejoined them. Kingston pulled his chair out from his desk and sat down, while Raymond perched on the edge of the desk, facing them.

'Your father took you around, didn't he?' Sydney asked. Raymond nodded. 'How was he?'

'He's great,' Raymond said. 'It was nice to see him in person.'

'How long has it been?'

'Years. He last visited around the time I turned eighteen.'

'How was Ireland?' Rita asked.

'Beautiful as always,' Kingston said.

Raymond narrowed his eyes as something dawned on him. 'Were you watching us through our GPS tracking devices?'

Jake looked guilty, which told Raymond everything he needed

to know. Jake had arranged for them to get the trackers after everything with Marcus. That way, should either end up kidnapped again, Jake could locate them. It was easier than hacking into the CCTV network.

'I knew your itinerary, remember?' Rita said.

'That doesn't mean you weren't tracking us.'

'We did both,' Jake admitted.

'Did you take many pictures?' Sydney asked. 'I would love to see them.'

'A few,' Kingston said. 'I promise we will share them with you, although achieving good photos with the crowds was difficult.'

'The Vatican was a disaster,' Raymond said. 'My father tried to talk us out of going. We should have let him.'

'It was wonderful that you got to spend time with him,' Sydney said.

'Yeah, it was,' Raymond said. He missed his father again. Even though his father had been absent most of his life, they still had a bond. They shared their interest in history, even if Raymond focused on buildings and his father on languages.

'Think you'll be able to get back to work?' Rita asked.

'Oh, I never stopped,' Raymond said.

Rita frowned. 'What do you mean?'

'I took one of Redmond's journals with me.'

'That's risky,' Jake said. 'You could have lost it.'

'Trust me, I wouldn't lose it.'

'What did you find?' Sydney asked.

Raymond glanced back at Kingston and saw him nod. 'Well, the journal focused on Ballarat. It's a town in Victoria.'

'I think it's classified as a city these days,' Rita said.

'Either way, I came up with a list of locations. And most of the buildings are still standing.'

Sydney perked up. 'You think the keys are still there?'

'Only one way to find out.'

Rita sighed. 'I guess we know what you're doing in your two weeks before you return to work.'

Raymond nodded, looking back at Kingston again. 'What *we'll* be doing.'

'You're more than welcome to come with us,' Kingston said. 'We can make it a team outing.'

'I can't,' Rita said, shaking her head. 'My family get-together is in a week. You know I can't miss it.'

'I'll have to check the schedule,' Jake said.

'Me too,' Sydney said.

'Look into it this afternoon and get back to me,' Kingston said. 'I can make the bookings tonight.'

'Why the rush?' Rita said.

'Because Ballarat has a heritage week next week,' Kingston said. 'Many of the buildings will be open for tours.'

'Well, that explains why you cut your vacation short,' Rita said.

Kingston nodded. 'It was a far too opportune moment to pass up.'

'I'll go look at the schedule now,' Jake said. 'Short notice, though.'

'Yes,' Rita said. 'You should have given us a heads up.'

Kingston shrugged. 'We couldn't risk someone intercepting our message.'

'I keep telling you our email is encrypted,' Jake said. 'You've got to be really good to hack it.'

'Don't underestimate my people.'

'Anyway, we should get back to work,' Rita said. She looked at Kingston. 'We have some things we need to go over.'

Kingston reached up and rested a hand on a stack of files on his desk. 'This, no doubt.'

'Yes.'

'I'll leave you to it,' Raymond said, shifting off the desk as Jake and Sydney stood up. 'I must let Mother know we're back.'

Raymond looked back, smiled at Kingston, and nodded in

farewell, getting one in return. He turned and followed Sydney and Jake from the room. As they made their way down the stairs, Jake looked back at him.

'Seriously, though, your tan is amazing.'

'It's going to make me stick out like a sore thumb,' Raymond lamented. 'Everyone else is pale from the winter.'

'It looks good on you,' Sydney said with a shy smile.

'Thank you.'

CHAPTER 3

SYDNEY hadn't taken a single sick day since she had started working at the hotel. Being the manager had its perks, and she noted that no one else had any time off scheduled, so she could allocate herself a week to accompany the team to Ballarat. She felt a little guilty doing it on such short notice, but after talking with the other team members, she found they were all okay with it.

By the time she finished for the day, she'd arranged for everything to be taken care of while she was away. She would not need to worry about anything, and she sent a message to Rita to let her know. She felt a sense of thrill at the prospect of a group excursion. It would allow her to redeem herself after the mess with Marcus. That hung over her like a dark cloud that she couldn't shake.

Stepping out of her office, she was surprised to find Jake in the hallway looking tired. She knew it wasn't a good sign. 'What's up?'

'I can't take the week,' Jake said, shaking his head. 'We're short-staffed right now.'

Sydney sucked in a breath as she realised it would be just her, Kingston, and Raymond. She felt disappointed that neither Jake nor Rita could go. She'd hoped to bond with them. 'So you couldn't take it off even if you tried?'

He shook his head. 'I knew we were short. I didn't realise how bad.'

As the head of security, Jake could see the files of the other workers. It must not be good if he couldn't manage even a week. 'You have days saved up, though, right?'

'Oh yeah,' he said, nodding. 'I have over a month of days saved up. It's just ... now isn't a good time.'

'I'm sorry,' she said. 'I wanted you to come.'

He looked up at her. 'You can?'

She nodded. 'I've already cleared everything.'

'Well, at least one of us is going,' he said. He ran a hand through his blond hair, messing up the spikes. 'You can keep Kingston and Raymond in line.'

She blinked. 'Do I need to?'

'Those guys are magnets for trouble,' Jake reminded her. 'I guess Rita and I can cover things from this end. I'll at least be able to watch the portals while you're gone.'

Someone needed to guard the portals. There had been enough attempts to reach them, though things had calmed since Marcus died. But they could start up again at any moment.

Footsteps rang and Kingston joined them. Sydney had to admire his tan. He wasn't a man who got out in the sun very often. It looked good on him, and she wondered how much of it covered him. She instantly shook the thought off. Kingston was technically her boss. She shouldn't think about things like that.

'Evening, Miss Madinah, Mr Peterson,' he said. 'What's the situation?'

'I'm in,' Sydney said with a smile.

'I'm out,' Jake said. Sydney could tell he was disappointed.

Kingston frowned at him. 'I believe you had days saved for such an occurrence.'

'Doesn't help when we're short.'

'Ah.' Kingston nodded. He also looked disappointed. 'So it will be three of us.'

'Looking that way.'

'That may work out in our favour,' Kingston said. 'Rita could only arrange for a two-bedroom suite.'

'Huh.' Jake frowned. 'Where would I have stayed if I could have come? Or did Rita forget about me again?' He waved it off. 'So it'll be you and Raymond in one room and Sydney in the other?'

'Indeed.' Kingston looked at Sydney. 'If that is acceptable.'

'It'll be fine,' Sydney said, a thrill of excitement shooting through her. She wasn't just going on a trip with them; she would be living with them for a week.

'It'll be a great chance for you all to get to know each other,' Jake commented, reflecting precisely what Sydney had been thinking. Aside from a few dinners, she hadn't really sat down and talked with Kingston and Raymond. Most of their discussions had been about the keys and portals.

'I have to agree,' Kingston said. He turned to Sydney. 'Our suite will have a kitchen, so we'll be able to do all our own cooking.'

'Oh, yikes,' Jake said.

Kingston frowned. 'What?'

'I've heard about your cooking,' Jake said. 'You put tomato sauce in everything.'

'Has Rita been outing my secrets again?'

'I didn't know it was a secret.'

Sydney hoped it wasn't true. She wasn't mad about sauce. There was only one way to find out, and she felt she was going to. She was more than prepared to team up with Raymond if it were the case.

'Anyhow, we leave in two days,' Kingston said, turning back to Sydney. 'I'm afraid the back seat of Raymond's car isn't very … roomy.'

'It's primarily a two-seater,' Jake confirmed. 'Plenty of room in the front, but it's not made for a carload of people.' He paused. 'Another reason it's probably a good thing I'm not going. I would have demanded you hire a bigger car.'

'What kind of car does Raymond have?' Sydney asked.

'Nissan GT-R,' Jake answered.

Sydney's eyebrows shot up. That wasn't a cheap car. From what they said, she had thought it would be a tiny two-seater runabout. Raymond had expensive taste. 'Is it his car or his mother's?'

'His,' Kingston said. 'His mother refuses to drive.'

'Lucille has to be driven,' Jake confirmed.

'Will I be fine in the back seat?' Sydney asked. She wondered about legroom. She wasn't the tallest person, but it didn't help that both Kingston and Raymond were over six feet.

'We'll give you ample room,' Kingston promised her.

'Just kick the back of their seat if they don't,' Jake joked.

'I'm sure Raymond would love that,' Kingston deadpanned.

It would leave scuff marks. Not what you wanted in a car like that. She most definitely would not kick the back of their seat.

'What do I need to bring?' Sydney asked.

'A good pair of walking shoes,' Kingston said. 'And warm clothing. It is winter.'

'You might want to check the weather report,' Jake said. 'In case it's going to rain.'

'Rita already has,' Kingston said. 'It's going to be cool but fine. Perhaps a little windy.'

'So maybe a scarf,' Sydney said. 'And gloves.'

'That sounds ideal.' Kingston smiled. 'The hotel Rita found us is in the city's central region. Many places will be within walking distance.'

It sounded perfect. What sort of hotel would it be? She doubted it would be as grand as the Medina Hotel. Would it be a modern or historic hotel? She couldn't wait to find out.

'I can have Rita put together a list of things you will need,' Kingston offered.

'That would be great, actually,' Sydney said. 'I've lived out of a suitcase before, but this is a different sort of trip.'

'You have?' Jake asked.

Sydney nodded. 'When I first moved to America. For the first month, I had to move from place to place until I found somewhere permanent to stay.'

'That would have been annoying.'

'It wasn't that bad.'

'I will update Rita on who is coming,' Kingston said, glancing at his watch. 'She will want things confirmed before she goes home for the evening.'

'Which is soon,' Jake observed.

'Five minutes.'

'Have a good evening,' Sydney said.

'You as well.'

Kingston turned and headed back towards the staircase. Sydney looked at Jake, noting the wistful look in his eye. 'I wish you could come.'

'Yeah, me too.' Jake shrugged it off with a sigh. 'Maybe next time.'

Sydney nodded. 'I'll see you tomorrow?'

'Bright and early.'

Rita had emailed a list of things she would need by that evening. Sydney had to admire her organisational skills. Sydney dug into her closet and found her luggage bag. The last time she'd used it was when she'd been moving to Adelaide. She packed everything she could that night, checking things off the list as she went.

The next day after work, she stopped at the supermarket for a travel toiletry bag. It was the last thing she would need. The toothpaste and shampoo that came with it would easily last her a week if she were careful. If not, she could always buy a new one while in Ballarat.

She still had to wrap her mind around the fact it would only take her just over an hour to get to Ballarat from Adelaide. For most people, it was easily a day trip to get there. But with the portal, it shaved off hours. She lamented portals weren't the standard form of travel for the country. Were they for Kingston's home planet? Sydney would have to ask him if she got the opportunity.

The excitement bubbling beneath her skin was barely contained. Jake still lamented that he couldn't come, and after some digging, she found out why they were short-staffed. One of the security guards was on paternity leave. Another had recently gotten sick and was recovering at home. While it didn't mean extra shifts for anyone in the office, it meant that no one could have time off until at least one of them returned.

Rita seemed indifferent about the entire thing, but that was just Rita. She rarely conveyed how she was feeling and wasn't one to wear her heart on her sleeve. After some prying, Jake told her Rita wanted to go, but the family get-together was an unavoidable annual affair. If the timing had been any different, she would have joined them.

They arranged to meet at the Medina Grand Hotel on the morning of the trip. Sydney dragged her suitcase along on its wheels and shouldered a purse. She wore walking shoes and comfortable clothing. Raymond had insisted they leave early to beat the traffic rush.

The night manager welcomed her into the hotel. She called up to Kingston's room to let him know she'd arrived, and he came down to meet her with his luggage bag. Had he even bothered to unpack from his trip to Europe?

'Morning, Miss Madinah,' Kingston greeted.

'Good morning, Mr Kingston,' she replied. She noted he also had a carry bag and wondered if she should have brought one.

'Shall we?' he asked, gesturing towards the stairs that led down to the vaults.

She nodded, leading the way. He was always the gentleman, so ladies first. They made it down the stairs with little hassle, and when they reached the door to the portal room, Sydney took out a keycard to open it. They had given her a key to the door only a few months ago. She'd been honoured that they trusted her with it, and she guarded it closely.

They stepped into the small room with the portals, Kingston double-checking that the door locked behind them. Sydney took a steadying breath.

'Still worried about the portal?' Kingston asked her.

'I've seen someone vaporised,' she reminded him.

He chuckled. 'Not you. You'll be fine.'

She nodded, but it didn't ease the tiny amount of fear she always felt walking through the doorway. The memory of the man walking through and disintegrating was burned into her memory. That had been the day she'd discovered the portal and had been thrown into the world of hunting for the keys.

Sydney knocked on the door to Melbourne out of habit. She opened it and stepped through. She felt the air shift slightly as she walked into Melbourne. It was the only thing that changed, otherwise portals felt like walking through a normal doorway. It was hard to believe someone could die crossing through. She'd seen it. A man atomised because he didn't have the right DNA.

They were deeper underground here, so the air felt thicker. Sydney couldn't even imagine living down here. She needed windows.

'I'm almost ready!' Raymond called from somewhere in the homestead.

Kingston checked his watch. 'We're five minutes early.'

They could hear Raymond moving around, and after a moment, he appeared from the doorway that led to his bedroom. He looked immaculate, as if it wasn't early in the morning. It wasn't as early here as it was in Adelaide. The sun would be almost up here, whereas it was still dark in Adelaide. Wrapping her mind around the different time zones was another thing she needed to get used to.

'Ready?' Kingston asked.

'Ready,' Raymond confirmed, pulling his luggage bag with him and closing the door to his bedroom. He straightened his jacket and then his glasses. 'No issues?'

'None.'

'Nice.' Raymond grabbed the handle of his bag and pulled it, leading the way down the hallway. He stopped at the bottom of the steps. 'We should get out before the morning rush.'

'That was the plan.'

Raymond nodded and led the way up the stairs. Sydney struggled with her bag as she trailed behind them. She wished the Barrys had an elevator but knew that would raise questions about an elevator to a floor that shouldn't exist. She wondered how many people had known about the homestead when it was built. How many people know about it now?

It was quiet when they entered the library. It was before opening time. Raymond led them through the corridor of the catacombs, up another flight of stairs, and into the library proper before taking them to a side door. The old building felt ominous, and its tall walls held history. It reminded her greatly of the old treasury building in Adelaide.

When they finally stepped out onto the streets of Melbourne, Sydney was surprised by how busy it was. Even for the early hour, people were everywhere. Melbourne was a hive of activity compared to Adelaide. It was almost jarring. If she had to pick a city, she'd pick Adelaide in a heartbeat.

Raymond led the way to the parking garage. Sydney couldn't imagine how much it set Raymond back to have a space. Did Lucille's place on La Trobe Street have assigned parking? This car park was closer to the library where Raymond primarily lived. That was no doubt why he'd chosen it.

She sucked in a breath as she spotted the car for the first time. It was sleek and low and a beautiful shade of midnight blue. It reminded her a little of his eyes, although they were lighter blue. If anything, his eyes were the colour of the sky. She shook the thought off. She needed to stop spending so much time thinking about his eyes.

'There it is,' Raymond confirmed, stopping next to the car and hitting the button on the remote to open the boot. 'There should be room for all our luggage if we cram it in there.'

'I think our smaller bags might need to go in the car,' Kingston said.

They shuffled their bags around, trying different ways of putting them in until all three fit. Good thing their bags weren't any bigger than they were. It was going to be interesting trying to get them back out. Kingston was right – their extra bags would need to go in the car.

'Sit behind me,' Kingston told her. 'I'll move my seat forward for you. Raymond's going to need the legroom.'

Sydney waited until he'd moved the seat so she could slide into the back. They handed her the bags, and she piled them onto the seat beside her. It was a little squishy in the back seat. Kingston moved the seat back so he could get in, then shuffled it forwards to give her more legroom, thus shrinking his own.

'Maybe we should have gotten a hire car,' Kingston said.

'It's not far,' Raymond said, closing his door. 'Next trick is getting out of the CBD.'

Sydney buckled herself in and sat back as the car hummed to life. A thrill washed over her at the sound. It practically purred. She couldn't believe she was sitting in a car like this.

'Raymond?' she asked.

'Yes?'

'How much is a car like this?'

There was a long pause. 'Enough.'

She frowned, pulling her phone out of her pocket and looking up the cost as he drove them through the city. She gaped. Given that the car didn't look old, she knew he'd have had to buy it new. How could an archivist afford such a thing? She put her phone away and overheard Raymond and Kingston talking about the location of the keys.

'It makes sense that one would be there,' Raymond said. 'Redmond oversaw the trials of the miners.'

'What miners?' Sydney asked.

Raymond glanced back at her in the mirror. 'The miners who fought in the Eureka Stockade.'

Sydney tried to think of her history and realised she was drawing a blank.

'It was a standoff over mining licence fees,' Raymond explained. 'The miners marched, built a stockade, and were attacked by red coats. Many people died, and they placed the miners who survived on trial. Redmond Barry was one of the judges.'

'He was an important judge,' Sydney said.

'He also oversaw the Ned Kelly trial,' Kingston said. 'It was quite remarkable.'

Raymond glanced at him. 'You say that like you were there.'

'I was,' Kingston said. 'Redmond invited me to sit amongst the civilians. He thought I would be interested.'

'You saw Ned Kelly?' Sydney said, surprised.

'He was quite a common-looking man. But his words had brevity. It was not long after that Redmond passed away.'

'I still think someone killed him,' Raymond said.

'As do I.'

CHAPTER 4

THE rest of the drive to Ballarat was spent in conversation about their trip. Kingston and Raymond were happy to fill Sydney in on the places they had been and the sights they had seen. Sydney decided she would visit Europe and see all the places for herself when she saved up some money.

'Ireland seemed particularly important to you,' Raymond said to Kingston as Mount Warrenheip came into view. 'It's like you view it as your homeland.'

'It almost is,' Kingston admitted. 'My home away from home.'

'Not Adelaide?' Sydney asked.

'I spent most of my years in Ireland,' Kingston said. 'My father had a home there. I lived there much of my time.'

'Is it still there?'

'Where we stayed when we went,' Raymond said. 'It was beautiful if dated.'

Kingston looked at him. 'Dated?'

'It doesn't look like you've updated it since 1850.' Raymond shrugged. 'Apart from the lighting and other things, I mean.'

'It has everything you need to live there.'

'Maybe. But new wallpaper couldn't hurt.'

'You did not complain while we were there.'

'I didn't want to be rude.'

Sydney had to hide her smile. Kingston glared at Raymond, who kept his eyes firmly on the road. They fell silent until they passed the 'Welcome to Ballarat' sign. A giant miner greeted them further along the route. Soon enough, Raymond took the exit off the highway and drove them over a hill, the city coming into view.

'GPS to the hotel?' Raymond asked Kingston.

'Yes,' Kingston said, taking out his phone. Sydney stared out the window as they came down the highway. It amazed her how many trees there were. She was used to city living. New York had been a concrete jungle. Adelaide had its ring of green, but nothing like this. Ballarat felt nestled in the bush from where she was looking, although the trees got farther apart as they drove.

The GPS's sound cut into the silence, Kingston holding his phone up so Raymond could hear it. As they entered the city centre, Sydney couldn't help but marvel at all the historic buildings. It felt like she was stepping back in time. How many of them hid the keys they were searching for?

Eventually, Raymond turned off Sturt Street onto a side street, and Sydney got her first look at the hotel. The grand nature of the building captured her imagination. It was heritage, which fit with what they were doing. Raymond pulled them into a car park out front and killed the engine. Kingston put his phone away, and Sydney hesitated as they opened their doors.

'Maybe I should stay with the car to guard the bags,' she said.

'I doubt anyone will steal them,' Kingston said.

'I'm just being careful. This car stands out.'

'It does a bit,' Raymond admitted.

'We won't be long,' Kingston told her.

Sydney nodded, settling back into her seat. Her legs wanted her to get out and stretch them, but she knew a few more minutes in the car wouldn't hurt. Again, she admired all the trees around her as Kingston and Raymond disappeared into the building. Turning, she looked out the back window to find a historic church. There *had* to be a key in there. She was sure of it.

Kingston and Raymond returned, and Raymond held a small placard to go in the car's window. They climbed back in, Raymond backing up and then driving them down a narrow driveway to the rear of the building. There were numbered car parks. Raymond moved into one, setting the placard in his window.

Kingston moved his seat so Sydney could squeeze out. Her body thanked her as she stretched out the kinks. They gathered their bags, Kingston leading the way back into the hotel. The interior was tastefully decorated, with a focus on the building's heritage. They found their way through the building to their door, which Kingston unlocked with a key.

Sydney realised it was an apartment. Like the rest of the building, it rode the line between heritage and modern. A little kitchen was next to a dining room and a small lounge with a flat-screen TV. The entrance had a corridor with rooms off it, she guessed, that led to the bedrooms and bathroom. It had a homely feel, and she could almost see herself living there.

'Apparently, this place has a spa,' Raymond commented.

'Single occupant only,' Kingston lamented.

Sydney chuckled. She'd have to check it out after a long day of walking. She was sure the two men would have shared if it were big enough.

'We should unpack,' Raymond said.

Sydney nodded then frowned as she realised it was still early in the day. She checked her watch. 'Isn't check-in supposed to be at two p.m.?'

'Rita used her influence to convince them to allow us to check in earlier,' Kingston said. 'They did not book the room last night. I believe we now owe favours.'

That woman could negotiate with anyone and get her way. She knew they could never have checked in so early had the room been booked the night before. Rita had probably booked that night just so the room would be empty for them when they arrived.

They headed back to the corridor, finding the rooms. Sydney was pleased to see that her bed was decently sized. She'd been worried it would be a single bed, but instead, she found a queen. A wardrobe with sliding doors and hangers allowed her to unpack her clothes.

Once done, she returned to the living area and sat on the couch to wait for the other two to finish. There was a book on the coffee table, much like the one they provided at the Medina Grand. She leafed through it, noting all the places of interest in Ballarat. There was so much heritage, it was overwhelming. How could they possibly go to all these places in a week?

She looked up at the sound of footsteps and spotted Raymond coming down the hallway. She smiled at him as he explored the kitchen area.

'Looks like we've got everything we're going to need,' he said to her. 'Except a kettle. I do not see a kettle.'

'Have you tried looking in the cupboards?'

He went through the cupboard, Sydney watching as he inspected the contents. He made a sound of discovery and pulled a kettle out.

'There should be some supplied packets of coffee and sugar, too,' she said. 'Maybe a couple of tea bags. We'll have to buy the rest.'

He looked back at her. 'How … oh, that's right, you're a hotel manager.'

She shrugged her shoulders and smirked. She returned to the book, finding a page about a deal with a local restaurant. They could get a discount if they ate there. She'd have to bring it up. Just because this was a working trip didn't mean they couldn't take some time out for leisure. She also found a theme park that sparked her interest.

'We've definitely got to go to Sovereign Hill.'

Raymond glanced back at her. 'Why?'

'Wouldn't it be interesting to see what life was like when Redmond Barry and George Strickland Kingston first came to Australia?'

'Yeah, it would actually,' he agreed. 'Add it to the list.'

Excitement zapped through her. Sydney couldn't remember the last time she'd visited a theme park. Living in Brisbane, her parents had an annual pass to the theme parks there. They'd go often, usually during the off-season when there were fewer tourists. She doubted this one had rollercoasters or anything of that style. It was more about the experience than anything.

'How are we looking?' Kingston asked as he joined them.

'We need groceries,' Raymond said, eyeing the coffee packets. 'And decent coffee.'

'That will be our first task,' Kingston said. He looked at Sydney. 'Does the book mention where to buy them?'

'It's mostly restaurants and attractions,' she said.

'That's what the internet is for,' Raymond piped up.

'We have a card for the Wi-Fi,' Kingston said, pulling it out of his pocket. 'If you want the code.'

'I'll get my computer,' Raymond said.

Sydney frowned as he headed back down the corridor. 'He brought his computer?'

'We thought it would be easier to research rather than crowding around a small phone screen,' Kingston explained.

That made sense. Sydney wished she'd had the foresight. Raymond returned with his laptop and set it on the small dining table. He took the card with the Wi-Fi details from Kingston, and it soon connected them to the hotel's broadband. A quick search found the location of the major supermarkets. It would be a short drive to them.

'Nothing within walking distance,' Raymond lamented.

'At least they're next door to each other,' Sydney said.

'We should write a list,' Kingston said, picking up the hotel-provided notepad.

They put together a shopping list and planned their meals for the week. Sydney mentioned the restaurant deal, so they factored that into their plan. While they were at it, they looked up the Heritage Week event page, noting what days it was on.

Kingston offered to do the groceries while Raymond assembled their week's itinerary. It surprised Sydney to see Raymond hand over the car keys. She hadn't expected him to be so quick with a car like that. Sydney also didn't know that Kingston could drive. She'd never seen him do it before.

'Just remember it's Australian road rules,' Raymond said. 'Left side.'

'Just like Ireland,' Kingston said.

He must have a car in Ireland. He offered to have her come with him, and Sydney took him up on it. They headed out of the apartment and down to the parking lot. Sydney was excited to sit in the front seat. Kingston connected his phone to the car to direct them to the nearest supermarket.

'Will we spend every day looking for keys?' she asked.

'The idea will be to find as many per day as possible,' he said. 'We brought a small lockbox to keep them in once we find them.'

A smart idea. Some people would try anything to get their hands on the keys. Guilt washed over her as she remembered how she had been so willing to hand them over to Marcus to get Raymond back. She kept quiet as they drove.

They zoomed around the expansive supermarket, collecting what they needed. They were spoiled for choice with coffee selection. Kingston found a particular brand and explained that it was a favourite of his and Raymond.

They loaded up the car and returned to the hotel to find Raymond exactly where they had left him, hunched over his computer and scribbling on the notepad.

'How'd you go?' Kingston asked him.

'I think I've got it all worked out,' Raymond said. 'I'll run you through it.'

'We'll just put these away first.'

They put the shopping away and then joined Raymond at the table.

'I've divided it by days,' Raymond explained. 'Some places are open every day, but a couple are only open on specific days. We'll have to hit those then.'

'Anywhere in particular we need to look?' Kingston asked.

'Definitely the School of Mines,' Raymond said. 'Redmond was heavily invested and involved in that school. I've got a feeling it will not be original on the inside.'

'What makes you say that?' Sydney asked.

'Because many of the buildings aren't,' Kingston explained. 'Thankfully, Redmond seemed to pick places where they wouldn't change much, or he hid them outside.'

'We've only come across one building where the key was on the outside,' Raymond reminded him.

'But your notes indicated some were. You mentioned it earlier.'

'The town hall,' Raymond told Sydney. 'There are at least two keys hidden there. One of them is meant to be outside near the front entrance.'

'Wouldn't that make it easier for someone to find it?' she asked.

Raymond nodded. 'And create a greater risk of the little hidey-hole popping open by itself because of the weather.'

'Hidey-hole?'

'That's right; you don't know.' Raymond grabbed a fresh piece of paper and drew a small box with a symbol. 'This is what we're looking for. It's a tiny, barely noticeable box. It has a little catch you need to press to open it, usually hidden along the edge.'

Sydney studied the picture. 'How big?'

'Big enough to hide a key.'

'Wouldn't that be hard to spot?'

'Redmond's notes usually include where to search,' Raymond said. 'He was a stickler for detail. He tried to make it as easy as possible.'

'Considering how long it has taken to break the code, I would not call it "easy",' Kingston said.

Raymond shrugged. 'Anyway, the School of Mines is open in two days. It includes all the original buildings. By my estimate, there should be about three keys there.'

'Redmond did like that place,' Sydney said.

Raymond nodded. 'It will depend on how heavily modified the buildings are. I've looked at some photos, and it's not looking promising.'

'Where else?' Kingston asked.

'The town hall, like you said. That's open all week.' Raymond tapped his pen against the notepad. 'The Highlander Hotel. The Ballarat Railway Station. I feel the area we need to look at isn't open to the public. We won't know until we get there.'

'Where else?' Sydney asked.

'The Mechanics' Institute will be open for tours in three days,' Raymond said. 'I think a lot of that building is still original. There are several churches, including the one across the road. We should do them tomorrow. Two other hotels still exist: The Unicorn and Craig's. I think one of them has been heavily modified.'

'Which one?'

'The Unicorn,' Raymond said. 'It's sitting empty. We could probably break in, but my research shows that the area we want to look at might have been demolished. We'd need to go there and see.'

'That's a lot of keys we're looking for,' Sydney said.

'I haven't even mentioned the old Post Office yet,' Raymond said. 'It's open the same day as the School of Mines. We should try that one in the morning and then spend the afternoon at the School of Mines.'

'Is everything central?' Kingston asked.

'Central enough. We could probably walk between them if that's what you're asking.'

'It is.' Kingston frowned and tapped a day on the plan. 'What's that?'

'Oh.' Raymond smiled and shrugged. 'Sovereign Hill.'

'There are keys there?'

'No. Sydney and I want to go, that's all. And we could do with a day off.'

Kingston looked confused. 'Why do you want to go to Sovereign Hill?'

'We want to see what life was like when Redmond came to Australia,' Sydney said.

'Smelly,' Kingston answered. 'Although I doubt they will have recreated that aspect.'

Sydney wanted to ask what he meant by that. He probably meant the horse manure from all the horses. She shrugged it off and surveyed Raymond's plan. One day had nothing scheduled. 'There's a day free.'

'I'm still studying the journal,' Raymond admitted. 'That's in case I find any other possible keys.'

'If we don't, we can use that day to enjoy the city,' Kingston said. 'We'll look at the Heritage Week schedule and see what to do.'

'That sounds great,' Sydney said.

'As for the rest of today, we should settle in,' Kingston said. 'And, Raymond, walk us through where we need to look at each building.'

'I'll brief you tonight over dinner,' Raymond promised.

CHAPTER 5

'NO,' Raymond said, reaching for the bottle in Kingston's hand. 'No, no, no. You are not putting sauce in there.'

'Why not?' Kingston asked, dodging Raymond's grab and holding the bottle out of reach. 'It'll add a little flavour.'

'There's adding flavour, and there's what you do,' Raymond countered. 'You'll dump the whole bloody bottle in.'

Sydney watched as they danced around in the kitchen area from her spot at the table. Raymond was trying to grab the bottle out of Kingston's hand, who was successfully avoiding him. It was so domestic that Sydney couldn't help but think how cute they were. It was obviously an old argument. She bit her lip to fight the grin.

'Just put the bottle down,' Raymond said, making another lunge for it and missing. 'I'm not letting you ruin this meal.'

'I never ruin meals,' Kingston countered.

'Don't even get me started.'

Sydney couldn't hold it in any longer and laughed. That got their attention, the two seeming to remember that she was there.

'It's seriously no laughing matter,' Raymond pouted.

'I'm sorry, it's just…' Sydney tried to control herself. 'It's so domestic it's adorable.'

Both their eyebrows shot up, the two men exchanging a look. She swore Raymond started to blush while Kingston averted his eyes. She wondered if anyone had called their relationship adorable before.

'Serious question,' Raymond said, pushing his glasses back up his nose from where they had slipped down. 'Sydney, how much sauce do you deem to be appropriate?'

'Well, that depends,' Sydney said. 'Just having it as a side dish is enough for most meals.'

Raymond looked smug and gave Kingston a pointed look.

'But…' Kingston pressed.

Sydney shrugged. 'If it's chips, you drown them.'

It was Kingston's turn to look smug.

'Okay, fair enough,' Raymond said. 'Chips are the only exception, though.'

Sydney frowned as Kingston uncapped the bottle and took a swig of sauce directly from it. She was about to question it when he put the cap back on and set the bottle down.

'I propose a truce,' Kingston said. 'The sauce will go on the side of the dish.'

'Good,' Raymond said, turning to face him.

Kingston gave him a sweet smile. 'Kiss and make up?'

Raymond rolled his eyes but stepped towards him. Sydney, suspicious of Kingston's plan, clapped her hand over her mouth to quieten her giggles. Kingston kissed Raymond firmly, and it was clear it wasn't just on the lips. Straight away, Raymond made a sound of protest and stepped back, sputtering and wiping his mouth.

'What the hell did you do?' Raymond protested. 'Swig the sauce bottle?'

'Perhaps,' Kingston said sweetly.

It was the final straw for Sydney. She burst out laughing. It was perfect revenge, and mentally, she gave Kingston a point for creativity. It wasn't the sort of thing she would do, but it was brilliant. She imagined his mouth still tasted strongly of the sauce.

'First, that is unhygienic,' Raymond chastised. 'Second, ew.'

'It is a bit unhygienic,' Sydney said between her laughs.

Raymond slapped Kingston lightly on the arm and stepped away from him. Kingston mocked being hurt.

'That's domestic violence!' Kingston protested.

'Suck it up,' Raymond said. 'You just kissed me with sauce in your mouth.'

A fresh round of giggles overcame Sydney as Raymond slid into the seat beside her at the table, leaving Kingston to finish preparing their meal. Raymond took his phone out of his pocket. Glancing over, Sydney saw that he was checking his social media. She wondered if he'd posted anything about their location. Jake grilled her about giving away their location, since anyone could follow them. No doubt Raymond had gotten the same lecture.

'I swear if you put sauce in the food, I'm getting takeout,' Raymond said.

'I just said I wouldn't,' Kingston said as he stirred the pan. 'Besides, we're on a budget.'

'You can afford it.'

'So can you.'

Sydney's ears pricked. She thought about Raymond's car and the fact that Kingston was a silent partner in the hotel. She looked over at Kingston.

'I don't mean to pry, but… how much money do you both have?'

Kingston and Raymond exchanged another look. Kingston raised a brow and got a shrug in return. He turned back to Sydney.

'I have a small fortune,' he admitted. 'It's been building up since I first came to Earth. Between investments and good financial decisions, I'm rather comfortable.'

'But wouldn't people get suspicious of you?' she asked.

'I move my money around,' Kingston admitted. 'Every ten years, I transfer it to a different institution or account. I make it look like I'm inheriting it. So far, no one has suspected anything.'

'That's probably smart,' Sydney agreed. 'What sort of investments?'

'The stock market,' Kingston said. 'I lost much of it in the crash in 1929.'

'So did everyone,' Raymond said.

Kingston nodded. 'After that, I've invested much of my money into gold. It holds value more than stocks and shares, although I still hold some of those.'

Sydney nodded, then looked at Raymond. 'What about your family?'

'We're… okay,' Raymond said. 'We're very similar. There are a lot of investments. My grandfather in particular was very good at reading the market and buying into startups during the dot-com era. Invested in two little companies called Apple and Microsoft.'

Sydney's eyes widened. If Raymond's grandfather had invested in those companies early, they would have a lot of money.

'How about crypto?' Kingston asked.

'I've… made some investments,' Raymond admitted. 'Not all of them work out, but a couple did.'

'Which ones?'

'Bitcoin,' Raymond said. 'I bought into that when it was fairly new.'

'How much is your portfolio worth now?'

It was clear Raymond didn't want to answer that. 'Let's just say my mother and I don't need to work. We just do because we'd go nuts if we didn't.'

A *lot* of money, then. It dawned on Sydney that she might be staying with two millionaires. She instantly felt humbled. She thought about her tiny flat in Adelaide and how she had to budget to cover rent, utilities, and meals. Sydney didn't even have a car to maintain. She hadn't gotten around to getting one yet. She was still saving up.

Not that she needed one, as everything was within walking distance of her flat, and she didn't have any hobbies outside of work. All she did was walk between work and home, with the occasional side quest to buy groceries and the odd time the group went out for drinks on a Friday night at the local pub. She really needed a hobby.

Kingston seemed to read her. 'That doesn't change your opinion of us, does it, Miss Madinah?'

'I mean… I didn't realise how successful you both were,' she said. 'I should have guessed. You part own a hotel in the heart of Adelaide, and Raymond has an expensive car and an apartment in the CBD…'

'We try not to flaunt it,' Raymond said, getting up to retrieve three glasses for their drinks. 'Most people don't suspect.'

'Do Jake and Rita know?'

Raymond's and Kingston's eyes met. Raymond shrugged while Kingston frowned.

'I'm not entirely sure,' Kingston admitted. 'I would not be surprised if Rita knew.'

'She does manage your books,' Raymond said.

'Not all of them,' Kingston said. 'Only the business-related ones.'

'So I might be the only one that knows?' Sydney asked. She felt as if they had entrusted her with another deep secret. She would guard this one as much as she guarded the other. If they wanted people to know, they would have told them themselves.

'What about yourself?' Kingston asked as he stirred the pan. It was a stir-fry with honey sauce. Not something you wanted tomato sauce in.

'I'm trying to save up,' Sydney said. 'I rarely have much left over after rent and bills.'

'You live in the CBD, don't you?' Raymond asked.

'Just on the outskirts,' Sydney said. 'Walking distance from the hotel.'

'Saves on parking.'

'That's why I chose it. I was fortunate to find it when I did.'

'Big?'

She shook her head. 'It's three rooms. Bedroom, combined bathroom/laundry, and a combined kitchen/living room.'

'All you need.'

'Considering I spend very little time there.'

Raymond frowned. 'How come?'

'Work,' she said. 'My hours are long, remember? It's part of being a hotel manager.'

'But you'd have time off,' he said. 'Weekends.'

'I spend those at home,' she admitted. 'I catch up on TV and read.'

'Got a favourite show at the moment?'

'A few,' she said. 'They're all between seasons. I like romantic comedies and just comedies in general.'

'I don't watch a lot of TV, so I wouldn't know what's on,' Raymond admitted. 'Between work and the journals, I don't have much free time.'

'This is done,' Kingston said, taking the pan off the stove.

Raymond fetched three plates, and Sydney felt useless as they served everything. She'd insist on cooking tomorrow. They sat around the small dining table. It had four seats but was a squeeze with just the three. Sydney didn't know how many more people would fit there. She watched as Kingston drowned his meal in tomato sauce, Raymond glaring at him and gently inching his plate further away from Kingston's.

'How long has the sauce thing been going on?' Sydney asked.

'Forever,' Raymond said.

'It's a preference,' Kingston said.

'Is it because you're an alien?' Sydney asked.

Kingston looked uncomfortable. 'I prefer the term "immigrant".'

Sydney made a note of that. 'What was the food on your planet like?'

'Processed. Very heavily processed.' Kingston sighed, stirring the sauce into his meal. 'The environment was destroyed long before I was born. You could no longer grow crops, fruit, or vegetables. Our livestock was on the verge of extinction. Everything we ate was fabricated. Being part of the elite meant we had a superior product. They tried to infuse it with taste. The common people had more bland meals.'

'It must have been amazing tasting actual food for the first time,' Raymond said.

'It was an apple,' Kingston said. 'That was the first thing I ever had. My father handed it to me so casually. He asked if I was hungry, and when I said I was, he took it from his pocket. I had tasted nothing like it.'

'And now you drown everything in tomato sauce,' Raymond chastised. 'Which destroys the taste.'

'Tomato sauce is delicious.'

'Mm-hm.'

Sydney smiled, taking a bite out of her meal. She took a moment to savour the taste. She'd never really thought about how good they had it on Earth. Kingston's planet sounded horrid. She still couldn't wrap her mind around the fact that one of her ancestors had come from that planet. She wondered which one. Sydney would have to track her family tree.

'So your planet was polluted,' Raymond said between bites.

'Lierdan went through an industrial age much like Earth,' Kingston said. 'They had the warning signs but ignored them in order to continue to profit. Then genetic modification became popular, and soon every child was being modified, which extended our life expectancy.'

'Which led to overpopulation,' Sydney said.

'We had a strict one-child policy which had existed for several generations,' Kingston said. He frowned. 'There was also forced sterilisation amongst the lower class. My mother very much opposed that.'

'They sterilised people?' Raymond asked.

'At birth.'

'That's sick.'

'It has happened here,' Kingston pointed out. 'Look into your history.'

'It doesn't happen anymore,' Sydney defended.

'That you are aware of.'

Raymond met Sydney's gaze. Sydney could see that Raymond was thinking the same thing as her. The need to defend their planet while thinking how barbaric Kingston's planet was. Sydney was glad she never had to go there. Marcus had wanted to take her, but it sounded like a horrible place to live.

'If you had to choose,' Raymond asked, 'between here and Lierdan–'

'Here,' Kingston cut in. 'I don't understand why anyone would want to return there.'

'Marcus did,' Sydney reminded him.

'He had a very rose-coloured view of the planet,' Kingston said. 'We didn't have to work there. Those that did chose to do so. Primarily out of sheer boredom.'

'What sort of jobs?'

'Teaching. Science. Mathematics. Technology.'

'So basically STEM,' Raymond said.

'Very much so.'

'Do the lower class work?' Sydney asked.

'Waste disposal and manual labour,' Kingston said. 'They often received only the most basic of educations. Enough for them to work.'

'Please tell me there was no child labour,' Raymond said.

'There was no child labour,' Kingston said. 'There were more than enough adults.'

They ate in silence for a while, Sydney eyeing Kingston's meal, confused by how he ate it with so much tomato sauce. She remembered how Jake had commented about Kingston cooking with a lot of sauce. Had Kingston ever subjected Rita to any meals with it?

'Did your planet have coffee?' Sydney asked.

'We had other stimulants,' Kingston explained. 'They were taken in pill form.'

'You were druggies,' Raymond observed.

'No.' Kingston narrowed his eyes. 'They had the same effect as coffee and energy drinks, only they were completely manufactured. No natural stimulants remained.'

'Did you ever have anything like coffee?' Sydney asked.

Kingston thought for a while. 'No, I don't believe we did. Maybe once, but I certainly do not remember reading about it.'

'I'm guessing you had the best education,' Raymond said.

'I was part of the elite. Of course I did.'

'What job did you have?' Sydney asked.

'I didn't have one formally,' Kingston said. 'I managed my father's finances and business investments on Lierdan, particularly in his absence.'

'What was your planet like?' Sydney asked. 'Did it have continents and oceans like Earth?'

'It did once,' Kingston said. 'It all became one giant city. The Elites lived at the top. The poorer you were, the further down you lived.'

'Sounds like Coruscant from *Star Wars*,' Raymond observed.

'Not far from the truth, actually,' Kingston said. 'Sometimes I wonder if George Lucas knew about our world.'

'I think giant cities are quite popular in dystopian science fiction,' Sydney said.

'Probably how this planet will end up,' Raymond said.

'It is on a similar path,' Kingston said. 'We discovered genetic modification early. That sort of thing is outlawed here.'

'I bet people are trying it.'

'No doubt.'

'So I'm guessing the poor people had no sunlight,' Sydney said.

'None at all,' Kingston confirmed. 'There was limited sunlight towards the top as well. The planet was covered in a shroud of smog.'

'How did you breathe?'

'Recycled air,' Kingston said. 'The air filters amongst the elite were near perfect. The less money you had, the poorer the quality. That's why disease was so rampant amongst the poor.'

'Wouldn't that control the population?' Raymond asked. Sydney shot him a glare at the insinuation of population control. He raised a hand in defence. 'I'm just throwing it out there.'

'Yes, it did,' Kingston said. 'That's why they did not try to prevent it.'

'But wouldn't it spread?' Sydney asked. 'You all live on the same planet. Surely the elite were affected by the disease as well.'

'Better doctors,' Kingston said. 'Limited mingling with the "undesirables".'

'Except for your mother,' Raymond said.

'Yes.' Kingston sighed. 'She disagreed with the stance taken by the elite. She felt we should look out for those less fortunate. That is why she tried to help as many as she could. Sadly, it cost her her life.'

'What was your stance?' Sydney asked. She couldn't imagine Kingston choosing to ignore the poor.

'I supported my mother,' Kingston said. 'But I will admit I was far more interested in my father's endeavours.'

'Coming to Earth.'

Kingston nodded. 'He was a businessman – a very successful one. Many looked up to him. When the time came to choose who would come to Earth, he was among the first selected. He established himself quickly. When Australia was discovered, and the plan came forth to centralise the portal network, he was chosen to be Protector because of his success.'

'So he came to Australia intending to become Protector,' Sydney said.

'Just as Redmond was to be the Keeper.' Kingston sipped from his drink. 'Redmond was a lawyer on our planet. One of the most respected. He was a very, very smart man, so it made sense for him to be chosen as Keeper.'

'But you didn't know about Kian,' Raymond pressed.

'Nothing,' Kingston confirmed. 'They kept the Overseer quiet. All I knew was that he was one of the first to set foot on this planet. He was the one who established the portal network and the one who saw about it becoming centralised.'

'Is it possible there are portals that aren't centralised?' Sydney asked.

'You'd have to ask Kian,' Kingston said. 'From the way it was explained to me, no. Something about them being overridden, so they all link back to the doorway in Adelaide.'

'The door between Adelaide and Melbourne exists,' Raymond pointed out. 'If that one can exist, then odds are that others exist.'

'It also doesn't require a key,' Sydney said, thinking back to the door in question. She'd never seen a key in the lock.

'True,' Kingston said. 'That is true.'

They finished their meal, Sydney insisting that they let her help them wash up. They'd done the cooking, so it was only fair that she helped with the cleaning. Afterwards, they retired to their rooms, Sydney curling up on her bed and pulling out a book she'd brought with her to read. It was a book on Redmond Barry. The man fascinated her as much as his successor. She wondered what Raymond would think if he saw her with the book.

She heard a television coming from Kingston and Raymond's room. That wasn't fair. She read a chapter of the book before retiring for the night. It was going to be a long day of walking tomorrow, so she wanted to be rested. She settled into the strange bed, switching off the bedside light. She fell asleep to the mumbling of the distant television.

CHAPTER 6

ST Patrick's Cathedral was a beautiful bluestone building surrounded by a large garden and a green wrought-iron fence. It was a tall building but had no steeple. Raymond had expected a steeple. That would have been the logical place to hide the key, but he knew from the journal that it wasn't the location.

The heritage week tours began at nine a.m., so they'd had breakfast and watched some morning news broadcasts until the time to leave rolled around. It had been a short walk across the road and down the block to find where a scattering of people were waiting for the event to start. The heavy doors were still closed when they arrived. Raymond checked the program and noted that there were both guided and self-guided tours available.

Not wanting to look out of place, he'd brought a camera with him. He'd never been much of a photographer; he'd never had a firm grasp on how to balance the light. Andrew had taught him a few things back when they were at university. Andrew was a hobby photographer who loved still life and portraits. Tanya was his favourite model, and Raymond had allowed himself to be Andrew's 'inspiration' for a while. The attention had been off-putting. Raymond was used to being ignored.

The camera had been a gift from Andrew before they embarked on their Europe trip. He'd made Raymond promise to document his travels and share a photo journal when he returned. Admittedly, Raymond had forgotten to take the camera with him on some of their adventures. He hoped Andrew didn't mind.

'Should I have brought a camera?' Sydney eyed his little camera bag.

'Most people use their phones,' Raymond reminded her.

'We should ask before we take any photos,' Kingston said.

'The program notes it as a photo opportunity,' Raymond assured him. 'But yeah, we probably should double-check.'

Other waiting people also had cameras, so he wasn't too worried. Some people were already photographing the exterior of the building. Raymond took his camera out and photographed the heavy doors. He wouldn't want to get through them in a hurry. He glanced up at the sky and noted it was a perfect shade of blue. The weather was perfect despite being winter. The only reminder was the chilly breeze that made him glad he'd brought his jacket.

'Nice day,' Kingston commented.

'It is,' Raymond agreed. 'Hopefully, it stays this way.'

'I think it's supposed to be a pleasant week,' Sydney said. 'People online commented that it usually rains when something is on in Ballarat.'

'Murphy's Law,' Raymond said.

'Hm?' Kingston said.

Raymond looked at him. 'You've never heard of Murphy's Law?'

'If something can go wrong, it will,' Sydney explained.

'That's a pessimistic outlook on life,' Kingston said.

'True, though,' Raymond said.

'It seems a bit that way with you two,' Sydney said.

'It is true of our first meeting,' Kingston said. 'We were attacked on the way home.'

Sydney's eyes widened. 'Bad?'

'We took care of it,' Raymond said, not wanting to drag the memory back up. He still felt ashamed of how he'd reacted that day. He'd been forced to kill someone for the first time and had gone into shock.

Sydney nodded, her eyes narrowed. It was clear she would dig into that later.

They looked up as the cathedral doors opened and a few people emerged. Several, no doubt the tour guides, wore Heritage Week shirts. The other people waiting around moved towards them. Raymond hung back. He wanted the tour guides occupied before he began poking around in the building.

'Where are we looking?' Kingston asked, pressing into Raymond's side.

'Near the entrance,' Raymond said. 'It should be low to the ground.'

'Is it a panel or…?' Sydney pressed.

'Place like this, I'm guessing a brick.'

'Stone,' Kingston corrected.

'You know what I mean.'

They wandered in behind the crowd, the heavy air weighing on Raymond the second he stepped into the cathedral. There was always something grand about places like this. He'd never been religious, but most old holy buildings left him with a sense of awe. They were beautiful in their architecture, and this one was no different.

He was instantly drawn to the stained-glass windows. They looked like little from the outside, but inside they were amazing. He snapped a picture as he followed Sydney and Kingston around the building. They followed a tour group, Raymond absently listening as the tour guide explained the building's heritage. His ears pricked when he heard the mention of renovations. That was never a good sign.

He took several photos, knowing that Andrew would be interested in them. Raymond would have to upload a few of them to his Instagram for him. He rarely posted much on there unless he thought Andrew would like it.

They eventually made their way back to the entrance, Raymond searching for the symbol on the stone. Further into the building, someone played the pipe organ. It was a cheery hymn that sounded lovely in the open space. He frowned as he saw that there had indeed been work done on the building. Everything looked fresh and clean. They did several laps at the entrance. Raymond felt his heart sink; they would not find what they were looking for.

'I think it's gone,' Kingston said, saying what Raymond had been thinking.

'They probably thought it was a loose brick and fixed it,' Sydney said. 'Or it's hidden behind something.'

'It's definitely not here,' Raymond said. It was a gut feeling. He couldn't put his finger on it; he just knew. It was like doing a wordsearch and realising the word wasn't in the puzzle. You just knew.

This wasn't how he'd wanted to start the day. He'd had high hopes of them finding the key. Renovation was proving to be as much of a problem as demolition. He had a list of Ballarat buildings that no longer existed, meaning their keys were long gone. It was just like Melbourne and Adelaide. The belief in 'modernisation' that had been prevalent in the sixties and seventies had done serious damage to his job.

'One last lap,' Kingston said.

It was pointless but Raymond went with it. A few of the other visitors shot them strange looks. He guessed it would look odd for them to focus on just the entrance when the rest of the building was more photogenic. After the lap, he knew it wasn't there. They headed back outside into the cool air, Raymond letting out the breath he had been holding. He felt deflated.

'That's unfortunate,' Kingston said.

'Is this what it's normally like?' Sydney asked.

'You mean disappointing?' Raymond asked.

She nodded.

'Yeah.' He gestured back towards the building as they walked to the main gate. 'Places like this get renovated, and when they do the renovation, they will often move or destroy the location without knowing it.'

'It's either that, or they destroy the building in its entirety,' Kingston said. 'We needed to break the code several decades ago before the demolition boom.'

'My great-grandfather did,' Raymond reminded him.

Guilt flashed across Kingston's face. He still blamed himself for what had happened to Raymond's great-grandfather. While they were on vacation, Raymond gently quizzed him about what had happened. They had been at Werribee Manor when a gang had set upon them. Raymond's great-grandfather had somehow worked out which door was the portal in the building and unlocked it with the key, shoving Kingston through it and locking it behind him. By the time Kingston had taken a taxi back to the location, it had burned to the ground, and his team was gone.

Raymond knew his mother blamed Kingston, but after hearing the story, he realised Kingston wasn't at fault. Raymond didn't know why his great-grandparents hadn't just followed Kingston through the portal. Something else must have been going on, or they had tried to distract the attackers. Raymond wondered if his great-grandfather had known Kingston was an alien.

'How far away is the next location?' Sydney asked.

'It's a short walk up Sturt Street,' Raymond said.

'How many places do you intend to visit today?' Kingston asked.

'Four in total,' Raymond said. 'All churches.'

'Then onwards we go.'

It was a simple yet pleasant walk to St Peter's Anglican Church. They arrived to find the building open and people walking in and out. In terms of size, the church was smaller than the cathedral, but unlike the cathedral, it had a tower. Like St Patrick's, it was made of bluestone and surrounded by a green wrought-iron fence. Perhaps that was the fashion in Ballarat. He wondered where they had sourced the bluestone from.

Eyeing the tower, Raymond noted it was a bell tower. Would they ring the bells for Heritage Week? A greeter at the gate handed out pamphlets, so they each took one. It was a self-guided tour of the church, including its history and highlights. He skimmed it and found a reference to the bells, so his assumption was correct.

The feel inside the church was more comforting than grand. It had a welcoming air. People were inside, taking photos of the stained-glass windows and the pulpit. The pews looked like they dated back to when the church had opened. Raymond could imagine people in their Sunday finest sitting on those seats.

'Where?' Kingston asked in a hushed voice.

'Redmond is very fond of entryways,' Raymond answered.

'We should probably look around first,' Sydney said.

Kingston and Raymond nodded their agreement, and Raymond took out his camera again. He snapped a few photos of the windows. He was glad the sun shone as it made the windows come to life. The building was indeed smaller, so it would be harder to hide the fact that they were searching for something.

'There is something, though,' Raymond said, looking down at the pamphlet. 'Redmond's journal never mentioned a tower.'

'So it's been modified,' Kingston said.

'It looks old,' Sydney said. She skimmed through the pamphlet. 'Here. The tower was added in 1891.'

'After Redmond died,' Raymond noted.

'And the tower is the entryway,' Kingston said, looking back towards it.

'Which means the entryway has been altered,' Sydney concluded.

Raymond's heart sank. After the disappointment of the cathedral, he'd hoped to have more luck at the Anglican Church. He also couldn't help but notice that the walls inside the church were smooth rather than stone – another bad sign.

'We should still look,' Sydney said. 'There might still be something.'

Raymond nodded, his knuckles white in their grip on his camera. He forced himself to relax, sucking in a deep breath and then letting it out slowly. He took a few more photos as he scanned the area around the entrance, trying to work out where the building's original entrance had been. As Kingston and Sydney walked around, Raymond could see they were studying the building's details.

'I wish I knew more about churches,' Kingston said.

'I don't think that would help us,' Raymond said.

'You'd need to have been here before they changed it,' Sydney agreed. She looked around. 'It is a beautiful church.'

'Most of them are,' Raymond said.

After another lap, Raymond had all but given up hope. He chalked it up to another failure. Odds were that the key had disappeared back in 1891 when it had been modified. Raymond was ready to leave. He snapped another couple of photos to give Andrew, this time of the pews and the pulpit. He started when Sydney grabbed his arm.

'Could that symbol you drew be on edging?' she asked.

'It could be anywhere,' he replied.

She pointed.

Raymond followed her finger, noting she was pointing towards the ground. It took him a moment before he spotted it. It was barely noticeable under a few layers of paint, but it was definitely the symbol, its lines etched like a strange-shaped R. He shot

Kingston a look, walked over to it, and then bent down to pretend to fix his shoe. He pried at the edging, finding it stuck with paint.

Kingston and Sydney shielded him as Raymond removed his switchblade and cut at the paint to loosen it along the grooves. Soon enough, it was free, and Raymond pulled at the edging and found the little groove with the button. It popped open, revealing the tiny space. He fished inside it, fingers finding brass. As he dug out the key, he grinned and sealed the space again. He pocketed his knife and key before standing.

'Got it,' he whispered to them.

'Oh my god,' Sydney breathed.

'An excellent observation,' Kingston praised her. 'Time to leave.'

They did another lap of the church before Raymond put his camera away, the three of them stepping back out into the sunshine. Adrenaline buzzed through Raymond. He'd gone from a major low to a full-blown high. His hopes lifted, and he was excited to get to the next location.

'I can't believe we found it.' Sydney practically bounced towards the gate.

'That's just one,' Raymond reminded her. 'And it might be the only one we find.'

'Don't be a pessimist,' Kingston said. 'You have a long list of locations. There is bound to be at least one more key.'

'Do you have somewhere safe to keep it?' Sydney asked.

'I've found a good hiding spot until we leave,' Kingston said.

He hadn't even told Raymond where he'd hidden the lockbox. Raymond had seen the box and knew it was only a small one. It was big enough to put several keys in but small enough to hide in a corner. Raymond just hoped Kingston didn't dig a hole in the wall to put it in. That would be awkward to explain if it were ever found.

'Do you want it now?' Raymond asked.

'You're the Keeper,' Kingston said. 'I trust you to keep it safe until we return to the hotel.'

Raymond moved things around in his pocket. It had a little space sewn into it where he kept his blade. He slid the key into it then zipped the area up so it wouldn't accidentally come free.

'I'm glad you have it and not me,' Sydney commented. 'I'd be scared to lose it.'

Raymond didn't want to tell her he was the same. The key felt like a lead weight in his pocket, and he became highly aware of his surroundings. They trekked back down Sturt Street, dodging pedestrians and finding it hard to talk over the din of traffic. Ballarat was alive with people. He saw many carrying pamphlets for Heritage Week, but most were not.

'Where to next?' Kingston asked.

'Ebenezer St John's Presbyterian Church,' Raymond said. 'It's a bit of a walk.'

'Easier to drive?'

'We should be fine. It's only about half an hour away if we walk quickly.'

'That's not that far,' Sydney said. 'I've walked further.'

'Ballarat is reminding me of Adelaide,' Kingston said. 'Everything seems to be within walking distance.'

'We've just gotten lucky so far,' Raymond said. 'Some of the locations are scattered a little further apart.'

'We'll deal with them when we come to them.'

Raymond checked to ensure his camera bag was closed then pulled out his phone to bring up the directions to the following location. 'Are you ready?'

'Onwards,' Kingston said.

CHAPTER 7

THEY took in the city's sights on their walk to the church. It was a stark difference between Melbourne and Adelaide. Few buildings seemed to be over two stories, with only the occasional three-story building thrown in. There was an even mix of older and newer buildings, with the newer buildings standing out like a sore thumb. Sydney couldn't help but wonder what the city would have been like when it was first established. It was a gold rush city, but surely the gold had long run out.

Sydney was riding high from finding a key. She'd barely noticed the marking on the edging, and it had shocked her to spot it. She'd been sure she was seeing things. She worried that they'd lose the key somewhere on their walks. It was taking all her willpower not to keep asking Raymond if he still had it.

They discovered a market as they were walking. It was situated outside Central Square, the town mall, along a closed road. They had draped a banner advertising Heritage Week between two buildings, and Sydney could see that much of the merchandise was old-school crafts like woodwork and crochet. They slowed to take everything in. Sydney was half tempted to buy something.

They finally made it to the end of the market. It had been busy, with many people gathered. It must be a novelty to have a market there, only running for Heritage Week and then disappearing, like an old-timey circus coming to town. There was even a jumping castle at one end for the children. She couldn't remember the last time she'd been on a jumping castle. She wished she still could.

'That's the School of Mines,' Raymond said, pointing to a collection of buildings as they passed them. 'The back of it, anyway. The buildings we're looking for are the next street over.'

'Tomorrow,' Sydney said.

'Yes.'

Most of the School of Mines was made of red brick, but the back wall sealed most of it from sight. A large chimney poked out over the top of the wall. Had the building been repurposed from something else? She didn't know much about the school. It was certainly large enough and centrally located in the city. People were walking in and out of a rear entrance.

Given that it was a working university, it made sense that it would only be open on selected days. Her heartbeat quickened. There was bound to be a key there, given Redmond had supposedly been so heavily involved. She'd have to look into it more. Given Ballarat's distance from Melbourne, she wondered how Redmond had become involved with the city.

They finally found themselves at the church. After the previous two churches, this one seemed a little underwhelming. It was still beautiful, but it was significantly smaller. There was no steeple or tower to this church. Nestled between a mixture of modern and older buildings, it wasn't the sort of place you'd expect to find a church.

The doors were open, so they walked in. Like the previous church, a greeter handed them a pamphlet about the building. The inside was much more modest than the last two buildings, but it was still welcoming. Sydney had once visited a church that had made her uncomfortable, but the ones she had been in today had felt like they were embracing her for being there.

'Entrance?' Kingston asked Raymond.

'Entrance,' he confirmed.

There were two buildings – a bluestone building and a brick building. Sydney felt the bluestone building would be where they would have the most luck. Still, they went to the brick building first and looked it over. The red carpet felt soft beneath her feet as they walked the pews, taking in the sights. The stained-glass windows were less elaborate but still as mesmerising as the previous two buildings.

'This all looks original,' Kingston commented as they moved around.

'It does,' Raymond agreed. 'I have a good feeling.'

They finished inspecting the building and moved to the bluestone church next door. This one was larger, with a second floor for pews. It was just as lovely in its own way as the previous buildings. They wandered around, Raymond taking photos to maintain their cover. Fewer people were visiting this church. Where earlier buildings had more than a dozen people, there seemed to be only one other person.

'This place isn't as popular,' Sydney observed.

'It seems less iconic,' Kingston said.

'It's also not on the main street,' Raymond said. 'Fewer people probably pass it during their day and don't think about coming to look inside.'

'That's sad,' Sydney said. 'It's been here just as long.'

They walked down the pews, eventually returning to the entranceway. They tried to keep the greeter out of sight as they inspected the walls, looking for any sign of the symbol. As Kingston had observed, the church appeared to be in its original state. Someone had well cared for it, but it had little work done.

'It's in the corner,' Kingston said, breaking the silence.

He gestured, Sydney spotting the symbol the second he pointed it out. Raymond put his camera back in his bag and headed over to it. He knelt, Sydney watching as he fumbled with the corner. She tried to read his body language, seeing him perk up a little as he opened the hidden box then suddenly slump. Dread filled her as he returned everything to how it was, standing back up.

'What's wrong?' Kingston asked. He must have picked up on Raymond's body language as well.

'Whoever put the key in was in a hurry,' Raymond said, opening his hand and revealing the key.

Sydney gasped as she looked down at the old-fashioned key. The black brass was bent, and she couldn't figure out how they managed it. She didn't think the old keys bent like that. It was right at the business end of the key, which meant there was no way it could go in the lock.

'So we found it, but it's useless,' Sydney said.

'It appears that way,' Kingston agreed.

'At least we found it,' Raymond said, sliding the key into his pocket with a sigh. 'We might be able to try to bend it back.'

'That would risk breaking it,' Kingston said. 'Metal fatigue at the bend location.'

'It's useless anyway,' Raymond said. 'So it couldn't hurt. I'll give it to my grandfather.'

Sydney frowned at that. 'Why him?'

'He took up metalworking as his retirement hobby,' Raymond said. 'It would mean having to go to Bendigo to see him.'

'He lives in Bendigo?'

Raymond nodded. 'My grandparents wanted out of the city and chose Bendigo. They have a little place on the outskirts. Miner's cottage with a large shed that he works out of, making metal sculptures.'

'It is a rather drastic change of profession, going from archivist to metal worker,' Kingston said.

'He's self-taught, too,' Raymond said. There was pride in his voice. 'Well, he watches a lot of YouTube videos. He's part of the local men's shed.'

'Letting him try to fix the key would be the best course of action,' Kingston agreed. 'He has the best chance of repairing it.'

Raymond smiled tightly. 'Bet it doesn't work, anyway.'

'Only one way to find out.'

They headed back outside onto the street. Sydney glanced at her watch and noted that it was lunchtime. Her stomach grumbled as if to rub it in. She looked around and couldn't see any sign of a place to eat where they were. They would need to walk back towards the town centre to find something.

'Lunch?' Kingston asked as if reading her mind.

'I could go for a drink,' Raymond said. Kingston cast him a look, to which Raymond narrowed his eyes in response. 'Not that sort of drink.'

'I was going to say it's too early,' Kingston said.

To be honest, Sydney could go for *that* sort of drink. A nice glass of wine wouldn't go amiss after their morning. Sydney sometimes had a glass of wine after work to decompress. It was one of the few luxuries she afforded herself. A little something to relieve the stress. One functional key was okay, but she'd hoped they'd have at least three by now. She wondered where else Raymond intended to take them that day.

'I say we walk back to Central Square and see what's in the food court,' Raymond said.

'There was a food truck at the market,' Kingston reminded them as they walked.

'Last resort,' Raymond said.

'You're not a food truck fan?' Sydney asked.

Raymond shook his head. 'Not really, no.'

'As Jake would say, Raymond's a food snob,' Kingston teased.

'No, I'm not,' Raymond defended. 'I've just never found a food truck that I've liked.'

'Hot jam doughnuts from most food trucks are nice,' Sydney said.

'If you say so.'

'We definitely need to take you for hot jam doughnuts.'

'I'm pretty sure the food truck we saw at the market didn't have them.'

'That doesn't mean we can't find one.'

Raymond shrugged it off. Kingston chuckled. It surprised Sydney that Raymond didn't enjoy food trucks. She'd heard stories about Melbourne and food truck festivals. Next time there was one, she would insist that they go. She was sure she could get Jake on board with her. Maybe even Kingston, too. She wasn't sure about Rita. She couldn't imagine Rita eating from a food truck.

'Let's just get lunch over with,' Raymond said. 'I have one more church I'd like to go to today.'

'Is it far?' Kingston asked.

'Not really. Everything is pretty central.'

Sydney hoped their luck would be better at the next church.

They found a Gloria Jean's coffee shop at Central Square. Sydney was glad to have some coffee along with her meal. They sat at a small table with leather seats that were cracked and pinched when you sat on them. They ate and people-watched. Central Square proved to be a busy shopping centre. It was only small compared to the centres in Melbourne and Adelaide, but it was well patronised. It was two stories with an escalator in the middle, and two anchor stores surrounded by little stores.

As they ate, Sydney looked out and saw someone with a Myer bag. 'I couldn't help but notice that the Myer building looks heritage.'

'There's no key there,' Raymond said before she could ask.

'You're sure?'

He nodded. 'I checked every location. It was never mentioned.'

'Should we look anyway?' Kingston asked.

'It's probably been heavily renovated,' Raymond said. 'I doubt anything of the interior is original.'

'Which is what you're worried about with many of the buildings,' Sydney said.

He nodded again. 'It's the case with a lot of buildings. They must keep the exterior original, but the interior is fair game.'

'That's kind of sad.' Sydney stirred her coffee with her wooden spoon. 'I imagine they used to have beautiful interiors.'

'You should see some buildings they demolished,' Raymond said. He pulled out his phone, typed something into it, then set it on the table. Sydney looked down and found a picture of a beautiful old building. It was stunning, and Sydney wished she could visit it. 'There wasn't a key there,' Raymond said. 'The building came after Redmond's time.'

Kingston leaned over and looked at it. 'That's the Federal Coffee Palace.'

'You know it?' Sydney asked.

'I went there once,' Kingston said. 'In about 1940, with one of Raymond's ancestors.'

'Of course you did,' Raymond sighed.

'What happened to it?' Sydney asked.

'Demolished in the seventies,' Raymond said. 'You want to know what they replaced it with?'

She nodded.

He returned his phone, typed some more, and showed her a picture of a crude concrete office building. She sucked in a breath, unable to believe they'd knocked down such a beautiful old building to replace it with… that. She hated it. It almost made her want to cry.

'Mind you, they're upgrading it right now,' Raymond said. 'What they intend for it is better than what it was.'

'Why did they knock down so many beautiful old buildings?' Sydney asked.

'Modernisation.' Kingston sipped from his drink. 'They felt that the cities were too old-fashioned and needed to be updated.'

'The original stuff is much better than what they have now.'

'I agree with you,' Kingston said. 'There was a lot of protest at the time, but no one of importance cared for the history.'

'Of course, it makes my job much harder,' Raymond said. 'Nearly every time I find a key location, I look it up, and the building is gone. Ballarat's been the luckiest I've had.'

'That doesn't mean all the keys are there,' Kingston said.

'No, but at least the buildings are,' Raymond said. 'That's a start.'

'The building still standing is a help,' Sydney agreed. 'Were there any Ballarat buildings that were gone?'

'A few,' Raymond said. 'But Ballarat seems to have preserved its history much better than Melbourne.'

'And Adelaide,' Kingston said.

Sydney nodded. She wished she could go back in time, find the people deciding, and talk them out of it. She was sure there were people at the time who had rallied to save the old buildings. She would have joined them in their protests. Sydney was fast discovering that she loved heritage. She'd never paid much attention to it before learning about the portals, but now that she was immersed in it, she found it fascinating.

'There is one thing that makes me curious,' Raymond said. 'And that's Redmond's house.'

'What about it?' Kingston asked.

'I'm certain he had keys hidden there,' Raymond said. 'And that he moved them before he gave the site to the Royal Children's Hospital.'

'He never mentioned it,' Kingston said.

'It happened before you arrived,' Raymond said.

Sydney shook her head, still trying to wrap her mind around the fact that Kingston was over one hundred years old. She didn't know how Raymond was so okay with it. If she'd found out her boyfriend was so old, she wouldn't know how to handle it.

'Was there anything in the journals?' Kingston asked.

'Not that I've found so far,' Raymond said. 'I'm still looking. He'd well and truly hidden the keys when his house was demolished.'

'Was he still alive?' Sydney asked.

Raymond nodded. 'He gave the manor away five years before he died.'

'What about Valetta House?' Kingston asked.

'Haven't even seen it mentioned.'

Sydney looked between them. 'What's Valetta House?'

'It was where Redmond lived when he died,' Raymond said. 'It's been sitting empty for years. My grandfather took me there when I was training to become Keeper.'

'I didn't know that,' Kingston said.

'Between the vandalism and the renovations on it over the years, there's little chance any keys are there,' Raymond said. 'Or if there were, they're long gone.'

'Did George Kingston ever have any keys?' Sydney asked.

Kingston shook his head. 'They were completely Redmond's responsibility. My father was only tasked with guarding the portal and keeping Redmond safe.'

'Until someone took them both out,' Raymond said.

'It does appear that way.'

They finished their coffee and lunch, tidying the table to make it easier for the server to clean. Sydney double-checked she had her purse before standing. Raymond led the way out of the coffee shop. Out of curiosity, they exited Central Square via Myer, finding that it had indeed been modernised. That ruled out the possibility of a key in the building.

They walked down Sturt Street. Sydney took in the buildings as they passed them. Raymond pointed out a few locations they needed to check in the coming days, including the Unicorn Hotel and Mechanics' Institute. Sydney marvelled at the city's history. She could almost imagine the horse-drawn carriages on Sturt Street, waiting outside the historic buildings. She was sure the roads back then would have been sand or gravel, not the concrete they were now.

They reached the bottom of the hill and found a street mall. They had bricked the road to turn it into a pedestrian-only area but seemed to be converting it back to a street. Nearly all the storefronts looked relatively new with their large glass panes. It would be hard to tell if any heritage buildings existed among them. There was decent foot traffic, and most stores were occupied.

'It's not too far from here,' Raymond said. 'It's just up the hill at the end.'

'Where are we going?' Kingston asked.

'St Paul's Anglican Parish,' Redmond said.

'We're covering all the dominations today,' Kingston joked.

'It is a bit that way,' Raymond said with a smile.

They found the church up the hill and around a corner. Sydney was almost surprised when they came upon it. She hadn't expected it to be there. She noted that the pub on the corner nearby also looked old, but when she pointed it out, Raymond shook his head. There was no key there. She wondered if Redmond just had a thing for churches.

Like the previous places they'd visited, they found a greeter at the door handing out pamphlets. There were a few more people at this church. Sydney skimmed through the booklet and was surprised to see a mention of the Eureka Stockade. The miners had met at a location behind the church before their march. She couldn't believe how much history this place had.

'Let me guess,' Kingston said.

'Entrance,' Raymond said before he could finish.

Kingston nodded.

'Maybe Redmond thought the entranceways would change the least if the churches were updated,' Sydney said.

'Or it was the easiest place to hide the keys,' Kingston said.

'The entrances are a little less sanctified than the main building,' Raymond said. 'Maybe he thought it was less sacrilegious to put the keys there.'

'All possible.'

They stepped into the main building and took in the area. It was a decent-sized church; Sydney guessed it could seat a couple of hundred people. Raymond took his camera out to snap some photos, playing the tourist. This church felt warm, like the previous ones, and there was a history in the air. If only the walls could talk.

'You're taking a lot of photos of the windows,' Kingston noted.

'They're the main eye draw,' Raymond said. 'Besides, Andrew will be interested in them.'

'Why?'

'He just finds that sort of thing fascinating.'

Andrew. Sydney frowned, remembering the man from when Raymond had been abducted. He was Raymond's friend from university. Sydney would have loved to have spent more time with him picking his brain about Raymond in his university days, but Andrew and his wife Tanya had gone home once everyone had been confirmed safe.

They walked a lap of the church's interior, taking in everything. Sydney admired the pipe organ built into one wall. No one was playing it, but it was as if she could hear the echoes of its notes in the confines of the church. Raymond snapped a few more pictures before they circled back to the entrance. Almost immediately, Sydney spotted it, simultaneously seeing Kingston grab Raymond by the back of the jacket.

'That's an easy one,' Kingston said.

'I see it,' Raymond said.

The symbol looked like poorly etched ancient graffiti along

the edging. It was out in the open, making it harder to retrieve. Raymond did his trick by pretending to tie his shoe again. Sydney and Kingston crowded up behind him to block the view. Sydney scanned the area, looking back into the church. Someone was watching them. It was an older gentleman sitting on a pew, his cane set in front of him. She gave him an easy smile as the man frowned and looked away.

Abruptly, Raymond stood again, his hand in his pocket.

'Well?' Kingston asked.

'Got it,' Raymond said, putting his camera back into its bag. 'Let's go.'

CHAPTER 8

THEY took their time heading back to the hotel. Raymond's adrenaline slowly eased down. The three keys in his pocket felt heavy. The lack of a key at the cathedral still disappointed him, and the bent key was a mystery to him, but finding two keys in one day was an accomplishment they hadn't yet matched.

They passed many people with pamphlets about Heritage Week. It seemed to have brought the tourists out in droves. The walk back was mostly uphill, and he was feeling it. Melbourne had its hills, but the ones in Ballarat felt steeper and larger. You could get fit just walking the streets of Ballarat. It really worked your calf muscles.

'Does Melbourne ever do something like Heritage Week?' Sydney asked as they passed Central Square again.

'Melbourne Open House,' Raymond said. 'You hear hordes of people in the catacombs of the library when they do.'

'Finding a key during that time would be quite difficult,' Kingston said. 'It is very well attended.'

'There are waiting lists,' Raymond confirmed. 'And lotteries to get on the waiting lists.'

'Oh, wow.' Sydney's eyebrows rose as her eyes widened 'I didn't realise that sort of thing was so popular.'

'People like to see what happens behind the scenes,' Kingston said. 'To look beyond the facade.'

'They should do something like that in Adelaide,' Sydney said. 'I'd love a tour of the town hall.'

'It's nothing remarkable,' Kingston said. 'Although they may have changed it since I was there last.'

'Your half-brother was a politician, wasn't he?' Raymond said.

'Whom I never met, yes.'

'He was premier,' Sydney said. 'A really successful one.'

'He gave women the vote,' Kingston agreed.

'Does it bother you that you never met him?'

'It does.' Kingston frowned, pushing his hands into his jacket pockets. He did that when he was uncomfortable. 'I would have loved to have sat with him and talked about our father. My known existence would have raised too many questions.'

'But you still have his name,' Sydney said.

'We passed it off as a coincidence,' Kingston said. 'We pretended we were distant relatives from Cork. After my father died and the new Barry couldn't break the code, I went to Ireland for a while.'

'To avoid the questions,' Sydney said.

He nodded.

'I'm surprised your Irish accent isn't stronger,' Raymond said. 'Given how many years you spent in Ireland.'

'It can be if I want it to be.'

'What do you mean?'

Kingston gave him a broad smile. 'I was trained in linguistics,' he said in a thick Irish accent.

'Oh God, no,' Raymond said, cringing. 'Don't do that.'

Sydney laughed. 'That's amazing!'

'We adapt our speech pattern to where we are,' Kingston said in his normal voice. 'Although we always had an accent, no matter where we went.'

'What is your native language?' Sydney asked.

'Not far removed from your English,' Kingston said. 'Which is why we could adapt to your language so easily. Lierdan's vocabulary is closer to Latin in regards to pronunciation. The Earth scouts obtained books, and our technology translated them and created training for us to learn to speak the way you do. We can also speak Irish.'

'Which makes sense, given the first portal was in Ireland,' Raymond said.

'Indeed.'

'How did your people find Earth?' Sydney asked.

'That information was classified,' Kingston said. 'I don't think even my father knew. There's a chance that Kian himself does not know.'

'But he's the Overseer,' Raymond said.

'Of the centralisation project,' Kingston said. 'Not of the original settlers.'

'Someone must know,' Sydney said.

'Odds are they're no longer with us,' Kingston said. 'The knowledge of how the portals work was reserved to the highest classification of secrecy. Some people would kill for that knowledge.'

'Considering what they would do just for the keys,' Raymond said, his hand absently going to his pocket. He could feel the outline of the keys in their hiding place. They were jingling slightly against each other and his pocketknife.

He saw Sydney shudder, hugging herself. He frowned at her reaction. Jake had commented that Sydney had tried to save Raymond, but he'd never gotten the full details. He'd have to ask her about it, but it was hard to find an appropriate moment to bring it up. How do you ask someone what they were doing while you were being tortured?

They finally made it back to the hotel. They stepped inside, Raymond's feet telling him he needed to sit down while his throat told him to get a drink. He first headed to the bedroom to put his camera away and remove his shoes. Kingston followed him, gesturing with a hand out. Knowing what he wanted, Raymond took the keys out of his pocket and handed them to him. He frowned as Kingston disappeared out the door and into the bathroom. Why ask for the keys and then go to the toilet?

Raymond wandered back out to the kitchen and opened the fridge to grab a can of soda. Sydney appeared from her room sans purse and shoes. He gestured if she wanted a drink, and she nodded, so he pulled another can out and handed it to her. She thanked him, retreating to the couch and opening it as she sat down.

'We should call and update Jake and Rita on the day,' Kingston said as he rejoined them. He got himself a glass of water.

'Probably a good idea,' Raymond said, joining Sydney on the couch.

He scooted over a little so that Kingston could sit down with them. The couch was big enough for the three of them, but it was a squeeze. Raymond found himself caught in the middle as Kingston took out his phone, dialled a number, placed it on speakerphone, and set it on the coffee table in front of them.

After three rings, it picked up.

'Kingston,' Rita said.

'Good afternoon, Miss Taylor,' Kingston said. 'Any chance you could summon Jake so we can speak to the two of you?'

'Just a second.'

They were put on hold. Raymond realised Kingston had called his office number rather than Rita's private phone. He checked his watch and saw it was still well within working hours. Getting Rita on the office phone when she was working was easier. She ignored her personal phone until after business hours.

The sound of classical piano drifted from the phone. If Raymond had to describe it as anything, it was 'elevator music'. He got fidgety. Kingston rested a hand on his knee after a moment, and looking at him, he saw Kingston silently telling him to calm down. He nodded, resting back against the couch. Raymond had never been a fan of waiting around. He always needed to be doing something.

'Jake would still be working,' Sydney said, looking at her watch. 'He might not get away.'

After a long while, the hold music cut out, and Rita returned to the line.

'I have you on speaker,' she said. 'Jake's here.'

'Hello, all,' Jake chirped. 'How's your holiday?'

'It's not a holiday,' Raymond said.

'It's been productive,' Kingston said.

'So you found some?' Jake said hopefully.

'Three,' Raymond confirmed. 'Although one is damaged.'

'How damaged?'

'Bent in a bad spot.'

'How the hell did that happen?'

'No clue.'

'We will try to have it restored,' Kingston said. 'But yes, we found three out of the four stops today.'

'That's a good hit rate,' Rita said.

'It could also be all we find,' Raymond reminded her.

'Don't be a negative nelly, Ray-Ray.'

Irritation flashed in Raymond. He knew there was nothing malicious behind the nickname. He thought of Rita as an annoying older sister. She certainly teased him like one.

'We plan to attend two places tomorrow,' Kingston said. 'One of them will take some time.'

'Is it big?' Jake asked.

'Big enough.'

'How's Syd holding up?'

'I'm fine,' Sydney said, leaning towards the phone so it could catch her voice. 'There's a lot of walking involved, but I brought good shoes.'

'We all did,' Kingston said.

'We certainly are getting our exercise in,' Raymond said. He shifted his legs a little, feeling them burn slightly. It was more walking than he was used to. He walked around Melbourne when he wanted to go somewhere, but Melbourne was relatively flat. Ballarat had hills.

'How's the weather holding up?' Rita asked.

'It's beautiful,' Sydney said. 'The sun has been shining all day.'

'Send it our way,' Jake said. 'It hasn't stopped raining here.'

'I think your weather will come our way,' Raymond said, thinking of Adelaide's location relative to Ballarat. He hoped they didn't send the rain. He hadn't brought an umbrella and wasn't a fan of them.

'How are things at the hotel?' Kingston asked.

They were met with silence. A thread of dread crept in. Raymond could just imagine Rita and Jake looking at each other, trying to work out how to word things.

'What happened?' There was an edge to Kingston's voice. He'd picked up on it, too.

'We, uh... had an issue overnight,' Jake said.

'What sort of issue?' Sydney asked, sitting up straight in her seat, switching into manager mode.

'Someone smashed several of our front windows.'

'When?' Kingston asked.

'About three a.m. We got them on camera, but they were wearing a balaclava.'

'So, no face.'

'No.'

A sound came from the back of Sydney's throat. 'Maybe I shouldn't have come here,' she said.

Raymond saw the worry and guilt on her face. 'It would have happened anyway,' he said. 'You wouldn't have been able to stop it.'

'But I could handle the clean up,' Sydney said. 'Now the temp has to deal with it.'

'I've got it sorted,' Rita assured her. 'Jake and I handled the police reports.'

'Do you think it's connected to that problem guest?' Kingston asked.

'It might well be,' Jake said. 'The police are looking into that lead.'

'He was threatening to come back,' Sydney said. The guilt on her face was growing. Her whole body looked stiff. 'It was a bad time for me to leave.'

'As I said, we have it handled,' Rita said. 'The windows have already been repaired, and the glass cleaned away.'

'How did they break them?' Kingston asked. 'I thought that glass was reinforced.'

'Crowbar,' Jake said. 'And a lot of effort.'

'They ran away after they did it,' Rita said.

'Do you think they'll be back?' Sydney asked.

'I'm staying tonight just in case,' Jake said. 'Hope you don't mind me taking your couch, Kingston.'

'It is fine,' Kingston said. 'You're free to use my food. My bed as well.'

'Nah, I'd rather not sleep somewhere where you and Raymond have…'

Raymond bit his lip, glancing at Kingston and seeing his warning look. Better not to tell Jake about the couch. He saw Sydney give them a suspicious look and shrugged it off with a smile. A flicker of realisation flashed through her eyes as they went wide. Beside him, Kingston pressed a finger to his lips, Sydney nodding.

'So, where are you going tomorrow?' Rita asked.

'The old post office and the School of Mines,' Raymond said, glad for the subject change. He didn't want to traumatise Jake. The man had taken the news about Kingston and Raymond well, but

Raymond knew it was probably better to spare him the details. Jake hadn't asked. None of them had. The person who'd probed the most about Raymond and Kingston's relationship had been Raymond's mother.

'I remember you mentioning the School of Mines,' Jake said. 'Didn't you say Redmond had a connection to that place?'

'Yes, he did,' Raymond confirmed. 'We're hoping to find a couple of keys there. It will depend on how much they've renovated the place.'

'Which will probably be a lot,' Rita said. 'Is it still a working school?'

'TAFE,' Raymond confirmed. 'It's part of Federation University.'

'Won't the university still be open?'

'I believe so, which is why they're only open for Heritage Week for one day. We'll try to join the tour groups and use them to see what we can find.'

'Sounds like you've got it all planned out,' Jake said.

'Raymond put together a schedule,' Sydney said.

'It amazes me that you found the location of so many keys over six months when it took you so long just to find the ones we already have,' Rita said.

'It just worked out that way,' Raymond said. 'I'm getting a better grasp on how the code works. And this journal in particular had a lot of keys hidden in it. It was like he tried to compact all the Ballarat keys into one journal.'

'Which makes it easier for you,' Sydney said.

'A lot easier.'

'Does this mean you will be faster at finding other keys?' Rita asked.

'Not necessarily,' Raymond said. 'Not only do I have to find the code, but I also have to research whether the building still exists. That takes time.'

'And you had plenty of time on your break,' Jake said.

'Exactly.'

'He spent an awful lot of time working on the journal,' Kingston said.

Raymond frowned at the comment and looked at Kingston, seeing a half-exasperated look. Kingston had said nothing about Raymond spending too long on the journal. Raymond would need to press him about it later.

'Well, we've had a great success rate so far,' Sydney said cheerfully. 'Raymond's amazing at what he does.'

'I wouldn't go that far,' Rita said.

Raymond preened a little at the praise from Sydney, looking at her and seeing her grinning at him. He returned the smile even as he ignored Rita's comment. Rita liked to drag him down. Raymond got little praise in his life, so he'd take it where he could get it. His mother certainly didn't praise him. She was consistently critical.

'Let us know if you require any help with the hotel,' Kingston said. 'We can always return if you need us.'

'We've got it covered,' Jake assured him. 'Right, Rita?'

'It was rather simple,' she agreed. 'It was just formalities.'

'Have a good evening,' Kingston said.

The others echoed his goodbyes before they ended the call.

The rest of the night went smoothly. Raymond went over the plans for the next day with them. Sydney asked permission to try out the spa. They reminded her she didn't need permission but gave her space and privacy. Kingston and Raymond curled up on the couch to watch television while drinking celebration beer. They limited themselves, intent not to get drunk.

After Sydney rejoined them, they prepared dinner, Sydney insisting that she do the cooking that night. They helped her, and soon they had a meat and vegetable meal, sided with some wine.

After they'd eaten and cleaned up, they filled in the evening talking. Kingston and Sydney talked about the hotel while Raymond listened in.

Finally, it got late, so they retired to their bedrooms. Raymond got ready for bed, his feet still hurting slightly from the walking. He was looking forward to climbing into bed and resting. The adrenaline had long worn off, leaving him exhausted. Knowing he had another long day of walking ahead made him feel even more tired.

'You haven't noticed yet, have you?' Kingston said, breaking his silence as he turned down the bed.

'Noticed what?' Raymond asked as he pulled on his sleeping shirt.

'Sydney's crush on you.'

Raymond stopped dead. He ran through all his interactions with Sydney and tried to figure out what Kingston was talking about. Nothing jumped out at him. 'No, she doesn't.'

Kingston gave him a knowing smile as he climbed into bed.

'You're delusional,' Raymond concluded.

Kingston shook his head as he settled in. Raymond finished dressing and turned off the overhead light, leaving the room lit only by the bedside lamps. He joined Kingston in bed and frowned as he saw that same look on his face.

'She doesn't have a thing for me,' Raymond argued.

'I think she used to like both of us once,' Kingston said. 'But she seems to have settled on you.'

'Sydney is strictly professional,' Raymond said. 'She's just friendly.'

'She's smitten.'

'I think you're confusing me for Rita and Sydney for Jake.'

'It is much like that, yes,' Kingston said. 'Complete with you being oblivious.'

Rita was oblivious to Jake's feelings. That much was true. But

Raymond didn't think Sydney had a thing for him. There were just no clues. He could remember how Andrew and Tanya had acted around him when they had been wooing him. Sydney was doing nothing like that.

'What makes you even think that?' Raymond asked as he wiggled between the sheets. The bed was soft, and the sheets were welcome after a long day of walking.

Kingston curled into him, tangling their feet together. Kingston's cold feet were a shock to his system, but Raymond bit his lip to avoid complaining. Kingston draped an arm around Raymond's waist and rested his head against his chest. 'It's the way she looks at you. The way she goes out of her way to speak highly of you.'

'Friends do that,' Raymond said. 'Sydney's a friend.'

'She'd like to be more.'

'I doubt it.'

'Pay attention to her,' Kingston said. 'You'll see it.'

Raymond sighed, sliding his fingers in circles over Kingston's back. 'Are you feeling threatened by her or something?'

'No,' Kingston said. 'I trust you.'

Well, that was something. 'Yet you never trust me when it comes to taking care of myself as the Keeper.'

Kingston huffed. 'You're never going to let that go.'

'You keep locking me up,' Raymond said. 'I don't like being locked up.'

'I hadn't noticed,' Kingston said drily.

'Not to mention you keep locking me up with Mother,' Raymond said. 'I'd rather be locked up with a rabid fox.'

'Why don't you get along with your mother?' Kingston asked.

'You know why,' Raymond said. 'Because she always saw me as an object. A means to an end. She doesn't see me as anything more than a tool.'

'She does care about you,' Kingston said. 'She proved that.'

'No, she was just worried she'd wasted all her hard work on training me,' Raymond said.

'She's your mother.'

'She's an egg donor,' Raymond said bitterly.

Kingston pushed himself up to look at him, concern clouding his eyes. 'Do you really view her like that?'

'She never allowed me to be a child,' Raymond said. 'She trained me from the second I could walk and talk. She isolated me from everyone.'

'Do you resent her?'

'All the damned time.'

Kingston simply nodded, dropping his head back onto Raymond's chest. Raymond couldn't help but wonder what that line of questioning was about. He brought his hand to the back of Kingston's head, gently massaging his scalp. He felt Kingston smile and pull him closer.

'Do you resent your job?' Kingston asked after a while.

'I resent that I didn't get to choose it,' Raymond answered. 'It's a family curse.'

'I wouldn't call it that,' Kingston said. 'Good things do come out of it.'

Raymond was ready to question what, but the answer flashed before he could. Their relationship. 'Yeah, some things do.' He pressed a soft kiss onto the top of Kingston's head, Kingston's hair tickling his face. He could smell Kingson's fruity shampoo. Raymond settled back against the bed, holding Kingston close and closing his eyes.

CHAPTER 9

THE morning brought new opportunities. Sydney had slept well, tired from all the walking the day before. She dressed quickly, her hopes riding high for finding another few keys that day. She felt good after their success the day before. It didn't bother her that one key was damaged and another hadn't been found. Three keys was a great tally.

She practically bounced into the main room, finding she was the first one up. She made herself breakfast, switched the kettle on so they could have coffee, and turned the TV on to catch the news. The weather report stated it would be a colder day. It was still sunny, but there was a cool breeze. They'd need to rug up.

She was buttering her toast when Kingston stepped into the room, brushing his fingers through his damp hair. He must have showered. She'd heard the water in the pipes, but the problem with hotels was that you could never be sure which room the water was servicing.

'Good morning,' she said cheerfully.

'Good morning, Miss Madinah,' Kingston replied, a warm smile spreading across his face. His eyes found the television. 'Anything interesting?'

'Just that we should probably wear jackets or coats today,' she said. 'It's going to be cool.'

'Easily done,' he said. He joined her in the kitchen, taking out two mugs – his and Raymond's, she realised. It was so domestic.

'It's the post office first today, isn't it?' Sydney asked.

Kingston paused for a moment. 'I believe so. And then the School of Mines.'

'I love seeing all the old buildings.' She brought her mug and toast to the table. 'There's so much history here.'

'There is,' he agreed. 'Today's buildings rarely have the same charm as the ones of old.'

'I know, right? Some modern buildings are just glass and concrete monstrosities.'

'There are some that are interesting,' Kingston said. 'Artwork, even.'

'But they just don't have the personality of the old buildings,' Sydney said. 'It's why I love working at the Medina Grand. There's just so much history there. You can practically feel it when you walk in.'

'It is a lovely building,' Kingston said. 'I was pleased when they announced it would be a hotel rather than an office building. Being a hotel suits it.'

'Did you have any say in the decision?'

'No.' Kingston made his toast, sipping on his coffee as he waited. 'I purchased into it after the decision had been made.'

'How long have you been a partner?'

'Since the hotel's early stages,' Kingston said. 'They were reluctant to allow me to join. Money has a way of talking.'

Intrigued, Sydney wondered how much Kingston had sunk into the hotel. It would have had to be overhauled entirely on the inside. Then a thought occurred to her: 'Do you think there's a key in the Medina Grand?'

'I somehow doubt it,' Kingston said. 'It's too close to the portals.'

'So there wouldn't be any at the State Library of Victoria either.'

'Most likely not.'

There was movement in the hallway, and Raymond appeared. His damp hair hung over his forehead. Sydney had to tear her eyes away and forbid thoughts of him washing. Her cheeks flushed as she focused on her breakfast. She had looked long enough to note the sour expression on his face.

'Are you awake yet?' Kingston asked Raymond.

'Getting there,' Raymond said, taking the coffee held out to him. He took a long drink, Sydney watching from the corner of her eye. 'Needed this.'

'Raymond's not a morning person,' Kingston told Sydney.

'I get up when I have to get up,' Raymond said. 'Just doesn't mean I have to like it.'

Sydney smiled. She understood that completely. There had been a period in her teens when she'd never wanted to get out of bed. Her parents had ensured she was always up, and she'd eventually broken the habit. She took another bite of her toast and paid attention to the news, listening for any stories about Adelaide. She doubted there would be, given they were in Victoria.

'Post office this morning, correct?' Kingston asked.

'Yeap.' Raymond grabbed some bread to drop into the toaster. 'Same as yesterday. Everything opens at nine. We do the post office first, giving us more time to explore the School of Mines.'

'You think we'll find more keys there?' Sydney said.

'I'm hoping,' Raymond said. 'Given Redmond's involvement in the school, I hope to find at least a couple. It's all going to come down to how much they have renovated the place.'

'We'll see when we get there,' Kingston said as he joined Sydney at the table.

Not long after, Raymond joined them as well. Sydney had finished her toast by then but stayed sitting at the table to finish her coffee.

She looked out the window that overlooked St Patrick's Cathedral. She wished they had found a key there. It was disappointing that they hadn't, but three keys were better than none. That was a better hit rate than they'd had before now, even if one was bent. If only their luck was always this good.

'Is it far to the Post Office?' Sydney asked.

'Not far,' Raymond said. 'And you saw where the School of Mines was.'

She nodded. 'I hope we find another three keys today.'

'Or we could find none.'

'Optimism, Raymond,' Kingston chastised.

Raymond narrowed his eyes and glared.

It wasn't far to the old Post Office. It was a beautiful cream building, with long ramps leading up to the two doors. The building was now part of the university and had been converted into a gallery for the art students. When they arrived, they found others waiting to get in, and Sydney spotted a notice requesting no photography inside the building. She pointed it out to Raymond, who nodded and kept his camera in its bag.

'I wonder why they don't use it anymore,' Sydney said, looking up at the old building.

'Most likely a financial decision,' Raymond said. 'Might have been worth more to sell it.'

'Most decisions are financial,' Kingston agreed. 'Pity, though.'

'At least it wasn't knocked down,' Sydney said.

They waited until the doors opened. A guide stepped out and offered pamphlets to those entering while reminding them about no photography inside. Sydney took a flyer, finding it filled with the history of the building and a rundown of the exhibition that was currently on display inside.

Upon entering the building, Sydney instantly felt her hopes decline. It was clear that they had renovated it. The space was wide open, so the exhibits could be displayed, and there was nothing to show that it had once been the post office. She let her gaze explore the walls and saw that they were all plasterboard. Even the entrances seemed to have been renovated over the years.

'I have a feeling we won't find anything,' Kingston said softly as they walked the floor.

Raymond flipped through the pamphlet. 'Looks like it was all changed in 2002 when the university acquired the building.'

'We can still look, though, right?' Sydney said. 'There's still a small chance.'

'They change a lot of buildings on the inside, leaving the facade intact,' Kingston said. 'That is our concern with all of the university buildings.'

'What was that about me not being optimistic?' Raymond pressed, nudging Kingston with his elbow.

Kingston simply gave him a tired look.

The exhibition proved to be interesting. It was a photography exhibition themed on the city's heritage. Sydney marvelled at the old photographs of Ballarat, noting the horse-drawn carriages. It surprised her to find that a tram line had once run through the centre of town. There was no sign of it now.

'I wonder how many of these buildings held keys,' Kingston said, studying a photograph of Sturt Street. 'And how many are still there?'

'That one is,' Raymond said, pointing to a building. 'That's the Mechanics' Institute. Tomorrow's target.'

Sydney found the building in question beautiful. She couldn't wait to see the inside but reminded herself that they needed to take it one day at a time. She moved on to the next photograph, which depicted a parade with floats covered in flowers. The pamphlet declared it was related to the Begonia Festival, a major citywide celebration. She made a note to come to visit the next time it was on.

They made two passes around the inside of the building, just to be sure. Everything looked to have been redone. Sydney sighed, her small flame of hope flickering out. She knew Kingston was right – they renovated the interior of the building while leaving the facade. Even the Medina Grand was guilty of that. She very much doubted the treasury building had a pool when it first opened.

'I think we're done here,' Raymond said as they finished the second lap of the room.

'I believe you're right,' Kingston agreed.

Sydney nodded, eyes drifting towards the doorway. Time to move on to the next building.

The walk to the School of Mines was uneventful. They made it in good time and found that the university was a hive of activity. Sydney realised classes must still be in session. People of varying ages walked around, many holding the telltale pamphlet of Heritage Week – another self-guided tour.

At the gate, a gentleman handed them campus maps and eagerly greeted them. He suggested which buildings they should visit. Raymond was interested in the building immediately to the left. Sydney could tell just from how he was looking at it that this would be their first target. Looking at the pamphlet, she could see it was a decent-sized campus, but everything was compacted together.

'Where to?' Kingston asked Raymond.

'The main building,' Raymond said, pointing to the building on their left, just as Sydney had predicted.

A tour group was forming outside, and they joined it. They were led through the building, and it quickly dawned on Sydney that it was another situation like the post office. They had changed the interior of the building. She saw Raymond's face fall as he made the same conclusion. She resisted the urge to reach out and squeeze his hand.

The tour was still fascinating. The tour guide was knowledgeable, giving a history of the school. Her ears pricked at the mention of Redmond Barry and his involvement in the school's formation. She wondered what the tour guide would think if he knew he had a descendant of Redmond standing amongst them. She kept her mouth firmly shut.

Sydney felt her hopes fading as they stepped out of the main building and onto the street again. What if they had changed every building at the university? She looked around and noted that there were a couple more buildings further along that looked to be historic, so she put all her hopes on them.

'We should have lunch,' Kingston said.

'Yeah.' Raymond's tone was flat. She wanted to hug him and assure him that everything would be fine and that they were bound to find another key. She pressed her hands into her sides.

'Where to?' Kingston asked.

'I think the university has a cafeteria,' Raymond said. 'Maybe we can find it.'

Sydney pulled out her university map and studied it, pointing to the spot. 'It's here.'

'Then that's where we'll go,' Kingston said. 'Let's see what the students eat.'

CHAPTER 10

RAYMOND had high hopes for the School of Mines. Given how Redmond had been involved in its establishment, he'd thought they would have uncovered several keys by this point. But after seeing how the interior of the main building had been modified, his hopes dissipated. He felt they would find it at every turn in this place.

The cafeteria was crowded. They waited their turn in the queue, discovering that the university had a wide selection for them to eat. Raymond made his choice and paid then waited for Sydney and Kingston to gather their food before they found a table in the back corner. They settled in to eat, Raymond studying the people around them and trying to guess what each of them was studying.

'I wonder how many are here for Heritage Week,' Kingston said, looking out over the crowd. 'And how many are regular students?'

'I'm guessing the ones with bags are the students,' Raymond said.

'We have bags,' Sydney pointed out.

'A camera bag and a purse,' Raymond said. 'They have backpacks and business bags.'

'We had something like a university on my planet,' Kingston

said, picking at his food. 'Very small classes. You studied the field in which you intended to find work.'

'That's exactly what university is,' Raymond said.

Kingston shot him an irritated glare. 'I did what would constitute as business management on this planet.'

'That would help you with your job,' Sydney said.

'It does,' Kingston agreed. 'I also took a side course in finance. And, of course, language studies. They had a special class for anyone who intended to come to Earth.'

'So you always intended to come,' Sydney said.

Kingston waved his hand in a so-so gesture. 'I had a higher chance of being chosen, as my father was already here. For a long time, I was on the fence. I took it when he told me it would be my last chance to decide.'

'You being the last one through,' Raymond said.

Kingston nodded. 'They sealed the portal home after I left.'

'Except for the key,' Sydney said.

'Kian's key,' Kingston confirmed. 'My going through was the last scheduled opening from my home planet's side. Any future openings would have to come from Earth.'

'From Kian.'

'Given he holds the key, yes.'

'So there were scheduled openings before you arrived,' Raymond said. He hadn't known that.

'Once every three months,' Kingston said. 'At least, Lierdan's months. In Earth time, I think it would be closer to five months. Our planet's orbit was different, but not by much.'

'Huh.' Raymond hadn't even considered the planetary time differences. Just how different was it? Kingston rarely needed as much sleep as Raymond – he was always the last to fall asleep and the first to wake. Raymond would wake some mornings to find Kingston watching him. He wasn't a big fan of that.

'What university did you go to?' Sydney asked Raymond.

'Undergrad at Swinburne, post-grad at Monash,' he said.

Her eyebrows rose. 'You have a post-grad?'

He nodded. 'Needed it to become an archivist.'

'I tried to talk him into doing his masters and a PhD,' Kingston said. 'So I could call him doctor.'

Raymond winced. 'I swear that's a kink of yours.'

Sydney laughed awkwardly, while Kingston looked amused.

'What about you?' Raymond asked Sydney, needing to change the subject.

'Washington State,' she said. 'I got in straight after high school. I applied to a few different colleges, but they were the only one that accepted me.'

'Not your first choice?'

'I wasn't fussy.' She shrugged it off. 'I just wanted to go to America.'

'You're from Brisbane originally, aren't you?' Kingston asked.

She nodded. 'Born and bred. I always wanted to get out of the country, though. My parents encouraged me to live my dream.'

'What did they think of you coming back to Australia?' Raymond asked.

'They were happy, although I think it disappointed them that it wasn't back to Brisbane,' she said. 'I applied to a couple of hotels in Brisbane. I never heard from them.'

'Their loss,' Kingston said. 'Our gain.'

Raymond gave her a warm smile that she returned. He was glad she'd come to them. He couldn't think of their little group without her. Besides, the hotel manager's awareness of the portals made things much easier. They'd debated letting Nicholas in on it, and Raymond had always had his suspicions that the man had known more than he let on, but Nicholas had always kept to himself and insisted that he didn't need to know everything.

They finished their lunch, picked up their things, and threw their rubbish into a nearby bin. As soon as they left the table a group came over to claim it. Back on the main street, Raymond got his bearings, trying to work out where they should try next on their quest.

'Where to?' Kingston asked.

'The courthouse and the jail,' Raymond said.

Sydney looked up. 'The what?'

'Part of this place used to be the courthouse and the jail,' Raymond explained.

'The courthouse would make sense, given Redmond was a judge,' Kingston said.

'I doubt he ever presided there,' Raymond said. 'Even with the miners from the rebellion, they brought them to Melbourne.'

'He still might have had an affinity toward the building,' Kingston said.

'Only one way to find out,' Sydney said hopefully.

They walked around to the courthouse and found it open, with someone giving tours. Raymond surveyed the small size of the group they were in. They would have difficulty separating from the group to search for the key.

When they finally got inside, they found that they had changed the building again. No longer was it a courthouse, but now a theatre. Where the judge had once presided was now a stage, and they had even altered the area where the common folk could sit and watch, turning it into rows of seating.

'Where was it supposed to be?' Sydney whispered to Raymond.

'Behind where the judge sits,' Raymond answered.

'That does not bode well for us,' Kingston said as he eyed the stage.

'No, it doesn't,' Raymond agreed.

As the tour guide explained the building's history, they edged away from the group and towards the stage. Nothing remained of the original interior structure. If there had been a key there, it was long gone.

Raymond wished he could go back in time, find whoever had changed the building, and urge them not to do it. He had a feeling his pleas would have fallen on deaf ears. Progress was progress; if that meant changing history, so be it. He'd had high hopes for Ballarat, and now it looked like their luck the day before had been just that – luck.

'I don't think we're going to find anything here,' Kingston said softly.

'No,' Raymond agreed. 'It's long gone.'

'Maybe someone found it and tucked it away somewhere,' Sydney said.

'I doubt it,' Raymond said. 'It's lost to time. Like always.'

'Don't lose faith yet,' Kingston said. 'Didn't you say there was one more place you wanted to look?'

'The jail,' Raymond said. 'It should be just inside the entrance. I think I saw that the entrance bricks were still standing.'

'So there's a chance,' Sydney said with optimism.

Raymond wished he could share her outlook. They rejoined the tour group and remained for the rest of the tour. Raymond kept looking around, hoping maybe, just maybe, the key was hidden somewhere else in the building. Some of it looked at least a little original. He accepted that the key was long gone when they made it out of the building empty-handed.

'One more chance,' Kingston said. 'Be positive.'

Raymond didn't want to argue with him. He led the way back to the old jail. It was situated next to the courthouse, with red brick walls, towers, and bluestone gates. The heavy green doors were open and inviting, which was an odd thing to think about a jail. What would it have been like before it was modified to become the school?

'Where to?' Kingston asked.

'Inside the courtyard, next to the gate,' Raymond said. 'Right-hand side.'

'Facing inward or outward?' Sydney asked.

'Outward.'

They entered the courtyard and found a few students sitting around. Raymond eased off the path and hopped into the garden to inspect the wall. He had only a rough idea of where the hidden compartment would be. The bricks were weathered, but none stood out, so he moved further in, gazing at each brick and looking for the telltale marking.

Finally, he spotted it. His spirits lifted. He knelt, fingers tracing around the edges of the brick until he found the little impression. He pressed into it and felt it click. The compartment sprung open. With deft fingers, he searched the space and grinned as his fingers closed around the brass.

'I don't think you're supposed to be in the garden.'

Raymond jumped at the voice, quickly shutting the compartment and pocketing the key as he heard Kingston answer.

'We're just looking for a photograph spot,' Kingston said. 'Something more organic.'

Raymond whipped his camera out of its bag. He stepped out of the garden and found a well-dressed man standing there. He was rather nondescript, aside from his tailored suit and neat tie. He looked like he'd just stepped out of a meeting, with fashionable glasses on the end of his nose and a cane in one hand.

'It didn't really work,' Raymond said as he stepped back onto the courtyard bricks. 'The angle is all wrong.'

'You'd be better off from the other side of the courtyard,' the gentleman said. He ran his gaze over them. 'Are you here for Heritage Week?'

'Yes, we are,' Sydney answered. 'We're from out of town.'

'I'm here for the week as well,' the man said. 'I've always wanted to inspect the buildings.'

He was very well spoken. He reminded Raymond a little of Kingston with how he pronounced every word perfectly. Raymond couldn't place his accent. It was so faint that it made it impossible to tell what it was.

'You've never seen them before?' Sydney asked. She was looking at him like she had seen him somewhere before. Raymond would have to press her on it.

'Not from the inside. I've passed them many times but never seen the interior,' the man said. He nodded. 'John Smith.'

'Sydney Madinah,' Sydney said.

Raymond hesitated, unsure whether he wanted to divulge information so freely to a stranger. He glanced at Kingston and saw him nod. 'Raymond Barry.'

'Hm. Like Redmond Barry,' John said.

'It is similar,' Raymond admitted. He definitely would not tell this man that Redmond was his ancestor and that he was named after him.

'Kingston,' Kingston said.

The man seemed to wait.

'Just Kingston,' Kingston reiterated.

'A good name,' John said.

'And yours is quite common,' Kingston said.

Raymond winced. The way he said that sounded rude, but John didn't seem to mind.

'It has its uses,' John said with a tight smile. 'I'm a very hard man to search.'

'There must be a million search results,' Sydney said.

'And nearly all of them are not me,' John confirmed.

Raymond couldn't help but be curious. It was an interesting way of looking at things. Most people who researched themselves wanted to be found. This man seemed to be the opposite, wearing his anonymity like a badge. Raymond could see the uses for that. He wanted to blend into the shadows. The fewer people who knew about him, the safer he was. The same went for Kingston.

'That must make it hard if you're in business,' Sydney said. 'People wouldn't find your profile.'

'I don't really use social media,' John admitted. 'I browse it. I'm not really much of a poster.'

He was like Raymond. He'd happily browse Tanya and Andrew's pages, but his page was almost empty. It was part of the 'wanting to keep a low profile' thing. His mother and grandfather had drilled that into him during his training. He couldn't be internet famous even if he wanted to. It would paint a larger target on himself than he already had.

'So you're visiting the different sites as well,' Kingston said. 'Seen any interesting ones?'

'The town hall,' John said. 'I pass it every day, and now I've been inside.'

'We plan on going there,' Sydney said.

Raymond mentally told her to stop giving away their game plan. They didn't know this man. He seemed innocent enough, but they didn't need to broadcast their intentions in case someone was listening. Sydney's problem had always been that she was too quick to trust. That had happened with Marcus and Raymond knew all too well how that turned out.

'You don't seem dressed for walking,' Raymond pointed out, looking over John's attire.

'I have a meeting this afternoon,' the man said. 'I thought I'd visit here and then go straight there.'

That made sense. It certainly explained the suit.

'What do you do?' Kingston asked.

'I'd rather not divulge too much,' John said. 'I'm sure you understand.'

'Completely,' Kingston said. Raymond glanced at him, noting the tone of his voice. There was distrust there. Raymond and Kingston were on the same page.

'I should leave you to it,' John said with a smile. 'I hope you find what you're looking for.'

Raymond's ears pricked at that.

'Your photos, I mean,' John clarified. 'Again, I suggest trying from the other side of the courtyard.'

'Thanks,' Raymond said.

John moved away, heading out the gate. Raymond could tell from the way he used his cane that it was for aesthetic purposes only. He wasn't leaning on it and held it loosely in his hand. No limp indicated there was no injury. Raymond also couldn't help but wonder about the strength of his glasses. They were either very weak or, again, for look. There had been no distortion in them.

'He seems nice,' Sydney said.

'Yeah,' Raymond said. 'He does.'

Kingston met his eye. They were definitely on the same page.

'We should be careful who we speak to,' Kingston said.

Sydney looked up. 'Do you distrust everyone?'

'Pretty much,' Raymond said. 'Anyway, I should take a few photos.'

'Maybe you should try his suggestion,' Kingston said.

It couldn't hurt. Raymond headed to the other side of the courtyard and found it *was* a better gate shot. He could also angle things to avoid catching other people in the photo. After snapping a few pictures, he returned to Kingston and Sydney.

'Did you get what you were after?' Kingston asked.

Raymond heard the real question in those words. 'Yeah, I did.'

Sydney smiled. 'Really?'

He nodded. 'We should go.'

'Anywhere else we need to go today?' Kingston asked.

'Not today.'

'Then let us return to the hotel.'

CHAPTER 11

THEY took their time walking back to the hotel. They stopped at Central Square to have a look through the shops. Nothing caught their eye, as everything on sale was exactly what could be found in Melbourne. There didn't seem to be any difference in the pricing, either.

As they rounded the corner off Sturt Street to the hotel, Raymond caught sight of a man leaning against the fence of the church. He was looking up at the hotel through a pair of binoculars. Instantly, Raymond felt a rock form in the pit of his stomach, especially when the man looked up, saw them, and quickly hid the binoculars.

Raymond almost suggested they leave and come back later, but Kingston pressed a hand into the small of his back and gently pushed him towards the hotel. They headed inside and made their way up to their room. When they got there, Raymond took long strides to reach the window that overlooked the front street. Sure enough, the man had his binoculars out and looked up again towards their room.

'He's not very subtle, is he?' Kingston said, practically in Raymond's ear.

'No, he's not,' Raymond said.

'Is that the man?' Sydney asked, joining them.

'We should move away from the window,' Kingston said, pulling at the back of Raymond's jacket.

Raymond dropped onto the couch. Kingston joined him while Sydney perched herself in the chair. Raymond toed off his shoes, his feet throbbing from all the walking. He wasn't used to being on his feet all day. As an archivist, he mostly sat in a chair, scanning documents into the digital archive.

'We should have expected someone,' Kingston said as he removed his shoes. 'I'm surprised it took this long.'

'You thought someone would watch us?' Sydney asked.

'We always have to assume someone is,' Raymond said. 'There are a lot of people who want access.'

'But to sit outside the hotel with a pair of binoculars?' Sydney asked. 'You'd think they'd try to hide it better. The last guy did.'

'You still noticed him,' Raymond reminded her.

'Only because he was there every day,' Sydney said. 'Which was odd.'

'It does mean we have a new admirer,' Kingston said.

'True,' Raymond said. They'd gotten lucky so far. Marcus had been the only person who'd targeted them, and no one had followed them to Europe. But if they were here in Ballarat, someone had followed them here.

'You thought that would happen,' Sydney said. 'After Marcus.'

'We don't know how many people came through the portal,' Kingston said. 'And how many of them would seek to gain access to the portals.'

'What do we do about him?' Sydney asked. 'Do we confront him?'

'No,' Kingston and Raymond said together.

'Never a good idea,' Raymond continued. 'He may be armed.'

'He will already know we've seen him,' Kingston said.

'I think he wants us to know,' Raymond said.

'Which makes him dangerous.'

Raymond nodded his agreement. The man wasn't going out of his way to hide what he was doing. What was curious was that he seemed to know what room they were in. Raymond wondered whether others would call the police on him, perhaps even the hotel staff.

'I think we should contact Jake,' Kingston said.

'He'd know what to do?' Sydney asked.

'Perhaps.'

Kingston took out his phone and hit a speed-dial number. Jake was number three on Kingston's phone. Raymond himself was number one, and Rita was second. He hadn't looked to see if Sydney had made it into the speed dial. He'd have to ask Kingston about it later.

Knowing it was still working hours in Adelaide, Raymond half expected Jake not to pick up. After the fifth ring, he did, his voice hushed.

'Something wrong, Kingston?' Jake asked.

'Yes, as a matter of fact, there is,' Kingston said. 'We have an observer.'

'What?' Raymond heard the alarm in Jake's voice. 'Where?'

'Sitting across the road with a pair of binoculars,' Kingston said. 'He seems to be looking towards our room.'

'Well, that's not suspicious,' Jake deadpanned. 'How long?'

'Since we returned to the hotel. He was not there this morning.'

'Okay.' Raymond could hear Jake thinking. 'I'm not sure what I can do about it from here, though.'

'Is there any way you can hook into the surveillance here?' Raymond asked.

'I doubt it,' Jake said. 'I have enough trouble hacking into the surveillance here in Adelaide. Ballarat is a whole other system. I don't even know which company that hotel uses.'

'Perhaps Rita might know?' Kingston suggested.

'She might,' Jake said. 'I can check with her, but something tells me it will be a company I've never worked with. I'd be starting with a clean slate. It might take me a couple of days to get access, and that's only if she knows the company.'

'Which won't help us.' Kingston met Raymond's eye. Raymond could see what he was thinking. They needed to know right now. In a few days, they will have finished their search of Ballarat and be on their way back to Melbourne.

'I don't think I can help you,' Jake said.

'It was worth a shot,' Raymond said, shrugging.

'Is there anything we can do?' Sydney leaned towards the phone.

'Just stay vigilant,' Jake said. 'Keep an eye on the guy. If he's that obvious, he might try something.'

'I'm armed, as always,' Raymond said.

'I have mace,' Sydney added.

Raymond looked up in surprise. He didn't know that Sydney carried a weapon. Was it a recent development or something she'd picked up while living in New York? Raymond put his money on the latter. He doubted anyone would want to take the subway in New York without a little precaution, especially a woman travelling on her own.

'Perhaps I should invest in a weapon,' Kingston said.

'I can get you a taser when you get back,' Jake said. 'It won't pass any security checkpoints, though.'

'Neither would my switchblade,' Raymond reminded him.

'True.'

'So we can simply keep an eye on our admirer,' Kingston said. 'Has anyone been watching the Medina Grand?'

'Not that I noticed,' Jake said. 'But if you've got a follower, then the likelihood is good that someone could case the place. I'll keep an extra set of eyes on things.'

'Please do,' Kingston said. 'And be wary of Rita. I fear someone might try to abduct her.'

'Trust me; I won't let anything happen to Rita.'

Raymond knew that was the case. Jake had long had a crush on Rita. Raymond couldn't remember when it started, only Rita seemed utterly oblivious, while everyone else knew. Then again, Rita could be fully aware and hiding it. Both things were possible.

'We'll let you get back to work,' Kingston said.

'Be careful,' Jake said.

Kingston hung up the phone, slipping it back into his pocket. 'Not what I had hoped.'

'I kind of expected it,' Raymond admitted. 'As he said, we're a long way from Adelaide. He knows the systems there, while the ones here are completely foreign.'

'The hotel might also have an internal security system,' Sydney said. 'It might not be connected to the internet.'

'Very true,' Kingston said. 'We can't pry without it looking suspicious.'

Raymond settled back against the seat, noting for the first time that Kingston had an arm draped across the back of the couch behind Raymond's shoulders. It was slightly possessive. Raymond shot Kingston a look out of the corner of his eye, but he seemed lost in his thoughts. Raymond absently reached into his pocket, fingers playing with the hidden brass key.

'I should hide the key,' Kingston said, noticing what Raymond was doing. 'Before we lose it.'

Raymond took it out of his pocket and placed it in Kingston's palm. Kingston still hadn't told him where he was storing the keys. Raymond knew where they were in Adelaide: hidden in a locked safe deposit box under a pseudonym at a bank. They were well and truly secured away.

'It's my turn to try the spa,' Kingston said, pushing himself up. He slid his hand across Raymond's shoulders in a gentle yet possessive caress. Raymond smiled faintly at the move.

'Have fun,' Raymond said. 'My turn tomorrow night.'

'Only fair,' Kingston agreed. 'Shame the spa isn't bigger.'

Raymond shrugged it off, watching as Kingston headed down the hallway to their room. When he was gone, Raymond turned back and saw Sydney looking at him. He couldn't quite read her expression. He saw a little fear and put it down to their new observer.

'We'll be fine,' Raymond assured her.

'He's very blatant,' Sydney said. 'He's not even trying to hide the fact he's watching.'

'No, he's not.'

'The last guy disguised himself.'

Raymond nodded, recalling Jake's description of the man in the overcoat and hat. He'd tried to hide that he was watching the hotel. This guy made no secret of what he was doing. That made him more dangerous, and Marcus had been dangerous enough. Raymond's fingers twitched as he remembered Kendra pulling his nails out by the roots. They had grown back, but it had been painful for a long time, and he'd had to avoid infection.

'Not that it was a good disguise,' Sydney said with a frown. 'The coat was out of place for the season.'

'Which made him stand out,' Raymond guessed.

Sydney nodded. 'I noticed him the first day and thought it was weird, but he kept coming back. I'm sure he was connected to Marcus because he disappeared after Marcus…'

She didn't need to finish the sentence. Since Marcus had died. Put a bullet through his own skull. Raymond shuddered at the memory. It still haunted his dreams. He hadn't had to clean up, at least. He'd been more focused on cleaning himself up after being taken and tortured. That job had fallen to Jake, Kingston, and Kian. He felt for Kian. He couldn't imagine having to do that to your own child.

'Let's change the subject,' Raymond said, noting the distant look on Sydney's face and knowing she was lost in her bad memories. He worried she blamed herself for what had happened with Marcus. Marcus had used her, and she hadn't realised it until it was too late.

'Good idea,' she said with a curt nod. 'Tell me about your childhood.'

Raymond snorted. 'Not much to tell, really.'

She tilted her head in question.

'Mother homeschooled me,' Raymond said. 'She'd leave me with mountains of homework while she went to work and expected it to be done by the time she got home.'

'So you self-taught?' Sydney asked.

'Essentially.' He shrugged. 'I mean, she'd explain everything before she left. But I had to work it out for myself if I had questions.'

'Was it safe leaving you home?'

'Probably not. But my father was around for the first few years of my life,' Raymond said. 'I was eight when he left and permanently returned to Europe.'

'What's your father like?'

'A brilliant man. He knows his stuff.'

'I think Jake mentioned he taught dead languages.'

Raymond nodded. 'He was giving a talk here in Australia when he met my mother. He decided to stay and study the local Aboriginal languages. Sometimes I think he regrets staying.'

'Why?'

'They fought more than they agreed,' Raymond said. 'My father is fully aware of my role as Keeper. He never agreed with it. He thought I should be able to make my own choices, but in the end, he caved to my mother.'

Sydney leaned forwards, placing a hand at the base of her neck. 'He tried to stop you from being Keeper?'

'He thought I should have the choice,' Raymond said. 'Of course, under pressure from the Barry family, it was clear that would never happen.'

'Your grandparents.'

Raymond nodded. 'I think my grandfather knew he would make me Keeper much longer than he told anyone.'

Sydney nodded. 'How old were you when he told you?'

'Eighteen,' Raymond answered. 'I officially stepped into the role at twenty-one. That's when I met Kingston.'

'Love at first sight?'

'Attraction,' Raymond confirmed. 'From my side, anyway. He decided to stay in Adelaide because of me, but it took a while to break down his walls.'

'He does seem to be a very private man.'

'He is that.' Raymond looked at her. 'How about you? Fairly normal childhood?'

'Normal enough,' Sydney said. 'My parents are still together and live in Brisbane. They both still work. My mother is in hospitality, and my father is an accountant. They always encouraged me to make my own choices. Within reason, of course.'

'Of course,' he said. 'So you chose to become a hotel manager?'

She nodded. 'We stayed at hotels when we went on holiday every year. I became fascinated with them. There were so many different guests, and I wanted to know how things worked behind the scenes. The manager at one hotel took a liking to me and showed me some secrets. I knew pretty much right then what I wanted to be.'

'But you decided to go to America.'

'I did.' She shrugged. 'Another dream of mine. I wanted to get out of the country, and I had always had my heart set on America. I travelled a little when I wasn't studying. It's a lovely country. There's so much culture there.'

'Going to Europe was the first time I'd ever been out of the country,' Raymond admitted. 'It's amazing to see how other people live. It does make you miss home, though.'

'It does,' she agreed. 'I mainly came back because it was easier to get a job as a hotel manager here, but also because I missed Australia.'

'Do you think you'll ever go back to America?'

'I don't know.' She frowned at that, seeming to consider it for a while. 'The chain I worked at said that when I had some more experience, I would be welcome to come back and work for them.'

'That's a good sign,' he said. 'That means you're efficient at your job.'

'I certainly hope so.'

'Is working at the Medina Grand easier than working in New York?'

'Oh, by miles.' She nodded. 'I was at a major hotel in New York. It had hundreds of rooms. On a busy day, we could have a thousand guests.'

Raymond's eyebrows shot up. He'd never realised that hotels could get that big. 'Seriously?'

She nodded. 'You had to coordinate everyone. There were thousands of employees, although everything had its own hierarchy. I made it to assistant manager.'

'That's pretty good,' Raymond said. 'You must have been really good at your job.'

'I tried to be,' she said. 'I used every opportunity to learn. If something came up, I would jump at the chance to experience it. I rarely said no. Mind you, not having a family at home helped a lot.'

'It means you could do overtime,' Raymond guessed.

She nodded. 'It still does.'

'Do you want a family?'

She paused to think. 'Maybe. I don't know.'

'Mm.' He smiled tightly, thinking of Olivia. She wasn't planned, but he couldn't imagine life without her. He'd promised that, once things settled down, he'd bring her to stay with him on her school holidays. That he'd take her to see the sights of Melbourne. He was aware that he was the absent father in the situation, but he had no intention of being a deadbeat. He'd also accepted that Olivia viewed Andrew as her father and Raymond as her 'bonus dad'.

'Some jobs make it hard to have a family,' Sydney said.

'Agreed.' He looked up. 'My father's job, for example. He travels most of the year. Has for a long time.'

'Was he on break when you went over?'

Raymond nodded. 'Universities were on break, so he didn't have many speaking engagements. That's why he invited me and Kingston over. Kingston has been trying to convince me to go to Ireland for a while.'

'Because he wanted you to see his home?' Sydney asked.

'Partly,' Raymond said. 'Partly because Ireland was where the first portal opened.'

'Did you go there?'

'He's not sure where "there" is,' Raymond admitted. 'We keep meaning to ask Kian if he knows.'

'You don't really know much about the portals, do you?'

Raymond stopped short. She was right. He and Kingston had yet to learn how the portals worked, how they were constructed, or where they had originated. Only that they were alien technology from Kingston's planet. In reality, Raymond and Kingston were just the grunts who looked after the portals. Raymond wondered how much Kian himself knew. He oversaw the centralisation of the portals, but did he understand their actual workings?

'One day, we might find out,' Raymond said. 'Until then, we can just guard them.'

Sydney nodded. 'Because people want to use them for bad reasons. To exploit them to gain power.'

Raymond nodded. 'Well, you can kind of see why.'

'But most of the keys don't work,' Sydney reminded him. 'And the ones that do don't lead anywhere important.'

'So far,' he said. 'We don't know where they lead. That's the problem.'

She set her jaw. 'And that's why you have to find the keys.'

'Exactly. And relocate them somewhere they can't be found.'

'Are they safe?'

'Yeah. They're safe.'

'But what if something happens to you?' she asked. 'Who finds the keys then?'

Raymond winced. 'We'll worry about that if it happens. Which it won't. Not anytime soon.'

CHAPTER 12

AFTER their conversation, Raymond disappeared into his room. Sydney went to her own room to do some reading, but her mind was on the man outside the hotel. What did he want? Why was he here? It was obvious that he was watching them. There were a few rooms that overlooked the front street, but the direction of his binoculars had been towards theirs. Had he not known that they were out?

Sydney reread her page after she realised she had taken none of it in. When she got to the end of it again, she couldn't keep herself focused. Her mind was elsewhere. She set her book down and slipped out of her room, tiptoeing across the apartment to the window. The others were still in their room, and she could faintly hear the television.

Careful not to disturb the blind and give herself away, Sydney looked out onto the darkening street. There was a light breeze ruffling the trees and an almost mist in the air. She couldn't remember there being a prediction of rain, but this rain was so fine it was a creature of its own. Some streetlights were coming on, leaving a halo in the mist.

The man was still on the other side of the street. He was leaning back against the fence of the church, his binoculars tucked under his arm and his phone in his hand. He was typing something. If only she could see his screen. Who was he contacting? She thought of the man who had been watching them during the Marcus ordeal. In that case, the man had someone over him – Marcus. He had been the one giving the orders. Did this new man have someone over him?

The man straightened, slipped his phone into his pocket, and walked along the street. Sydney needed to know where he was going. Her shoes were still on, and her key card was in her pocket. Nothing was stopping her.

Without a second thought, she headed for the door, stepping out into the corridor. She hurried down the stairs and out the front of the hotel. Looking down the road, she spotted the man further down to the right. She crossed the street and walked briskly after him, glad she wasn't wearing heels and very aware of the sound her shoes were making on the pavement.

Everything echoed in the darkening evening. Behind her, the cars on Sturt Street were a constant stream, but as they got further away, they faded into background noise. Few cars came along their street, leaving them alone. She kept her distance from the man, not wanting him to notice her.

Up ahead, he turned the corner. Sydney worried he'd get away, and it took all her willpower not to burst into a run. She reached the end of the street, glancing up at the sign. Dana Street. To her left, she saw the man continuing without stopping. She followed, wishing she'd brought her bag with her so she'd have her mace.

The further they got from the hotel, the more it dawned on her what a bad idea this was. The man could easily overpower her, and she'd left Raymond and Kingston behind. She swallowed down the lump in her throat and resisted the urge to turn around. She wanted to know where the man was going.

There were more cars on this street, although not as many as on Sturt Street. He crossed another road. They were in the business district now, though an old school stood on the other side of the road. Sydney eyed it, wondering if there might be a key inside. Raymond hadn't mentioned any schools for their search. The school looked old enough.

A few people were milling around at the traffic lights at the next intersection. Sydney hung back, watching the man wait for the green man. When it lit up, she waited until he was halfway across before following. They walked past an entrance to a parking garage, and Sydney had to stop sharply as a car exited without stopping for pedestrians.

There was a lot more traffic here. The man continued, never looking back. She didn't know what she'd do if he saw her. The hotel and safety were getting farther and farther away, and the more they did, the more she questioned her actions. Was he heading towards a hotel? Or a house? He mustn't have a car nearby if he was walking this far.

They crossed another street and then another. Sydney frowned as she found herself at the top of an extremely steep hill. She glanced at the cars coming up it and worried about their brakes when they stopped at the roundabout at the top. There was a large brick church on the other side of the road, and as she walked down the hill, she passed a church-like bluestone building that seemed empty. A pity. The building had character and potential.

At the bottom of the hill, the man kept going, crossing another street. Then they passed one of the most hideous buildings she'd seen in a while. It was a modern monstrosity, and Sydney realised it was the police station. At least if something went wrong now, she knew where to run. The man continued. She swore he'd picked up his pace. Was he late to a meeting?

She followed him past the police station and across another street. After waiting for a truck to turn the corner, she realised in horror that he'd disappeared. Sydney quickly stepped across the street and looked around, trying to work out where he had gone. He wasn't walking across the car park, and she swore he hadn't crossed to the other side of the street.

The street in front of her was void of pedestrians, and there was no sign of him anywhere. Panic washed over her as she stopped on top of a bridge. A thought occurred to her, and she leaned over the side, spotting the entrance to a tunnel where a bluestone-lined creek disappeared. There was no way she was going down there.

She'd lost him.

Sydney stepped back into the apartment, carefully closing the door behind her. She tiptoed down the corridor to the living area and was relieved to find that it was empty. She could still hear the television in the far bedroom of Kingston and Raymond. They hadn't noticed she was missing.

Sydney went to her room to take off her shoes and retrieve her phone. She'd made the mistake of leaving it behind while she was gone. At least she'd remembered her key card. It would not have been very pleasant to have had to knock to be let back in. There would have been questions she wasn't prepared to answer.

Suddenly thirsty, she exited her room to go to the fridge and retrieve a soda. She popped open the can and took a long drink then retreated to the couch. Dropping onto it, she set the can on the coffee table and googled for tunnels under Ballarat. She discovered her suspicions were correct. There *was* a network of tunnels under the city. They covered a creek system and wound their way under the CBD.

That must be where the man had disappeared – he must have

entered the tunnels. Had he known she was following him? Where could he have gone? There were several entrances and exits to the tunnels all across the city. Any one of them could have been his destination. It was a lucky dip to work out which one.

Hearing a door open, Sydney looked up and spotted Raymond stepping out of the bedroom. He headed straight for the fridge and stood there for a moment before gathering some things for dinner. Sydney kicked herself. She could have been making them dinner. How would she explain why she hadn't?

Raymond glanced her way then did a double-take as he noticed her. 'Oh, hey, I thought you were in your room.'

'I was,' Sydney said. She picked up her can to show him. 'I needed a drink.'

'Fair enough.' He closed the fridge and grabbed a saucepan. 'Pasta sound good to you?'

'I'll eat anything. I'm starving.'

And she was. Her stomach growled at that moment to drive the point home.

'All the walking, right?' he asked.

'Right.'

She watched as he put the water on to boil and dropped the pasta in. He fetched another saucepan for the sauce. Sydney drank from her can, letting the fizz sit on her tongue a moment before swallowing it down. The reality of what she had done by following the man was slowly sinking in, and her hand trembled ever so slightly. She set the can back down before he could notice.

The door of the bedroom opened again, and Kingston came out, looking greatly refreshed. He'd dressed himself in a shirt and slacks, and regrettably, all the buttons were done up. Did he ever dress down? He always looked immaculate. He'd freshly combed his hair, too. She looked back at Raymond and noted he seemed a little rumpled. His shoulders were tight in his shirt as he worked, and she could see the outline of muscles. What she would give to see him without a shirt.

Kingston stepped up behind Raymond, resting a hand on his hip and gazing over his shoulder. 'Pasta?'

'That's the plan,' Raymond said.

'A fitting choice. We require the carbohydrates after our adventure.'

'No extra sauce.'

'I'll add it afterwards.'

He pressed a kiss onto the back of Raymond's neck, and it was so intimate it made Sydney blush. She'd never had anyone do that to her. A thought of Raymond kissing her like that came unbidden to her mind, and she quickly chased it away. No. Thoughts like that would have her blushing, and they might ask her why. She didn't want to have to explain.

'Ah, Miss Madinah,' Kingston said, spotting her for the first time. 'How have you pulled up after the walk?'

'I'm a little sore, but I'll live,' she said. She was sore, but not from walking with the others. More from her brisk pace to get back to the hotel before they noticed she was missing. The Dana Street hill had been a struggle. She couldn't remember if she'd ever been up a hill that steep before. She hoped they would avoid it while they were hunting for keys.

'How was your spa?' she asked him.

'I wish it were larger,' Kingston said. 'It was a little…'

'Cramped?' she offered.

'Very much so.'

He was right. It was only the size of a regular bath, and Kingston was a tall man. The spa was barely the right size for Sydney. Raymond and Kingston would struggle to fit in the water. But a spa was a spa, no matter how small. Even a foot spa felt good. She could go a foot spa right now for her aching feet. She rotated her ankles, trying to loosen the muscles.

'Are you looking at the news?' he asked her, eyes on her phone.

'Oh, no,' she said. 'I was just looking up interesting facts about Ballarat.'

'Anything good?' Raymond asked.

'Did you know there are tunnels under the city?'

Raymond turned to look back at her. 'Yeah?'

She nodded. 'They covered over a creek system. It stretches across the entire CBD.'

'Interesting,' Kingston said. 'There is a creek in Melbourne that was covered over in much the same way.'

'William's Creek,' Raymond said.

Kingston turned to him. 'You know of it?'

'It used to flood a lot,' Raymond said. 'Redmond mentioned it in his journals. It's on Elizabeth Street. They built over it after Redmond died.'

'After a great flood,' Kingston agreed. 'I believe it is now a stormwater drain.'

'Is it wise to build over creeks?' Sydney asked. 'Where does the water go?'

'Most people don't notice,' Raymond said. 'Only when it rains really badly. I remember my grandfather talking about a flood in Elizabeth Street in the seventies.'

'One I missed,' Kingston said.

'You were in Ireland?' Sydney asked.

'Yes,' he said. 'I spent several decades there before returning to meet Raymond.'

Sydney nodded. It was another reminder of how old Kingston truly was. How did he get away with staying in one place and not ageing? He had to move around. It sounded exhausting. Sydney looked back down at her phone and the map of the tunnel network. She noticed something she hadn't before.

'Ballarat used to have an extra A in it.'

'It did, yes,' Kingston said. 'B-A-L-L-A-A-R-A-T.'

'Huh,' Raymond said. 'When did they change it?'

'I'm not sure,' Kingston said. 'I believe it was recent.'

Sydney looked it up. 'Technically, 1994.'

'Our lifetime,' Raymond said.

'I wonder why they changed it,' Sydney said.

'No doubt to simplify it,' Kingston said. 'It happens in a lot of places.'

'It's an Aboriginal name,' Sydney said, continuing to read the article about it. 'It means "resting place".'

'Not very accurate for why we're here,' joked Raymond. 'We're certainly not resting.'

Sydney smiled.

'Ballarat is a place rich with history,' Kingston said. 'As we are discovering.'

Sydney liked the history. It always hurt her to see it being torn down or modified. She could understand why it bothered Raymond, as it made his job harder. She switched off her phone and set it beside her. Kingson took a seat at the table, leaving Raymond alone to cook. The food was safe from extra sauce.

She contemplated telling them about her adventure but decided against it. She knew they would chastise her. It had been a stupid idea. She was kicking herself. She licked her dry lips, eyes drifting towards the window.

'I'm sure he's still out there,' Kingston said. He must have seen her looking.

'No, he's gone,' Sydney said. 'I looked.'

Kingston frowned, head tilting. He got up and went to the window to peer out. 'You are correct.'

'It would be stupid to stay all night,' Raymond said. 'We're not going anywhere.'

'I had thought he would stay later. We might have gone out for dinner,' Kingston said.

'It looks damp out there,' Sydney said. 'Maybe he doesn't like the rain?'

Kingston peered out again. 'It appears misty.'

'I thought the weather was supposed to be fine,' Raymond said.

'During the day,' Sydney said. 'It's not really raining. Just misty.'

Kingston turned back to her. 'We cannot see that from here. Have you been out?'

Panic bubbled up inside her. She fought to keep her face impassive. 'No. It just gets like that sometimes in the evening in Adelaide when I'm walking home.'

He watched her for a moment then walked back to his seat. She'd gotten away with it. She let out a breath, careful not to make it audible. She picked up her can to drink and wash down the lump in her throat. She'd almost been caught.

'Anyway, this is almost done,' Raymond said. 'Who wants to set the table?'

CHAPTER 13

THE spa seemed to have set Kingston at ease. He was more optimistic and happier in the morning. Sydney noticed he was smiling despite them not having done well the day before. The same couldn't be said of Raymond, who looked defeated. Sydney just wanted to hug him. They needed a win.

Once again, the day started at nine a.m. They ate their breakfast and got ready. Raymond had charged his camera battery overnight, so it was prepared to go. Sydney decided that today she'd try to take some photos with her phone. She knew the building they were going to was lovely to look at, so she wanted to get some shots in. She remembered the other buildings she'd spotted while following the man. Ballarat was a photogenic city.

'What do we know about the Mechanics' Institute?' Kingston asked Raymond as they walked down Sturt Street.

'They built it in the 1860s,' Raymond said. 'Its primary use has been as a library and theatre. They also used it as a museum at one point. I think it's still used as a library and theatre today.'

'And where would the key be?' Kingston asked.

'The library,' Raymond asked. 'It's along one of the walls in the skirting board.'

'So it's going to depend on how much the library has changed,' Sydney said.

Raymond nodded. 'Hopefully, not much.'

Despite the mist the night before, the weather had blessed them with another sunny day, though clouds were on the horizon. Sydney hoped they stayed away. They'd heard a comment the day before that it was strangely fine for this time of year. Usually, it was overcast and raining, especially given that there was an event running.

They arrived at the Mechanics' Institute to find a small crowd. It appeared to be a popular building. Sydney put it down to the building's central location and its somewhat iconic status. She knew from looking at a photo of it the night before that it had a statue on the roof, but she couldn't see it from this side of the road.

'Are we going straight to the library?' she asked, eyeing the building.

'That's the plan,' Raymond said. 'And after this, we'll go to the Unicorn.'

'How far away is that?' Kingston asked.

'About two doors up.'

Kingston looked impressed. 'Close.'

'Very.'

The doors to the Mechanics' Institute opened, and a man in a familiar Heritage Week shirt came out. He announced they were offering tours, either led or self-guided. They opted to go self-guided, taking the pamphlet about the building and stepping inside. They found the way to the library, entered, and were instantly surrounded by books on metal shelving. Old books. Most of them had leatherbound covers. The scent of leather covers, dust, and old wood hit her. Of well-worn pages. It reminded her of an old bookstore.

'I could have fun here,' Raymond commented, eyeing the shelves.

'History?' Kingston asked.

'Definitely.' Raymond walked over to study the leatherbound covers. 'I could spend weeks in here.'

Sydney read the pamphlet, studying the section about the library. 'They have records of every newspaper ever printed in the town.'

'Really?' Raymond looked around. 'I wonder where.'

'Focus,' Kingston said, an amused sparkle in his eye.

'Yes, of course.' Raymond nodded, casting his gaze around the room again. 'While old, this doesn't look original.'

'No. The shelves look to be only a few decades old,' Kingston agreed. 'Original bookshelves tended to be wooden.'

'But we're not focusing on the bookshelves,' Sydney said. 'Didn't you say it was the skirting board?'

Raymond nodded. 'Main reading room. Close to the door.'

They wandered the rooms, soon finding themselves in the main reading room. It was a two-storey room with an upper balcony surrounding it. There were areas to read, and bookshelves and displays made up the outer ring. The tables and chairs looked to be original. They were beautiful old stained wood. Sydney wondered how many people had sat in them over the years. She could see the appeal. Raymond's eyes glossed over a little at the surrounding books. Kingston prodded him twice to keep him focused on the task.

Sydney looked around the doorway, eyes on the skirting board. It also looked original. It had seen some wear and tear, but it was well looked after. The entire building seemed to be looked after. It felt timeless, as if she'd stepped back into the past. The history of the walls was calling to her, making her want to pick up a book and settle in to read.

'Got it,' Raymond said, his eyes on the left side of the door. 'Cover me.'

Sydney and Kingston moved over to him as he did his shoelace trick. Sydney wanted to see how he got the key but kept her back to him and gazed out over the reading room. There were a lot of people there. Some were tourists like them, but others seemed to be genuinely there to read and research. She eyed the books on the walls and wondered what they were about. She felt they weren't fiction, but she couldn't be sure.

After what felt like forever, Raymond stood up again and joined them. 'I got it,' he said cheerfully.

Sydney's heart soared at those words. What an excellent start to the day. They moved away from the wall and further into the room. Sydney wondered if they would stay a little longer – she wanted to see everything the building had to offer.

'I suggest we stay,' Kingston said, answering her question. 'Look the building over.'

'Good idea,' Raymond said. 'There might be another key for all we know.'

Sydney hadn't even considered that. She nodded her agreement and took out her pamphlet to see what else was in the building. 'There are a few rooms open to the public,' she said. 'Should we look at those?'

'Of course,' Kingston said. 'We'll move through and see what we can find.'

They didn't find another key. They checked every room and found that a few had been 'restored', but otherwise, everything seemed to be original. The theatre impressed Sydney. It was interesting that it didn't have sloping seats like some of them, but she saw how that could be practical. You could take all the seats out and make it a ballroom, if needed, or an exhibition room.

It was nearing midday when they finally stepped back out onto Sturt Street. Raymond suggested they check the outside of the building to be sure. They inspected the brickwork and found nothing that stood out. Eventually, they accepted they would only find one key at the building.

'So, the Unicorn,' Kingston said, looking up the street.

'Yes,' Raymond said, patting his pocket where the key was, double-checking that it was still there. She was glad he had the key and not her. She worried that she'd lose it somehow.

They walked two doors up and found the front of the building. Sydney stopped to peer in the window, finding what looked to be the remains of a cafe. The shop was closed and long empty. There was dust on the surfaces that looked like it hadn't been disturbed in a while. She couldn't see a 'for sale' or 'for lease' sign on the building, so it was just vacant.

'We should try around the back.' Raymond nodded towards a side alley.

They joined him, walking between the former hotel and the bank. As they made their way around, Sydney was startled to find that the building wasn't deep. In fact, it looked like the rear of the building had been demolished and a new part added. Her heart sank at the realisation of this. She saw the concerned looks on Kingston and Raymond's faces as well.

'This doesn't bode well,' Kingston said as they walked around the back of the building, the gravel crunching beneath their feet.

'We need to get upstairs,' Raymond said.

They tried the rear door, finding that it was locked. Sydney had expected that. She hadn't expected Kingston to pull a lock pick out of his pocket and kneel to pick it.

'I keep meaning to learn how to do that,' Raymond said as he watched.

'I taught Jake,' Kingston said. 'It's really not that difficult.'

'I think you can buy kits online,' Sydney remarked, thinking about the kits she'd seen on slightly dodgy websites over the years. They were usually for padlocks, but she guessed they'd work on any lock.

She kept her eye on the alley in case anyone came around the corner. Looking behind them, she was surprised to find they were at one of the side entrances of Her Majesty's Theatre. She studied the large building, noting that it looked to be old as well.

'Raymond,' she asked. 'What about there?'

She pointed to the building, and Raymond turned to follow her gaze. He saw the sign. 'I thought about that, but no. I think it was built too late for Redmond to put a key there.'

'Huh.' She looked back towards the Unicorn. 'But this one isn't?'

'It was one of Ballarat's first hotels,' he said, turning back to where Kingston was still working the lock. 'I wouldn't be surprised if Redmond stayed here at some stage.'

'Which is why you want to look upstairs,' Sydney said. 'He hid it in a guest room?'

'Common area,' Raymond corrected.

'How did he manage to hide all these keys?' she asked. 'Someone must have noticed him doing it.'

'You'd think, yeah.' He shrugged it off. 'I don't know how he did it. I think he knew the builders in some cases. In others, I think people didn't question what he was doing. He was practically royalty by the time he died. Everyone knew who he was.'

'I would have been suspicious,' Sydney said. They were out of the sun here, and the air was cold, so she crossed her arms over her chest to warm herself. 'Royalty or not, I would have wondered what he was doing putting little boxes in buildings with markings on them.'

'Sometimes it's easier not to question,' Kingston said. 'I think I almost have it.'

'Should we be worried about alarms?' Sydney asked, eyes drifting towards the alarm box on the wall. The last thing they needed was for the police to arrive while they were in the building. While she was sure Kingston and Raymond could afford bail, she didn't want a blemish on her record to explain to any future employers.

'It doesn't look on,' Raymond said. 'I guess we'll find out.'

'If an alarm sounds, we walk away quickly,' Kingston said.

Sydney watched as he tinkered a little longer with the lock then pulled the door open. He stood, slipping the lock pick back into his pocket and opening the door properly. Sydney eyed the alarm and saw that the blue light didn't start flashing. It made no change at all.

'I don't think there's power to the building,' Raymond said.

'Lucky,' Kingston said.

They stepped into the building. They passed several side rooms, Sydney careful not to disturb the dust. She worried about their footprints. As they moved through the building, she couldn't help but notice how modern it was. They had completely converted it into a cafe, with no sign of the original purpose of the building at all.

Kingston gestured towards them. 'Found the stairs,' he said in a stage whisper.

They climbed the narrow staircase to the top floor, and Sydney's heart sank again. The top floor looked like they had converted it into office and storage space. They made their way through the building. Sydney noticed confusion etched on Raymond's face.

'I have no idea where the room is supposed to be,' he said, almost distressed. 'I think they've changed the layout up here.'

'They have demolished the rear of the building and added onto it,' Kingston pointed out.

'I doubt we're going to find a key here,' Raymond agreed. He sighed heavily. 'Why do people do this?'

'They only need to keep the facade,' Kingston reminded him. 'Everything else can be changed.'

'I hate that. The main part of the building is where the real heritage is.' Raymond thumped a fist against the wall in frustration. Not hard enough to do any damage, but it was loud enough to make Sydney jump. 'I think we can chalk this one up as a loss.'

'Agreed,' Kingston said. He turned back towards the staircase.

They made their way down and back out of the building. Kingston fiddled with the lock when they got to the bottom, and after closing the door behind them, he locked it again. Sydney had to commend him for doing that. It meant that people up to no good couldn't break in and smash the place up. There were always opportunists out there.

'Is that all for today?' Kingston asked Raymond.

'Yeah,' Raymond said. 'I'm trying to space it out to a couple of buildings a day.'

This was music to Sydney's ears. She could feel the adrenaline rushing through her. She didn't think her body could take the constant highs and lows during the day. It also meant they had more time at any particular building.

'Maybe we should go look at Her Majesty's,' Sydney suggested. 'We're right here.'

'That's a splendid idea,' Kingston said. 'I am rather fond of theatres.'

'You don't go very often,' Raymond said.

'I don't get the opportunity,' Kingston said. 'I keep intending to go more often.'

'Are you fond of theatre?' Sydney asked Raymond.

'Nah. I find it to be a bit pretentious,' he said with a shrug. 'I also don't like the crowds.'

'The atmosphere is part of the reason for going,' Kingston said as they walked out of the alley and around the edge of the bank onto Lydiard Street.

Raymond paused, pointing across the street. 'That's Craig's Hotel, by the way.'

Sydney looked across the street at the building. It was impressive to look at. It was painted a heritage grey colour and even had a tower. She couldn't wait to see inside. It reminded her a little of the Medina Grand.

'When are we going there?' Kingston asked.

'The plan is in two days,' Raymond said. 'That's when they'll be open for tours.'

'Shame it's not open today,' Kingston said. 'Given we are here already.'

'I know. They seemed to have spaced out the different days that buildings are open,' Raymond said. 'I guess that's both a good thing and a bad thing.'

'Good because we don't have to rush,' Sydney said.

'Bad because we can't do them in blocks,' Raymond said.

'Anyhow, let us see about this theatre,' Kingston said as they stopped in front of the building. It was an older, two-storey cream-coloured building with green doors. There was an awning over the entranceway. Sydney couldn't help but wonder if it'd ever had a verandah. A few people were standing outside, indicating that it was a building that had organised tours. 'I'm sure it's bound to be beautiful.'

Sydney couldn't wait.

CHAPTER 14

HER Majesty's Theatre turned out to be beautiful indeed. Since no show was currently playing, the tour took them to some backstage areas. Sydney felt small in the actual theatre itself. It surprised her that there was an organ in the orchestra pit that could rise and lower as needed. No one played it that day, but the tour guide invited them to come back when someone was. It tempted her to beg Kingston and Raymond to return.

The theatre was ornate and decorative. Every single inch was covered in some form of decorative plaster or sconce. The building looked like two storeys from the outside, but inside, the theatre was three storeys with two levels of balconies above the stalls. The raked stage itself was large, and a domed roof towered above all.

Sydney had snapped a lot of photos and saw Raymond doing the same. She listened to the building's history and noted that it was built before Redmond had died but possibly too late for him to have hidden a key there. That didn't stop her from looking for the little etching that signified the location of a key. She saw Kingston and Raymond studying the walls, so she wasn't the only one looking.

When they made it outside, they broke for lunch. They walked down Sturt Street to the mall, found a cafe and ate. Afterwards, they browsed the mall itself. The range of stores impressed Sydney, although she saw several empty storefronts. Given the foot traffic, it was a popular place for the locals, and she could honestly see why. It had a relaxed air to it.

Afterwards, they headed back to their hotel. The strange man was there, across the road from the hotel. He didn't even look at them as they rounded the corner. He hadn't been there that morning when they had left. Sydney wanted to walk up to him and ask him where he had disappeared to. Did he go into the tunnels? She glanced at Raymond and Kingston and knew they wouldn't agree to her approaching the man.

Entering their room, Sydney dropped onto the couch. Her feet hurt from all the walking she had been doing these last few days. She was used to being on her feet all day, but there was something different about standing around the Medina Grand and walking the hills of Ballarat. It worked different muscles. She'd thought she was fit, but now she questioned that.

'I say we go somewhere for dinner tonight,' Kingston said as he settled into the chair in the room. 'Make an outing of it.'

'There's the restaurant the hotel has a deal with,' Sydney said. 'You just have to show proof that you're staying here and you get a discount.'

'What sort of restaurant is it?' Raymond asked, joining her on the couch.

'I'm not sure.' She plucked the hotel guide up off the coffee table, flipping through it. 'It looks like it's also a hotel. It says here that the menu is standard fare.'

'I wonder if they have steak,' Kingston said.

'You up for some tonight, are you?' Raymond asked.

'It has been a while.'

Sydney noted it listed a website on the page, so she pulled out her phone to search for it. She found a menu available and, after skimming through it, nodded. 'They have steak. Eye fillet.'

'Excellent.' Kingston grinned.

Raymond leaned into her space to study her phone. Sydney felt herself heat at having him so close to her. She could feel his breath on her as he looked at the screen. 'Looks like they have quite a range of options,' he said. 'Fish and chips, risotto, steak, seafood, parmigiana, and even a stir-fry.'

Sydney wasn't sure what she'd get. 'We'll be spoiled for choice, although it looks expensive.'

'Don't worry yourself about that,' Kingston said. 'We've got you.'

Sydney looked up, ready to argue, but knew from the expression on his face that it would be a moot point. He'd already made his mind up. If there was one thing both Kingston and Raymond were, it was stubborn. Sydney was a little stubborn herself, but she knew when to pick her battles, and this was one she couldn't win.

Raymond settled back into his spot, moving away from her. He stretched his legs out and rubbed them. 'I call dibs on the spa tonight.'

'It's your turn anyhow,' Kingston said.

'That's right,' Sydney agreed, trying not to imagine Raymond in the spa. 'Kingston and I have both had our turns.'

'Is it any good?' Raymond asked.

'Not the strongest water jets, but it is relaxing,' Kingston said. 'Although there is not much room to stretch out.'

'It's only the size of a regular bath,' Sydney reminded him. Kingston and Raymond were not short men, so she imagined they would be cramped in the spa.

'Shame we don't have bath salts,' Raymond said, rubbing his thigh again. 'I'm starting to feel this week.'

'And here I thought you were fit and healthy,' Kingston teased.

'Melbourne's mostly flat,' Raymond reminded him. 'So's Adelaide.'

'There are a lot of hills here,' Sydney agreed. 'I spend most of my days on my feet, and I'm feeling it.' She didn't tell them about Dana Street hill. That was the worst hill she'd ever had to climb.

'I'm only teasing,' Kingston said with a smile. 'I'm feeling it, too. We've had it far too easy where we live.'

'Even the treadmill hasn't prepared you for it?' Raymond asked.

'There's something different about a treadmill and walking an actual hill,' Kingston said.

Sydney had to agree with him. Not that she ever used a treadmill much. She got her walk in at work, and going to and from it. She stretched her legs out and resisted the groan as her muscles twinged. 'Can we drive to the restaurant, please?'

'I was about to suggest that,' Raymond said. 'And I don't even know how far away it is.'

'I must agree,' Kingston said. 'I think we need a break.'

Oscar's proved to be an art déco building. Sydney had never been a fan of that type of architecture. She was more partial to heritage buildings, but she guessed it was interesting to look at in its own way. It made it hard to tell when the building was built. She knew they would not find a key there.

Kingston had called ahead and made a reservation to ensure they got a table. It turned out to be a wise move because there was a small line of walk-ins waiting to be seated. The server took their names and brought them to a reserved table. Sydney felt some of the walk-ins glaring at the back of her head. All she could think was that they should have planned ahead as they had.

'Popular place,' Raymond noted as they sat down.

'Which bodes well for the food,' Kingston said. 'If it were empty, I would be worried.'

They deliberated over their menus and Kingston insisted on

getting them all wine to go with their meals. Sydney felt terrible about not paying, but Raymond and Kingston assured her it was fine. After all, they'd been the ones who'd wanted to come to Ballarat.

Looking around, Sydney noted that most people were in casual wear. She'd put on a nice blouse and dress pants just in case, and now she felt overdressed. The interior was stylish and relaxed, with dark-stained wood tables and chairs. There were no tablecloths, and everything about the place seemed casual. It felt homely.

'Shame we're not staying here,' Raymond said. 'We could come here for all our meals.'

'We haven't tried the food yet,' Kingston reminded him.

'I'm just saying.'

'I imagine it would be expensive,' Sydney said. 'It's cheaper to make your own meals.'

'Fewer dishes, though.'

You couldn't argue with that point. Sydney didn't mind doing the washing up. Her parents had always said that dirty dishes were a sign of a fed family. She looked up as the server brought them their drinks. Sydney thanked him as he set her glass in front of her. They were each sitting on a side of the table. The tables weren't very big, and Sydney worried there wouldn't be enough room for the food.

'Well, I'd call this trip a success so far,' Kingston said, picking up his glass.

'We've had more misses than hits,' Raymond said.

'But we did have some hits,' Kingston said. 'Several, in fact. And we're only halfway through the week.'

'Not to mention it's been fun,' Sydney said.

Raymond pulled a face. 'I'm not sure all the walking is "fun".'

'But seeing the buildings is,' Sydney said. 'Learning about all the history.'

'I didn't know you were interested in this sort of thing,' Kingston said.

'Knowing the history can be important to my job,' Sydney said. 'But I am interested in it, yes.'

'I suppose I can see how it would be important,' Raymond said. 'If someone asked you about the history of the Medina Grand, you'd need to know it.'

She nodded. 'You'd be surprised how often people ask about the building. Especially about the vaults.'

'I still don't know why anyone would want a wedding reception down there,' Raymond said, pulling a face. 'No windows.'

'It's the novelty of it,' Kingston said. 'It's unique. And Simon is an excellent caterer.'

'He is that,' Sydney agreed. 'I don't know how he does it all.'

'Years of practice,' Kingston said. 'He's been working at the hotel for several years now.'

'I remember him saying,' Sydney said. 'He mentioned he was a restaurant's assistant chef before he started working for the Medina Grand.'

'At a prestigious restaurant,' Kingston confirmed. 'The Medina Grand was a step down for him.'

'Then why take it?' Raymond asked. 'Wouldn't you want to step up?'

'Sometimes a sideways step is just as important as a step up,' Sydney said. 'The Medina Grand has a very relaxed atmosphere. It wouldn't be as full during peak hour as a high-end restaurant.'

'And perfect to cut your managerial teeth on,' Kingston said. 'As you would know, Miss Madinah.'

Sydney nodded her agreement. The Medina Grand was technically a sideways step for her in her career. It might have been a step up from assistant manager to manager, but the hotel wasn't as busy as the one she'd worked at in New York. There certainly were a lot fewer rooms as well.

They sipped their wine. Sydney people-watched and observed the food around them. She had to admit that it all looked good.

She couldn't wait for their meal to arrive. Given how busy it was, she expected it to take a while. She looked at the two men beside her. Raymond was studying something on his phone, a frown on his face, while Kingston was people-watching like she was.

'You know, it's rude to be on your phone at the dinner table,' Kingston commented, looking back at Raymond.

Raymond snorted. 'Look who's talking.'

'What has you so engrossed?'

'Jake,' Raymond said. 'I sent him a message to see how that thing at the hotel was going.'

A wave of guilt wash over Sydney – she'd forgotten about that. It should have been the first thing on her mind as the hotel manager. *She* should have been the one messaging Jake and Rita. 'How's it going?' she asked.

'Apparently, the guy came back for round two,' Raymond said.

'What?' Alarm shot through her. 'Did he do it again?'

'Police got him before he could,' Raymond said. 'It was that drunk guy from last week.'

That didn't surprise her. The guy had vowed revenge for being thrown out. Sydney was glad they had caught him. 'Is everyone okay?'

'Just a little shaken up,' Raymond said, sliding his phone back into his pocket. 'Jake had been staying at the hotel in case something happened.'

She had to commend him for that. He didn't have to do that. He could pass it off to the night shift and deal with everything in the morning. Jake took his job seriously.

'I'm sure he's glad he didn't come here,' Kingston said.

'You'd have to ask him, but I bet you're right,' Raymond said.

They fell silent again. Sydney thought about how she would have handled the situation had she been there. In reality, not much different would have happened. The attacks occurred at night, so the night manager would be the one the police needed, and Jake would still have to talk to them. Rita would touch base as well.

Thinking of Rita, Sydney looked back at the two men. 'Rita didn't seem thrilled to be attending her family event.'

'That's because she hates it,' Raymond said.

'Rita does not get on well with her sisters,' Kingston expanded.

That surprised Sydney. She was an only child, so she didn't know what it would be like to have a sibling. She couldn't imagine dreading them so much that she'd want to avoid them. 'Why?'

'From my understanding, they are a rather competitive family,' Kingston said. 'They look down on her for not becoming a doctor and instead coming to work for me.'

'But she pretty much runs the hotel,' Sydney said. 'Her job's important.'

'They do not view it that way,' Kingston said.

'They avoid each other except on family day,' Raymond said. 'Their mother insists on it. You can only get out of it if you're in the hospital and dying.'

'Wow.' Rita would have preferred to come to Ballarat then. 'That bad?'

Kingston and Raymond nodded.

They were interrupted as their food arrived, the three sitting back in their seats so the server could place their plates. Despite the tables being small, there was enough room for all three. It might have been a tight squeeze had there been four of them. The food looked delicious, and picking up her knife and fork to eat, Sydney found it was.

'I stand by my point of wishing we'd stayed at this hotel,' Raymond said after he'd eaten a little of his meal.

'We'll see if that thought remains when we are given the bill,' Kingston said.

Sydney grimaced, reminded that they were shouting her meal. She was half tempted to insist that she pay her share. They hadn't let her chip in to buy the groceries for the week, either. They were paying for pretty much everything on this trip. She wondered what their budget actually was.

They ate most of their meal in silence, simply enjoying the food. Everything was cooked to perfection, and the taste was delicious. It went well with the wine that Kingston had chosen for them. Did he know much about wine? He had been raised as part of the elite of his planet, so fine dining had to be part of his curriculum.

'Did they have wine where you're from?' Sydney asked him.

'There was something similar once,' Kingston said. 'It was long gone by the time I was born.'

'Because everything was processed,' Raymond said.

Kingston nodded. 'No fields mean no crops.'

'Climate change?' Sydney asked.

'And acid rain,' Kingston confirmed. 'It killed the majority of natural plant life. Only that in climate-controlled greenhouses survived, and that was simply for looks.'

'How did you get oxygen?' Raymond asked.

'Technology,' Kingston answered. 'Air recyclers. We lived inside buildings and domes. Of course, the elites had the best air quality. We also had natural light. I could not say the same for the rest.'

'Did the rest have the same life longevity as you?' Raymond asked.

'No,' Kingston said. 'They generally only lived a couple of hundred years.'

Sydney nearly choked on her food. A short life was only a couple of hundred years? 'What's a long life?'

'I think our oldest was nearly a thousand,' Kingston said.

'That's a big difference,' Raymond said.

'It was,' Kingston agreed. 'But the elites didn't care about the lesser. They viewed their shorter lives as population control.'

'But you didn't,' Sydney said, noting the disdain in his voice.

Kingston shook his head. 'While I understand the need for

balance in society, what we had was far from balanced. My mother used to always say that one day the poor would realise they had greater numbers and rise against the elites. That would be the end of the planet.'

'You think that's what happened?' Raymond asked.

'We'll never know,' Kingston said, sipping from his wine.

It made Sydney very aware of the societal disparities on Earth. How the 'elites' in first-world countries lived compared to the poor in third-world countries. How companies were destroying the planet to make a profit and exploiting their workers to do it. It wasn't as bad in Australia as in other countries, but the imbalance remained.

'Do you think this planet is on the same trajectory?' Raymond asked, voicing what she was thinking.

'If the path doesn't change, then it could,' Kingston said. 'On the other hand, genetic modification of human embryos is outlawed. Rightfully so.'

'Which prevents a massive surge in overpopulation,' Raymond said.

Kingston nodded.

She hadn't meant for the topic to take such a dark turn. It made her bitter. She forced a smile and tried to enjoy her meal. Sydney wondered how much of Kingston was modified. She thought of the whole conspiracy about 'designer babies'. It reminded her of the movie *Gattaca*. She hoped the world never came to that.

They were finishing their meal when Sydney spotted a familiar face stepping through the restaurant. She caught Kingston and Raymond's attention, gesturing in the man's direction. They saw him just as he saw them. He smiled at them and headed to their table.

'Hello again,' John Smith said, resting his non-cane hand on the back of their empty chair. 'Enjoying your meal?'

'Didn't expect to see you here,' Raymond said.

'I regularly enjoy this establishment,' John said with a cheerful smile. 'How are you finding it?'

'Delicious,' Kingston said. Sydney could see the muscles tighten in his jaw.

'How did your photography go?' John asked Raymond.

'You were right. The other side of the courtyard had a better view,' Raymond answered.

'I thought as much,' John said with a serene smile. 'I dabble a little in photography myself. I take it you're not a professional?'

'No,' Raymond said with a shake of his head. 'I mainly only take photos for a friend.'

'A friend who didn't come with you?'

'No.'

Sydney noted Raymond was keeping his answers short and vague. Kingston had a look of distrust on his face. Her hackles raised. She knew nothing about John Smith. He was an enigma. Her eyes wandered down to the hand on his cane, spotting a large signet ring with a crest. She did not know what the crest was. It was some kind of shield. A family crest, maybe. She couldn't make out the details from here. She wished she could take a photo of it to look it up later.

'I won't keep you from your meal,' John Smith said. 'I was just leaving myself. Have a good evening.'

'You too,' Sydney said, planting a smile on her face and feigning a cheerful nature.

He turned and left them, heading out the door of the restaurant. Was that the way into the hotel, or was he going elsewhere first? Kingston and Raymond looked at each other. She wished she could read their minds. All she could see was that they weren't happy.

'That's the second time we've seen him,' Raymond commented.

'Technically, third,' Sydney said. 'I saw him at one of the churches.'

Raymond and Kingston turned to her. 'What?' Raymond asked.

'He was at a church watching us,' Sydney said. 'The one on Bakery Hill.'

'Is that so?' Kingston said. 'Either it's a small town, or…'

Sydney blinked. 'You think he's following us?'

'We can't know for sure,' Kingston said. 'But it is possible.'

'Or it could be a coincidence,' Sydney said.

'I don't believe in coincidences,' Raymond said.

'We will have to keep an eye out,' Kingston said. 'If he appears again…'

Sydney nodded. They'd have to look into him. It could be a situation like Marcus all over again. She shuddered, not wanting to be suckered twice. Sydney understood where they came from and why they had to be cautious. She just wished that it wasn't the case. It would be nice to find a friendly person and not anticipate they wanted something.

She went back to finishing her dinner, worry on her mind.

CHAPTER 15

RAYMOND had to drag himself out of bed the following day. He'd taken advantage of the spa the night before, and it had relaxed him so much that he'd fallen straight asleep the second his head had hit the pillow. His racing thoughts were unusually absent.

He noticed when Kingston left the bed to shower, as his warmth followed him. Raymond lay in bed for a bit longer until he heard the water cut off then slunk out from beneath the comfort of the blankets. He wanted nothing more than to stay there, his muscles screaming for him to crawl back into bed. They had two more places to visit that day, so he knew he wouldn't get a rest until at least that afternoon.

He grabbed his toiletry bag as Kingston stepped back into the room.

'You're up,' Kingston observed.

'Barely,' Raymond admitted, noting the way Kingston's curls fell over his forehead when it was wet. He wished the shower were bigger so they could take it together. Probably not a good idea to do that with Sydney staying with them. He didn't want to scar her. 'Sydney awake yet?'

'She showered before me,' Kingston said. 'She's an early riser.'

'Did you two leave me any hot water?'

Kingston gave him a measured look. Of course there was hot water. Raymond knew that, but he teased Kingston about it anyway. Kingston loved long showers, and Raymond would dig at him about using all the Medina's hot water. Raymond winked at Kingston and headed for the bathroom to take his turn in the shower.

After shaving and dressing, he finally made his way into the apartment's main living area. Sydney and Kingston were talking at the table over their breakfast, the television in the background tuned to the news channel. Raymond noted it was a weather report and frowned as he saw that afternoon showers were predicted. Hopefully, they made it back to the hotel before then.

'What's the plan for today?' Sydney asked him as Raymond dropped his bread into the toaster.

'The railway station and the town hall,' he answered. 'We should be back here by lunchtime.'

'I could do with a rest,' Sydney admitted. 'We can rest this afternoon, right?'

'I think we could all do with a rest,' Kingston agreed. 'Perhaps we can find a movie to watch.'

'Here or in town?' Raymond asked.

'Here.'

'That sounds good,' Sydney said. 'I like that idea.'

So did Raymond. It had been a while since he'd just sat down and watched a movie all the way through. He had a short attention span for these things. There were a few movies he wouldn't mind seeing. They'd have to make lists and see if they had any films in common.

Raymond lathered butter and Vegemite on to his toast and slumped into a chair at the table. Kingston slid a cup of coffee towards him. Raymond muttered his thanks and ate. He checked his watch – they still had over an hour until the Heritage Week event started for the day.

Sydney gazed out the window. 'It's very overcast today.'

'TV said showers are forming,' Raymond said. They'd been so involved in their conversation that they must have missed the report. 'The aim will be to make it back here before they set in.'

'Hopefully they're gone by tomorrow,' Sydney said.

'Time will tell,' Kingston said. 'If we need to buy an umbrella, we at least know where to look.'

That was true. Several of the shops they had been to sold them. Still, it would be a walk to those shops in the rain before they got them. Raymond had packed a coat, but it wasn't very thick and would only keep some of the rain off.

'Should we take our coats?' Sydney asked.

'That might be wise,' Kingston agreed.

It would be. Raymond wasn't a fan of coat-wearing, but he'd do it if it meant staying dry. Coats were bulky, and he didn't like how they looked on him. They made him look fat, despite his fit physique. Kingston could look good in anything, and he was sure Sydney was the same. Raymond always looked strange in certain outfits, and coats were among them.

He finished his breakfast and helped with the washing up. Raymond then grabbed his camera bag and finished getting ready, dragging his coat out of the bottom of his suitcase and putting it on. He hated it. It always felt weird, as if he were wearing too many layers. He was never big on layers.

'You're pouting,' Kingston observed.

'What? No, I'm not.'

'Yes, you are.' Kingston pulled his coat on, and sure enough, he looked perfectly dashing. 'Why?'

'Just not a fan of coats, that's all.'

Kingston narrowed his eyes but said nothing. Raymond could tell from his face that he wanted to comment but was biting the inside of his cheek. Not a good comment, then. Raymond chose to ignore him, grabbing his camera bag and slinging it over his shoulder.

'Let's go,' he said.

It was a bit of a walk to the train station. The station was a cream building with arches and a clock tower. It impressed Raymond when he saw it, eyeing the tower and admitting it looked good. He remembered from his research how a fire had once gutted the tower, but the structure had survived and been restored. The building was now well cared for and, no doubt, a landmark for the city.

He also admired the hotel sitting on the corner near the railway station. It was beautiful, with majestic arches and ornate brickwork. He knew there wasn't a key there, but he still wished to take it in. He snapped a photo while Kingston and Sydney were looking up at the railway station.

'Are you getting sidetracked?' Kingston asked.

'Just admiring the architecture,' Raymond said, turning back towards the station. 'I think they're doing self-guided tours here.'

'Shall we go look?' Sydney asked.

They walked up the driveway, avoiding the buses lined up waiting for passengers or dropping them off. And there were a lot of passengers disembarking from a recent train. Raymond noted that many of them were carrying camera bags like he was. More tourists coming to take in Heritage Week.

They didn't find anyone handing out pamphlets at the front of the station, but rather a display rack offered them. Because it was a functioning station, Raymond could see why they went with this route. If people wanted the pamphlet, they could take it, but if they simply were there to catch a train, they could ignore it.

He took a pamphlet detailing the building's history. Raymond found the part that mentioned the 1981 fire but noted that it was restricted to an extension built after Redmond had hidden the key. He studied the guide, trying to find where to start their search.

'So, where are we looking?' Sydney asked.

'I'm not 100% sure,' Raymond admitted. 'The journal just said the office by the line.'

'That does not help much,' Kingston said as they stepped into the station. 'There are two lines, and I imagine many offices.'

There were two platforms, one on either side of the station, and an old staircase joined them. The stairs of the staircase were so worn down that they were bowed in the middle. Raymond couldn't help but wonder if they were a safety hazard like that.

'As I said,' Kingston said as they looked around them. 'Many offices.'

'And most of them won't be accessible,' Raymond said as he looked at the closed doors. Kingston wouldn't be able to pick the locks without someone noticing. He could also see surveillance cameras covering every inch of the station.

'We're not going to find a key here, are we?' Sydney said sadly.

'It was a long shot,' Raymond admitted. 'I wouldn't know until we looked.'

'Let's wander around and see what we can find,' Kingston said.

They walked along the platform, Raymond taking the chance to snap a few photos while Sydney did the same on her phone. They found their way back out to the main foyer, took the stairs over the train line to the other side, and then inspected that side. Everything looked to have been upgraded over the years. Some of it had an older feel, but at the same time, it didn't look original.

'I think we can consider this one a loss,' Kingston said. 'Why did he choose a railway station?'

'It could be how he travelled to and from Ballarat,' Raymond said.

'The journals don't say?' Sydney asked.

Raymond shook his head. 'Rail would have been the fastest method, so I imagine that's what he did.'

'The other option being horse and carriage,' Kingston said. 'It would be a long trip. Cars were a marvellous invention.'

'Did you get around by horse and carriage?' Sydney asked.

'A few times,' Kingston said. 'I preferred to walk if the location was close enough.'

'Which you still do, old man,' Raymond teased.

Kingston narrowed his eyes at him, disdain sparking. Raymond quips about Kingston's age never got a positive reaction. It was clear Kingston didn't like to be reminded of how old he was; even though it sounded like, for his people, he was still relatively young.

'Where next?' Sydney asked.

'Town Hall,' Raymond said. 'There's supposed to be two keys there, but I've pretty much accepted that one of them is gone.'

'Why?'

'The interior of the building has been renovated a few times,' Raymond said. 'But the key on the outside might still be there.'

'On the outside?'

'That is unusual,' Kingston said. 'Redmond usually hid the key on the inside.'

'It should be by the front steps,' Raymond said. 'I don't know why this building is different, but given that they seem to leave facades untouched, it bodes well for us.'

'Shame he didn't hide more keys on the outside,' Kingston agreed.

'I'm just glad I brought my good walking shoes,' Sydney said, stretching her legs. 'I swear I'm going to lose a few pounds this week.'

'You and me both,' Raymond agreed.

They stopped several times on the walk back to the town hall to take in some buildings along the way. One of those buildings was the Ballarat Mining Exchange. It was open for tours, so they took advantage. It was built after Redmond died, so Raymond knew there wouldn't be a key there, but the history fascinated him. The building still had many original features, and he could see in his mind's eye the empty space being a hive of activity in its prime.

As they left, the air seemed heavier, as if rain was imminent, and it was accompanied by a distinct chill The coat shielded Raymond from most of it, but he still felt bulky with it on. He could only think about taking it off once they returned to the hotel. Sydney and Kingston didn't seem bothered by theirs. He was jealous.

They tagged onto the back of the next tour when they arrived at the town hall. Raymond knew that the key he doubted was still there was meant to be by the staircase. Stepping inside, it surprised him that more of the building was original than he had thought. There had been modifications, but much of the original interior was still in place.

When they stopped by the staircase, his eyes cast around for any sign of the etched symbol. The staircase still looked to have many original features. It had definitely had a fresh coat of paint over the years, and he doubted the carpet running up it was the original carpet.

He saw that Kingston and Sydney were also scanning the walls and skirting boards. Sydney seemed to have a good eye for these things, so if Raymond missed it, she might catch it. As they moved through the building, he snapped photos of the different items. The tour guide talked about the council's history, where the meetings were held, and how the town hall had once been used as a bank. Raymond would love to see the vault, but it and the collection were publicly off-limits.

By the time they made it back outside, it had started to drizzle. It was a fine mist of rain. Just enough to be annoying. Raymond pulled his coat tighter around himself as they stepped off to the side near the main stairs.

'I didn't see anything in there,' Sydney said.

'Nor did I,' Kingston confirmed.

'It was supposed to be by the main staircase,' Raymond explained. 'But no, I didn't see anything either.'

'What about this second key?' Kingston asked.

Raymond turned, scanning the wall near the front steps. He moved along to see if he could spot the small compartment. He wondered how Redmond would even get it into the bluestone brick. Raymond moved back towards the stairs to check there, finally spotting the mark on the side of the steps themselves.

He knelt beside the stairs, reaching for the area and feeling around the edges of the grove. Finding it, he pressed the catch and popped the compartment open. He grinned, reaching inside and faltering as he found nothing. He checked again, feeling around completely inside the box. The key wasn't there.

He shut the compartment and rejoined the other two.

'Did you get it?' Kingston asked.

Raymond shook his head. 'It was empty.'

'What?' Sydney said.

'It's definitely the compartment, but the key wasn't there.'

'That's… odd.' Kingston frowned. 'Do you think Redmond might have taken it out?'

'Or someone else,' Raymond said.

'Who?' Sydney asked.

'I don't know.' Raymond looked back at the little compartment. 'This is what we were afraid of. Someone else finding the spots and taking the keys before we can.'

'Let's not jump to conclusions,' Kingston said. 'It's possible the key was never put in there.'

'No, Redmond definitely put it there,' Raymond said, meeting his eye. 'The journal is pretty clear. He put the key there.'

'So now what?' Sydney asked.

Raymond shook his head at a complete loss. There wasn't anything that they *could* do. They had to chalk this one up to a loss.

'Hello again.'

The hairs on Raymond's neck prickled. Turning, he spotted John Smith standing a couple of feet away. He was still dressed in his immaculate suit, the cane in his hand and glasses perched on the end of his nose. Raymond was certain that those glasses were for show only, given they didn't distort John's eyes at all.

'Oh, hi,' Sydney said, surprised. 'I thought you said you'd already been to the town hall.'

'Oh, I did,' John Smith said, patting a small bag on his side. 'I came back for photos. You could say you inspired me.'

Raymond wasn't sure if he bought that or not. Strange how John kept popping up everywhere they were. Raymond had been raised not to trust anyone. Heck, he didn't completely trust Kingston not to lie to him. The fact Kingston hadn't told him his true age, or that he was an alien, had confirmed that.

'You came back for photos?' Sydney asked.

'It is a beautiful building, and I wouldn't miss such an excellent opportunity,' John said. He looked at Raymond. 'Did you find what you were after?'

There was something about the way he said that. Alarm bells rang in Raymond's head. He set his jaw. 'I got some great photos,' he answered.

'Excellent,' John said. He looked to the side. 'It seems the next tour is about to start. I'll be joining it. Have a great rest of the day.'

They watched as he wandered over to join the small tour group that was forming. Raymond noted that the cane seemed for looks, as he wasn't putting any of his weight onto the stick. A lot about the man seemed to be for show.

'We keep running into him,' Sydney said softly.

'Yes, we do,' Kingston said. 'Perhaps it's time we talked to Kian.'

Raymond frowned, puzzled. 'Kian? Why Kian?'

'It's possible he knows everyone that came through the portal from the home world,' Kingston said. 'He might know this John Smith.'

It was worth a shot. Raymond looked at his watch – by the time they got back to the hotel, it would be lunchtime in Adelaide, and Kian would no doubt be at his usual table at the cafe.

'We better head back,' Raymond said, putting his camera back into his bag.

'Indeed,' Kingston agreed.

CHAPTER 16

THE drizzle didn't let up as they walked back to the hotel. Sydney pulled up the hood of her coat to protect her hair. It wasn't a heavy drizzle but rather a mist, reminding her of the mist the evening she'd followed the man watching the hotel. Just enough to make things damp without making them wet. She couldn't wait to be out of it.

They rounded the corner to the hotel and found that the man watching the place was in his usual spot. She'd half expected him not to be there in this weather, but there he was. He was leaning against the church fence, wearing an oversized coat with the hood up, his binoculars in hand. He was typing something on his phone. As they crossed the road to the hotel, he glanced at them. It tempted Sydney to yell at him to go home, but she kept her lips sealed.

She was happy when they stepped inside. The hotel was warm and welcoming. They made their way up to their rooms, Kingston unlocking the door and letting them in. Stepping inside, Raymond quickly peeled his coat off as he walked towards his bedroom. He'd looked unhappy all morning. She'd wanted to ask him what was wrong. Did the coat bother him?

Sydney went to her room to put her bag and coat away, removing her shoes. Her feet and legs were hurting. She stretched them out, rotating her ankles to ease the pain. When this trip was over, she would sit down for a week. Sydney knew she had to go back to work, but she would find every excuse to sit down to rest her poor legs.

Heading into the main living area, she put the kettle on to make them coffee. She needed a warm drink after the cold outside. She also made herself a sandwich for lunch. Kingston and Raymond soon joined her, the three moving around the tiny kitchen. Sydney made them both coffee, which they took with thanks.

They retreated to the small dining room table to eat. Kingston took out his phone and then checked his watch. Did he still have it set to Adelaide time? She'd adjusted her watch on the car trip to Ballarat. Kingston dialled a number on his phone, Sydney noting that it was on speed dial. Jake's name appeared on the screen.

After a few rings, Jake picked up. 'Something wrong, boss?' Jake asked.

'I was hoping you might find Kian for us,' Kingston said, picking at his sandwich absently. 'We need to ask him about someone we keep running into.'

'The guy watching the hotel?'

'A different person.'

'I'll see if I can find Kian,' Jake said. 'He should be in the courtyard. You think this person is one of yours?'

'It's possible.'

There was silence. Jake was moving. His muffled voice indicated he was talking to someone. After a moment of the phone being fumbled, Kian's voice came on the line.

'How may I help you, Kingston?'

'We keep running into someone here in Ballarat,' Kingston said. 'A man named John Smith. I was wondering if he was from our planet?'

'The name is unfamiliar. I'm afraid I don't know everyone who came here before the centralisation. Can you describe him?'

'He's of average height. Brown, greying hair. He wears glasses.'

'I don't think he actually needs them,' Raymond said. 'I think they're for show.'

'That would be most likely,' Kian said. 'Our people didn't require glasses.'

'He uses a cane,' Kingston continued. 'Also possibly for show, and wears suits.'

'He has brown eyes,' Sydney added when she saw Kingston wasn't going to mention them. 'And a signet ring on his left hand. It has a family crest on it.'

'Interesting,' Kian said. He paused for a while. 'I'm afraid he doesn't ring any bells. As I said – I don't know everyone that came here. Most came before they put me in charge. I only oversaw the centralisation. Others were responsible before that.'

'So you do not know who he could be,' Kingston said. 'Or if he's one of ours.'

'I'm afraid not,' Kian said. 'The odds are likely that he has also changed his name. A name like that tells me he wants to blend.'

'A conclusion we have made as well,' Kingston said, looking at Raymond and Sydney. Raymond nodded.

'I'm sorry I can't be of more use to you,' Kian said. 'I take it you are in Ballarat for business reasons.'

'We are,' Kingston said. 'We have been successful so far.'

'Excellent news. Be mindful if you are being followed.'

'We always are.'

Kian bid his farewell, returning the phone to Jake, who came on the line.

'Tell me about him,' Jake said.

They repeated their description of John Smith. Sydney wondered if Jake was jotting it all down or if he was putting it all to memory. She could hear him moving, so it was more likely to be the latter than the former. After a while, Jake huffed.

'With a name like that, I would have thought he'd try to blend, but it sounds like he's pretty showy,' Jake said.

'He is a bit,' Raymond agreed. 'I think he wants to look distinguished.'

'I'll look into him,' Jake said. 'But I really need more to go on. Like date of birth or residency information. His name is really common, meaning there will be thousands of people with that name. Maybe a middle name will help narrow it down.'

'Many of my people didn't take middle names,' Kingston said. 'Especially those who wanted to blend. They thought it easier to go with the two names.'

'Wait, is Kingston not your real name?' Sydney asked.

'No, it's my real name,' Kingston said. 'However, it was not my father's.'

'And we don't even know your first name,' Jake said. 'Which makes you near impossible to look up.'

'Entirely intentional,' Kingston said.

Raymond smirked. Sydney had a feeling he knew Kingston's first name. She wished she could pry it out of him. It would be an older name, she thought. She would have to look up the popular names at the time he'd arrived on Earth. She wondered if she could guess it.

'Anyway, I need to get back to work. My lunch break is almost over,' Jake said. 'I'll try to look this guy up, but I don't have high hopes of finding anything.'

'Maybe we should sneak a picture of him,' Raymond said. 'Would that help?'

'It might, but if this guy wants to disappear, odds are he has no photos online.'

That made sense. Some people were camera shy, and it was logical to reduce any online presence if someone didn't want to be found. They bid Jake farewell. They finished eating lunch, all lost in their thoughts. Sydney wished she could get inside Kingston and Raymond's heads to see what they were thinking. Both their faces were impassive.

Sydney was worried about their watcher, and how John Smith kept turning up. She still sided with the fact it might be a complete coincidence. They had seen a couple of familiar faces at the different venues they had visited so far over the week. It made little sense that the guy interested in them would introduce himself. But then, Marcus had. Could it be narcissism?

Raymond got up from the table as soon as he'd finished eating and disappeared into his bedroom, returning after a moment with his computer. Sydney frowned, wondering what he was doing. He joined them at the table again, and Sydney couldn't help but notice that the background of his computer was a picture of an older gentleman.

'Is that Redmond Barry?' she asked.

'Hm?' He looked at her then at his screen. 'Yes.'

'Raymond likes to keep pictures of him around to remind himself of his role,' Kingston explained.

Raymond shrugged it off, opening up a blank document. 'Let's write everything we know about John Smith.'

'Well, there's everything we told Kian,' Sydney said. 'His height, suit, hair, et cetera.'

'Fake glasses,' Raymond said. His fingers flew across the keyboard. Sydney blinked at how fast he typed. He was a touch typer. Sydney was more on the slower side herself. She'd never been into computers and only really knew enough to get around her job and life. 'I doubt he needs to cane to walk.'

'He is a man of impression,' Kingston agreed. 'And very careful in his speech.'

'Kind of like you,' Sydney said. 'And Kian.'

'Habit,' Kingston said.

'I'd pay to hear you go full slang,' Raymond said with a half smile.

'I don't even know what the latest slang is,' Kingston admitted. 'It changes so frequently.'

'I can barely keep up with it,' Sydney admitted. 'Australians use a lot of slang.'

'Americans don't?' Raymond asked.

'They do. Most of it is based on locality. The slang from the south differs from that in the north.'

'Kind of like here.'

She nodded.

'Do you even know what a "dog and bone" is?' Kingston asked.

Raymond and Sydney stared at him blankly.

'Phone,' he explained. 'Although it doesn't work with modern phones.'

'Back to John Smith,' Raymond said, returning to typing the details on his document. 'Do we agree that his suits are tailored?'

'Definitely,' Sydney said as Kingston nodded.

'Although I couldn't see any branding,' Kingston said. 'Wherever he gets them made does not brand them.'

'Or he requests not to have branding on them,' Sydney said.

'Either way, I think this guy has money,' Raymond said. 'Either that or he spends most of his paycheque on his suits.'

'He has a way of holding himself that says he is very sure of himself,' Kingston said.

'He definitely has confidence,' Sydney agreed. 'He also mentioned he likes photography.'

'That could have been a lie,' Raymond said. 'I also think he was asking if I found the key there today.'

'And he already knew you hadn't,' Kingston agreed.

'You think he found it?' Sydney asked.

'It is likely,' Kingston said.

Sydney felt a wave of guilt wash over her as she realised she'd been the one to mention they were going to the town hall. 'You don't think… he looked there because of what I said, do you?'

'He said he'd already been there,' Raymond said. 'Although that could have been a lie as well. We don't know enough about this guy to know what the truth is and what he's making up on the spot.'

'I'm half surprised he doesn't have a hat,' Kingston said. 'He strikes me as the sort to have a top hat.'

'Maybe he stopped wearing it when it went out of fashion,' Raymond said. 'Same for the pocket watch.'

Kingston narrowed his eyes. 'Not everyone wore a pocket watch.'

'But you did, right?'

'Had to tell the time some way, and wristwatches had not been invented.'

Sydney blinked as she realised Kingston was older than wristwatches. Out of curiosity, she eyed him. 'When was sliced bread invented?'

That gave Kingston pause. 'Early twentieth century, I believe. Why?'

'Hang on.' Raymond's fingers flew over the keyboard, and Sydney could see he was searching for it. '1928.'

'Wow.' Sydney shook her head. 'You're older than sliced bread.'

Raymond smirked. 'So, is sliced bread the best thing invented in your life?'

'They have invented many great things in my life,' Kingston said. 'I'm quite fond of the sewage system myself.'

'Sewage systems are old.'

'Not in Australia. Not what we have today.'

'Back to John Smith,' Sydney said, not wanting to think about life before sewage systems. 'We think he has a job, right?'

'Not really,' Raymond said.

'He said he had a meeting the first day we saw him.'

'That does not necessarily mean a job,' Kingston said. 'It is possible to have meetings without one.'

'He was very cagey when we asked him what he did for a living,' Raymond remembered. 'Said something about not wanting to divulge too much.'

Sydney remembered now. John had gone out of his way not to give out any information about himself. 'We know he eats at that restaurant,' Sydney said.

'True,' Raymond added to their list. 'Although how often we don't know.'

Kingston slid out of his seat and came around to stand behind Raymond. He rested his hands on Raymond's shoulders. Raymond didn't move, as if he hadn't noticed what Kingston was doing. His entire focus was on what was happening on his screen.

'Is there anything else we know about him?' Raymond asked.

Kingston's eyes scanned the screen. 'I think we've covered everything.'

'Should we add that he seemed to already be in Ballarat and knows the area?' Sydney asked.

'That is something,' Raymond added to the list. 'Do we think he's a native?'

'We don't know where my people spread after they arrived,' Kingston said. 'They could well be all over this earth.'

'But originated in Ireland,' Raymond said.

'John Smith doesn't seem to have the accent,' Sydney said, looking up at Kingston. 'You, Kian, and Marcus all have a faint Irish accent. John Smith doesn't.'

'He could have lost it,' Kingston said. 'It would depend entirely on how long he has been here and whether he spent much time in Ireland.'

'So he could have come through the portal and come straight here,' Raymond said.

'Wasn't Ballarat founded in the 1850s?' Sydney asked.

Raymond frowned and looked it up. 'Technically 1938, but gold was found in 1851.'

'So he might have arrived then,' Kingston said. 'Although I doubt he would have been in Ballarat this whole time. Someone would have noticed that he doesn't age. The town is large now, but it wouldn't always have been that way.'

'What is the population?' Sydney asked.

Raymond searched. 'Last check, it was just over one hundred thousand.'

'Which is small compared to Melbourne,' Sydney said. 'Maybe he spent some time there.'

'Or he's been moving all over the state,' Kingston said. 'One way we avoid people noticing our age is to keep moving. We stay away from a place for a while and then return when people would think we are our own descendants.'

'As you did with my grandparents,' Raymond said.

Kingston nodded. He paused. 'Did you tell them?'

'Damned straight I did,' Raymond said. 'Grandfather's response was "I knew it".'

'You mean about Kingston's age?' Sydney clarified.

'Long family conspiracy,' Raymond explained. 'Because Kingston here was always the spitting image of his "father".' He made air quotes around the last word. 'And they were never seen together.'

'I should have known the Barrys would work it out,' Kingston said, a faint smile on his lips. 'You always were a bright bunch.'

Raymond smirked.

Sydney shifted her chair slightly to look at Raymond's screen properly. She scanned the list and realised how little they knew about John Smith. Everything they knew was superficial. They knew nothing about his habits, his history, or even if he was a local. That was just speculation.

'We need more,' she said out loud.

'It will be interesting to see if he appears again,' Kingston said. 'I have an inkling that he will.'

'We'll have to play our cards close,' Raymond agreed. 'If he worked out about the town hall so easily, he could work out the other locations.'

'Maybe we can feed him some fake ones?' Sydney suggested.

'That might be worth trying,' Kingston agreed. 'What do you suggest?'

'We could say the train station,' Raymond said. 'We already know that's basically a dead end. He might spend a few hours trying to find it there.'

'He's already been to the School of Mines,' Sydney said. 'Do you think he chose there because of the connection to Redmond?'

'That would be the obvious reason,' Kingston agreed. 'Should we suggest the Unicorn?'

'We could throw that out there,' Raymond agreed. 'Or some churches we've already been to and gotten the keys from.'

'This will depend on us seeing him,' Sydney said. 'And if he's actually the one behind the guy who's watching us.'

'Wish we could just walk over and ask the guy,' Raymond grumbled.

'You know he won't answer,' Kingston said.

'I can be persuasive.'

'Let's avoid violence.'

Sydney wondered what they meant. She couldn't imagine Raymond meant torture, especially after everything he'd been through with Marcus. Sydney's eyes drifted down to his hands, shuddering as she remembered how all his nails had been ripped out by the root. You wouldn't think it looking at them now. They were still shorter than they should be, but they at least looked normal.

'I think that's all we can do right now,' Kingston said. He patted Raymond on the shoulder. 'Send the list to Jake. He might use some of it.'

'Was planning on it.'

CHAPTER 17

KINGSTON turned in early for the night. He complained of leg cramps, so he went to bed early. They'd convinced him to take some painkillers before he went, Raymond teasing him a little about his age and earning a light swat over the ear. Sydney couldn't help but notice the fondness between them and the smile they'd shared before Kingston disappeared down the hall.

Sydney wasn't tired yet, so she commandeered the television and found a movie. After working on his computer, Raymond eventually joined her, and the two settled onto the couch to watch the film. It was an older film. Sydney wasn't sure if you would call it a 'classic' given she'd never heard of it before, but it was still enjoyable.

It was the sort of movie with the credits at the start, so when it ended, it went straight to commercials. She wondered when things had changed and they'd started putting the credits at the film's end. Sydney was glad they had. She couldn't imagine sitting through the credits to watch the movie. She voiced this out loud to Raymond.

'Well, most people didn't come at the film's start,' he said. 'You could walk in any time and leave whenever you wanted.'

She stared at him. 'Really?'

He nodded. 'I'm pretty sure Hitchcock was the one who changed that. He wanted his films to be viewed as a complete package.'

'That makes sense,' she said. 'I couldn't imagine missing the start of a film.'

'That's because we're used to it now,' he said. 'We can't imagine it any other way.'

That was true. She looked at him. 'How do you know that? About how things changed?'

'Tanya's a film buff,' Raymond said with a smile. 'She's a walking encyclopedia of film facts. I wouldn't be surprised if she's seen every movie in existence.'

Sydney nodded. She was curious, though. 'How did you, Tanya, and Andrew meet?'

'University,' Raymond said without hesitation. 'Undergrad. We were in the same classes. They're both librarians.'

'So, you just introduced yourself?'

Raymond snorted. 'More like they accosted me.'

'What do you mean?'

'Week two,' Raymond said. 'I always sat alone in the lecture theatre. They just came and sat down beside me. Andrew on one side; Tanya on the other. They introduced themselves as my new friends.'

'Just like that?' Sydney said, surprised. How could you say you were friends with someone when you didn't even know them?

'Just like that,' Raymond said. 'They'd noticed I was a loner and not mingling with the rest of the class and decided to fix that.'

'And they did?'

'Well, it worked.' Raymond smiled. 'We did end up becoming friends.'

'So, how did they do it?' Sydney asked. 'Just spent time with you in class?'

'They took me out for coffee,' Raymond said. 'And kept inviting me to come with them to things. Sometimes it was trips to different pubs. Sometimes it was to the museum. Sometimes it was back to their apartment. They were staying in the city near the university at the time.'

'They just got to know you slowly,' Sydney said. 'Were they a couple then?'

He nodded. 'They're childhood sweethearts. They got together at high school.'

'How does Olivia come into it?' She tried to work it out. She remembered Jake's comment when everything had gone to crap about the three of them being together, but she didn't see how it worked.

'Oh, they had their eye on me since day one,' Raymond said. 'They wooed me every time we went out, and eventually, I cracked.'

'And Olivia happened?'

'No, not straight away.' He shrugged. 'We were together for about three years. Of course, I never told my mother about that. She thought I was wasting my time with them while she was busy trying to hook me up with every girl she could find.'

'I remember,' Sydney said. Lucille had point-blank asked Sydney if she was single the first time they had formally met. She remembered being shocked by how forward Lucille was.

'Olivia happened on our graduation night,' Raymond said. 'We got completely wasted. One thing led to another, and… well. Olivia.'

'You're sure she's not Andrew's?'

'Definitely,' Raymond said. 'Andrew gets drunk and passes out. You could say he wouldn't have been able to perform. Also, Olivia looks more like me than Andrew.'

She did. Olivia had Raymond's eyes and hair colour. There was no mistaking the fact that she was his daughter. 'And Andrew was okay with that?'

'He was,' Raymond said. 'There's also the fact Andrew can't exactly have children of his own.'

'Why?'

'We didn't know at the time, but, well...' She could see him trying to form words. 'He shoots blanks. They found out when they tried to give Olivia a sibling. They settled with one after that. Olivia treats him as her main father anyway, and I'm perfectly okay with that.'

Sydney wondered if Andrew *was* actually okay with that. It must have been unpleasant to learn you can't have your own children. What must it be like raising another man's daughter as your child? She doubted Andrew would ever say anything to Raymond, but she would have been uncomfortable if she were in his shoes.

'Wait, if you were with Andrew and Tanya, how did you end up with Kingston?' she asked.

'We always had a spark,' Raymond said. 'After I met him, I told Tanya and Andrew about him. Then when they met him, Tanya was all, "You need to get with this guy". We agreed to end our relationship after that. Graduation night was meant to be our last night together.'

'You certainly made it memorable,' Sydney said. It sounded like a complicated mess. 'You wooed Kingston?'

'We flirted,' Raymond said. 'But he never made a move. Then one day, I had enough and kissed him.'

'What happened?' Something fluttered in her gut. She could only imagine Raymond doing that to her.

'He was shocked for a moment,' Raymond said. 'But he ended up kissing me back.'

'I bet he was,' Sydney said. 'Was it just out of the blue?'

Raymond paused to think. He had a faraway look in his eye, so Sydney knew he was remembering. 'We were walking alongside the Torrens,' he said. 'We went there a lot to talk. Still do. I just had a gut feeling that I had to do it, so I did.'

'Maybe Tanya and Andrew rubbed off on you,' she said.

'I hope so.' He chuckled. 'They're impulsive, that's for sure. They've mellowed out a lot compared to what they used to be.

Tanya and Andrew are the sort to decide to go skinny dipping in the middle of winter on an urge. They'd just look at each other and start stripping off.'

Sydney shuddered at the thought of going into the water in that weather. 'Did you go too?'

'Sometimes,' he admitted. 'Usually, I called them crazy while they tried to convince me to join them.'

'I'm sure having Olivia was what calmed them down,' she said.

'Definitely,' he said. 'Being responsible for another life makes you grow up a lot.'

'Did it make you grow up?'

'I was never a child,' he said, going serious. There was a dark look in his eye. It was clearly something that he hated.

'What do you mean?'

'I mean, my mother raised me to be the Keeper,' Raymond said. 'That included never being allowed to go out and play like other children.'

'What did you do instead?'

'Lots of research,' Raymond said. 'A heck of a lot of puzzle books. She wanted me to have an analytical and calculating mind. I can finish a puzzle book in under an hour these days. I don't find them fun or challenging. They bring up bad memories.'

She nodded. She didn't want to pry but was compelled to ask more about being the Keeper. 'What sort of training do you need to be a Keeper?'

'Being an archivist is certainly the top of the list,' Raymond said. 'You must know how to handle books correctly and understand how records work. That's at least a few years at university.'

'Including a post-grad,' she said.

He nodded.

'What else?'

'Lots of learning to solve riddles and puzzles,' he said. 'It helps with learning to break Redmond's code. And, of course, getting to know everything about Redmond's life intimately. You have to be able to think how he thinks. That way, you can get inside his head and work out how he hid the locations in the journals.'

She nodded. It sounded like years of work. 'Is that all?'

'Well, you need to be able to protect yourself,' he said. 'I know two different martial arts. I know how to shoot a gun. I've had some training with weapons, including knives.'

That didn't surprise her. 'I'm guessing being fit is part of it.'

'Definitely,' he said. 'I have a whole workout routine.'

She'd pay to see him working out. She'd pay double if it were shirtless. Heck, throw Kingston in as well. He was good to look at. 'Do you work out with Kingston?'

'Sometimes,' Raymond said. 'We use the gym at the hotel. Most of the time, I use a gym close to the State Library. I have a membership there.'

She'd have to dig at Jake to see if she could get the name of the gym and then sneak in to spy on him. That wouldn't be too creepy, would it? Maybe she could start working out there as well. She needed to get more fit. This excursion to Ballarat proved she wasn't as fit as she thought.

'Sounds like it's a lot of work becoming the Keeper,' Sydney said. 'Are you sure Olivia will catch up?'

A dark look crossed his face. 'Yes. And only if she wants to. I will not force it upon her like it was on me.'

There was an edge to his voice. Sydney wanted to shrink back into the couch. He was protective of his daughter, and his childhood resentment simmered at the surface.

'Just wondering,' she said. 'What did your father think of it?'

'He didn't agree with it, but he wasn't going to argue,' Raymond said. 'He knew before he had children with my mother what was to be expected. It was an unwritten contract.'

Her eyes widened. 'He agreed to it?'

'He understood,' Raymond corrected. 'As I said, he disagreed with it. He just knew what would happen.'

'So he knows about... everything.'

Raymond nodded.

'I'm sorry to say this, but that's kind of messed up,' she said. 'If I were in his situation, I would have refused.'

'Which is what I'm doing now,' Raymond said. He grunted. 'My mother has been harassing Andrew and Tanya about training Olivia. I had to call her several times while I was in Europe to tell her to stop.'

Sydney had expected that. 'Did she?'

'Of course not. Mother is a firm believer in responsibility before personal choice.'

That had Sydney thinking back to the situation with Marcus. 'But wasn't going to Werribee responsibility over family?'

That gave him pause. She could see him making calculations behind his blue eyes. 'You know, I'm going to use that next time we argue about it.'

'You're still arguing about it?'

'It comes up.' He rubbed his jaw. His stubble was a little longer than it had been that morning. What would he look like with a beard? She couldn't picture it. 'Mother holds grudges.'

Sydney nodded. Again, she could picture that. She felt Raymond was the same but knew better than to mention a similarity between him and his mother. There was animosity between them, although there was also a lot of respect. She remembered how Lucille had reacted when she'd thought Raymond was going to die. She wished Raymond could have seen it as well.

'You know, I know little about you,' Raymond said, turning the conversation around. 'Only child, right?'

She nodded. 'I have a couple of cousins who are similar in age, so I spent time with them.'

'Older or younger?'

'Older. Not by much.'

'What's America like?'

She paused to think. 'Well, I only saw a small section of it,' she admitted. 'Honestly, it's not that much different. We have better coffee, though. And our food is a lot less greasy.'

He smiled faintly at that. 'So, the culture isn't much different?'

'It's different,' she said. 'It's hard to explain. They follow different sports and have different tastes in music. That changes depending on where you go. Some people like baseball, some like basketball, and some like their version of football. Some people like all three.'

'New York is dangerous, isn't it?'

'Not if you're careful,' she said. 'There are places you don't go alone, but that's the same in every city. I always carry my mace with me. I can tell you our public transport is better. And our health care. Most people there don't even realise how bad they've got it.'

'Huh.' Raymond considered that. 'I didn't realise our health care is different.'

'It's hard for me to explain it,' Sydney said. 'You'd be better off looking it up online. But yes, their health care is pretty bad. I also get way more benefits working over here. More vacation time, sick days, et cetera.'

'Hours?'

'About the same,' Sydney admitted. 'Better overtime pay.'

'Do you do much overtime?'

'I try to avoid it.' Sydney shrugged. 'I want to have a life outside of work. Does that make sense?' Not that she had much of a life. Her spare time was mostly spent at home, but she wasn't going to tell him that.

'Perfectly,' Raymond said. 'I'm the same. Although I have a lot of difficulties making friends.'

'Why?'

'I'm just not that outgoing,' he admitted.

That surprised her. He came across as confident to the point of fault. But she knew from experience that interacting with people took a different type of confidence. Someone who enjoyed extreme sports and going to raves could still be an introvert.

'I'm also not easy to get along with,' he said.

'I don't know about that,' she said. 'I've had no problem.'

'You're the sort that gets along with everyone,' Raymond said. 'Which is exactly what you need to do your job.'

It was. You didn't get far in her field of work if you weren't a people person. She'd learnt how to read people, knowing what they would say before they made the request. It prevented surprises. She found Kingston and Raymond rather difficult to read. They played their cards close to their chest. So did Jake when he shut himself down, and he was a very outgoing, 'heart-on-your-sleeve' kind of guy.

'Did you and Jake click the first time you met?' she asked. 'He seems like he's a friend of yours.'

'We hit it off,' Raymond said with a nod. 'Jake's kind of like you. He gets along with everyone so long as they don't rub him the wrong way. He's good at reading people, too. The first time we went out for drinks, we discovered we had a few things in common, including liking the same band.'

'The Runaway Boys,' Sydney remembered.

He nodded. 'We both have every album of theirs. We see them every time they come to Adelaide or Melbourne. They've got a few hits but never really broke out of Australia.'

'I don't think I've ever seen them play,' she admitted. She knew their songs. She'd looked them up after discovering that Jake and Raymond were interested in them. They were good, but not her sort of music. 'You're a rock fan?'

'Definitely a rock fan,' he confirmed. 'You?'

'I prefer hip hop,' she said. 'With a bit of dance.'

'Very American,' he teased.

'Hey, I always liked it,' she said. 'I just got to hear more of it over in America.'

He accepted that, stretching his legs out. She could tell by the way he rubbed them they were hurting. It reminded her of her muscle tightness. She stretched out her legs to ease them a little. She could really go for a massage. Maybe when they returned to Adelaide, she would look up a massage parlour and book herself in as a reward.

'I think I might go to bed,' Raymond said, glancing back towards the door. 'See if Kingston's actually asleep or if he's just reading.'

'He reads?' Sydney asked.

'He reads a lot,' Raymond confirmed. 'He studies us.'

She frowned at that. 'What do you mean?'

'Humanity,' Raymond said. 'He reads a lot of books about humanity. Our history, our psychology and behaviour, all that sort of thing. I think he's trying to "get" us.'

'Or make sure he fits in,' Sydney said.

'He fits in,' Raymond said. 'Better than I do.'

'You fit in fine,' she assured him. 'Everyone likes you.'

'That's because they don't know me,' Raymond said. 'It's easy to like someone if you don't know their flaws.'

That was true. 'Some flaws are endearing.'

He snorted. 'Yeah, that's one way of looking at it.'

Sydney studied him. There were a lot of contradictions. He was both sure of himself and seemed to dislike himself. Raymond loved his job, but he hated it. He was outgoing but an introvert. One thing was for sure – Raymond Barry was a complicated man. And she liked that about him.

'I'll turn in as well,' she said. 'Need to rest up before tomorrow.'

'Our last day looking for keys tomorrow,' Raymond reminded her.

'Fingers crossed,' she said.

He nodded and smiled at her. 'Fingers crossed.'

CHAPTER 18

THEY were out the door before nine. They'd dragged themselves out of bed and had breakfast, going over the plan for the day before they left. The weather was overcast again, which meant it would be another day in coats, much to Raymond's annoyance. Kingston would insist he wore one, and if it started raining, Raymond was sure Kingston would hand Raymond his coat if he didn't have one. Kingston was a gentleman like that.

They made the walk across the centre of Ballarat towards the Highlander Hotel. Raymond wasn't sure what they would find at the former hotel. He knew it had undergone renovation over the years, but how much would determine whether they found a key. It was the same story as every other building they had visited. He cursed modernisation. He honestly preferred the original buildings.

That was something he had loved about Werribee Park Mansion when he and Rita had gone there searching for a key. It had been like stepping into a time capsule. The building had a history and a charm that many had lost. Even from the brief time he had been in there, he could tell a lot of the interior and furnishings were original. He longed to go back and explore that building properly but knew that both his mother and Kingston would freak out if he went back to Werribee.

Honestly, Raymond considered what had happened in Werribee all those years ago to be ancient history. Yes, his great-grandparents had died there, but that didn't mean he was cursed to the same fate. He knew it didn't help that Marcus' goons had accosted Rita and himself while looking for the key. Kingston had some form of PTSD from the experience in Werribee, but Lucille had no excuse for why she was so upset. From what he could gather, she hadn't even been that close to her grandparents.

They reached the Highlander Hotel after the start time of the day's event. There was a small gathering of people inside the building when they arrived. The building was usually closed at this hour. They were only open in the morning for people to come and see the building, and stepping inside, Raymond realised that where they wanted to go was not open.

'Where are we looking?' Kingston asked, studying the building's brochure.

'Upstairs,' Raymond said.

'But we can't go upstairs,' Sydney said.

'Yeah.'

'We can ask,' Kingston said, looking around and spotting the person in charge of the building.

They wandered over to them, waiting while the woman finished discussing the history of the building with another visitor. When she was done, she turned to them with a huge grin. It was genuine, too. Raymond could tell that she loved her job.

'How can I help you?' she asked.

'We were wondering if the upstairs area is accessible,' Kingston said.

'Not for today's opening,' she said. 'The business has requested that we keep things downstairs. I can tell you the history of the upstairs if you're interested.'

'Thank you,' Kingston declined. 'Although I do have to ask if it's original.'

'No, it's not,' she said. 'It's been used for many purposes over the years, so they have changed it for those different purposes.'

'Just like downstairs here,' Raymond said, looking around. Little of the room looked to be original. Maybe the brickwork, but even that looked like it had been touched up over the years.

'Exactly,' she said. 'It's had a variety of tenants and names and has served as a popular drinking spot for Ballarat since its establishment.'

'So very little of the interior is original,' Kingston confirmed.

'I'm afraid not,' she said. 'This is also not the original building.'

Raymond's ears pricked. 'What do you mean?'

'The original building was destroyed in a fire in 1885,' she said. 'It was rebuilt soon afterwards.'

Kingston looked at Raymond with a question on his face. Raymond shook his head. He hadn't picked that up in his research. He saw Sydney's face fall and knew she was thinking the same thing. They would not find a key here. He should have looked deeper into the history. He wondered how he had missed that critical piece of information.

They thanked the guide and moved away, heading back outside. Raymond heaved a sigh as he was hit by drizzling rain again. Sunshine was predicted for the afternoon, and it couldn't come fast enough. He pulled his coat collar up.

'You didn't know it had burnt down?' Kingston asked as they stepped to the side and away from the door.

'No,' Raymond said. He was disappointed in himself for missing that. 'It wasn't in the notes.'

'The key would have been lost then,' Sydney said.

Raymond nodded his agreement. 'It's the same with a few buildings. There's a hotel near the mall that was supposed to have a key, but when I researched it, I found out it had also burned down.'

'So that happens with a lot of buildings,' Sydney said.

Raymond nodded again. 'Too many. If it's not redevelopment, it's fire.'

'I remember the great fire of Melbourne in 1897,' Kingston said. 'An entire block went up in flames.'

'The one in Elizabeth Street,' Raymond said. 'I remember reading about that.'

'Melbourne had a huge fire?' Sydney asked.

'It was devastating,' Kingston said. 'The tallest building in the city at the time was destroyed. A beautiful building.'

'You went and saw it?' Raymond asked.

'Of course,' Kingston said. 'It was before I left for Ireland. I remained for a while after my father's death, but it became clear that the Barry family couldn't break the code, so I went to Ireland. They were the ones who told me about the building fire. I didn't see the fire itself, but I certainly saw the aftermath. Complete devastation.'

'Was fire common?' Sydney asked.

'Seems that way,' Raymond said. 'I'm guessing it's because they didn't have the safety features we have today. Sprinklers, alarms, that sort of thing.'

'It was shortly after that they installed the first automatic sprinkler system in one of the new buildings in Melbourne,' Kingston said. 'You could say the fire led to innovation.'

'Tragedy always does,' Raymond said.

'People learn from mistakes,' Sydney agreed. 'Where to next?'

'Craig's Hotel,' Raymond answered. 'Hopefully, we have more luck there than we did here.'

The drizzle didn't let up as they walked back to Craig's Hotel. Raymond had chosen to go there second, hoping the crowd would be less by the time they arrived. It proved accurate, as they found few people standing outside the building. They greeted the poor worker standing in the rain with pamphlets, who politely asked them to keep their photography discreet and not bother any guests who were staying in the hotel.

Stepping inside, Raymond felt like he was coming home. They had tried to keep the interior of the hotel authentic. It had a classical feel, and they made everything look like it had been there since conception. He knew it was all appearance because the original furnishings and interior would be well worn if it were true, and everything looked pristine and well cared for.

'Is it in the tower?' Sydney asked as they moved through the building lobby.

'No, the tower was added later,' Raymond said, gazing around the building. 'It's downstairs, near the staircase.'

'Not a room?' Kingston asked.

'No.' Looking at his pamphlet, Raymond could see that one room was open for them to look at. He was glad it wasn't a room that Redmond had hidden the key in, because their luck meant it would be a room different from the one on offer for photos.

'Any clue as to where?' Kingston asked as they made their way towards the staircase.

'Side panel on the right side,' Raymond said.

They moved around the staircase, Raymond taking his camera out to snap a few photos of the ornate structure that led the way upstairs. People were coming and going, so they tried to fit in as best they could. They inspected the side of the stairs, pretending to be looking at the woodwork.

'There!' Sydney said, pointing to a panel near the base.

Raymond followed her finger and saw the etching on the panel. Like the rest, it was small and almost hidden beneath the stain. They had painted it over a couple of times. He moved over to it, kneeling so he could reach it. His fingers traced the edges and found the compartment had been painted shut. He took out his knife and carefully cut it open, finding the switch that sprang it free.

He reached inside the compartment and grinned as he felt the cold brass of a key. Raymond quickly fished it out, deposited it into his pocket, and closed the compartment up again. He brushed at the spot to hide what he had done, put his knife away, and quietly joined the group again.

'Well?' Kingston asked.

'Got it,' Raymond confirmed.

'Nice.' Sydney grinned.

'Shall we go upstairs and inspect the room?' Kingston asked them.

'Might as well while we're here,' Raymond said.

They moved up the staircase. Stepping inside the room open for inspection, Raymond heard Sydney suck in a breath, and he found her eyes open with wonder. He could see what was catching her attention. The room was immaculate and straight out of the 1850s.

Everything about the room was ornate, from the decorative edging along the tops of the walls all the way down to the floral carpet. A four-poster bed sat in the room, and everything was colour coordinated. He snapped a few pictures, seeing Sydney do the same as they stepped around the room. He felt he had to be careful in here, as if he could somehow disrupt history.

'Their eye for detail is astounding,' Kingston said, pausing at the door to the bathroom. 'Sadly, the bathroom breaks the aesthetic.'

'How so?' Sydney asked.

'It's modern,' he said. 'An original bathroom would have a chamber pot.'

'I'm glad it doesn't,' Raymond said, shuddering at the thought. 'I wouldn't want to stay here if it didn't have a flushing toilet.'

'A luxury of the modern age,' Kingston said, stepping back into the room and inspecting the view from the window. 'I imagine this is one of the larger guest rooms.'

'The pamphlet doesn't say,' Sydney said, running her eyes over the piece of paper. 'It just says it's a feature bedroom.'

'"Feature" meaning they use it in all their publicity,' Raymond guessed.

'It is a gorgeous room.' Sydney snapped another photo of the bed. 'It's a shame the Medina Grand doesn't have a classic theme.'

'I'm rather glad it does not,' Kingston said. 'I prefer the modern style.'

'Well, you are an alien,' Raymond commented. Kingston narrowed his eyes at Raymond, only to be met with a smile and a wink.

They did a full tour of Craig's Hotel, complete with the function rooms and the currently closed restaurant. The hotel was a mix of classical and modern features. The furniture was antique, but screens and projectors were ready to go if needed. Raymond had a feeling the kitchen would be fully modern as well. The hotel was mostly about appearance and cashing in on the city's history.

As they returned to the foyer, Raymond heard Sydney make a half-surprised, half-distressed sound. She was staring at the door. Kingston went rigid, and before he even looked, Raymond knew who was there. John Smith.

The man had a coat on for the weather. It was more a trench coat that came down to his knees, and it also looked to have been tailored for him. Again, there was no sign of a brand, and Raymond noted that the cane he was using differed from the one they had seen him with last time. It was a similar style, but this one had an eagle head with emerald eyes.

Raymond was wondering if they could find a back door and disappear when John Smith saw them. He beamed at them, coming towards them, his cane tapping on the floor. His walk was better described as a strut, and Raymond was sure that if you balanced a cup on his head, he wouldn't spill a drop of water. Everything about the man screamed upper class.

'Hello again,' John said cheerfully. 'We seem to keep running into each other.'

'Indeed, we do,' Kingston said carefully. 'Are you here to photograph the hotel?'

'But of course,' John said. 'I've always wanted to peek behind the curtain at Craig's. Are many of the rooms open?'

'Only one guest room,' Sydney answered. 'And a few rooms here on the lower level.'

'I keep meaning to try the restaurant, but I haven't found a fitting occasion,' John said. 'A place like this should be saved for special moments.'

'You talk like a local,' Raymond observed. 'How you've seen the buildings from outside but never from inside.'

He was sure John Smith faltered slightly, but it was a blink-and-miss-it moment. 'Such buildings like this are quite well known.'

Raymond noted his avoidance of the unspoken question. He was certain that John Smith lived in Ballarat. That meant he most likely worked here as well. They could pass that information to Jake now they had confirmed it. It tempted Raymond to follow the man back to his car to get the plates, but he felt John Smith wouldn't allow that.

'I like your cane,' Sydney said.

'Yes, it is a favourite of mine,' John Smith said. That confirmed he had a collection of them. Another detail they could add to their list. 'Have you been here long?' John asked them.

'We were just about to leave,' Kingston said. 'We've done the full tour.'

'Photography?'

'Lots,' Raymond said, slipping his camera back into his bag and zipping it closed.

'I imagine you got some brilliant shots,' John said. 'Any suggestions?'

'I quite liked the guest room,' Sydney said.

'I was thinking more about the staircase,' John said.

Alarm bells went off so loud in Raymond's head that it was deafening. He forced himself to keep his face impassive and eyes straight. Out of the corner of his eye, he saw Sydney and Kingston doing the same.

'There is nothing truly remarkable about it,' Kingston said. 'It is old, but I have seen better staircases.'

'Such as?' John asked.

Kingston smiled and didn't answer.

'Many then,' John said. 'So, how goes your week? Any places left to visit?'

'We are thinking of going to the train station tomorrow,' Sydney said, falling into their plan. 'I've heard a lot about the tower.'

'It is quite catching to the eye,' John agreed. 'It's a shame they couldn't organise a steam train for the week. I believe they were trying but were unable.'

'That is a shame,' Raymond said. 'It would have been quite photogenic.'

'That it would,' John said. 'They bring them in from time to time. They always draw a large crowd when they do.'

Raymond wondered if he meant to give so much away about his life here in Ballarat. He simply nodded along, waiting for more.

'Anyhow, I shall not keep you,' John said. 'I'm sure you have places to be. Be mindful of the weather. It's a little damp out there. It can get so particularly in the evening, as I'm sure you've noticed.'

Raymond spotted the frown on Sydney's face. She must be wondering the same thing – why mention the evening?

'We'll be careful,' Kingston said. 'Enjoy your time here.'

They let him go, moving out of the hotel. They made their way along the street to Sturt Street, rounding the corner. Raymond glanced back and saw that no one was following them. He looked over at Kingston and gave him a nod. Kingston returned it. He'd noticed they weren't being followed either.

'Oh god,' Sydney breathed. 'He's everywhere.'

'He's definitely following us,' Raymond said.

'So it would seem,' Kingston agreed. 'I suggest we return to our hotel and fill Jake and Rita in on what is happening.'

Raymond nodded his agreement. Maybe Jake had something for them. He could only hope.

CHAPTER 19

THE man wasn't standing across the street when they returned to their hotel, much to Sydney's relief. She pulled her coat closer around herself to keep the cold out. It was still drizzling, but she could see patches of blue sky approaching them. It looked like it would fine up later in the afternoon.

As they stepped into the hotel, the receptionist came around towards them. 'Were you expecting anyone today?'

Kingston frowned. 'Why?'

'A man was trying to enter your room,' the receptionist said. 'One of the other guests noticed him trying to pick the lock and called me.'

Sydney's skin prickled, electricity shooting up her limbs. Could it have been the man who'd been watching them? That confirmed that it was them he was watching.

'What happened?' Kingston asked.

'He ran when I confronted him,' the receptionist said. 'Just so you're aware, I've let our security know about the incident.'

'Thank you,' Kingston said. 'No, we are not expecting anyone.'

'I didn't think so,' the receptionist said. 'You would have said something, and I doubt he would have run.'

'Thank you for telling us,' Sydney said.

The receptionist nodded and went back to her post.

They remained quiet as they made their way to their rooms. Kingston unlocked the door and admitted them all inside. Everything looked to be the way they had left it. It looked like the guy hadn't made it past the door before they caught him.

'Everything seems fine,' Raymond said, echoing Sydney's thoughts.

'We're going to need to be doubly sure that all we lock the windows and doors when we leave,' Kingston said. He huffed, disappearing back down the hallway.

'Where is he going?' Sydney asked.

'Probably to check on the keys,' Raymond said as he set his camera bag on the table. He patted his pocket. 'That's what the guy was no doubt after.'

Sydney nodded. Kingston came back down the hall holding a box. It was a small lockbox. Kingston opened it with a tiny key and tipped out the keys they had already found. They were safe.

'Well, that's good,' Raymond said. He fished inside his pocket and dropped the new key into the palm of Kingston's hand along with the others. 'One more for the collection.'

Kingston put them back inside the box, sealing it. 'I'll return this to its hiding spot.'

Kingston disappeared down the hallway. Sydney crossed over to the window. No sign of the man. She doubted he'd be back now that they had chased him away from the hotel. That was provided it was the same guy that had tried breaking in.

'What are you looking at?'

She jumped. Raymond's voice was in her ear and broke her out of her thoughts. 'Just seeing if the guy was back.'

'He doesn't appear to be,' Raymond said. Sydney could almost feel him against her back. As he moved away, Sydney quietly exhaled. 'If it's the same person, I doubt he'd want to be seen around the hotel.'

'I was just thinking that.'

Raymond set himself down on the couch. She contemplated joining him but made her way over to the chair. It was tight on the couch when there were three people. They could all fit but had to squish up against each other. 'Should we tell Jake about what happened?'

'We most definitely will,' Kingston said as he rejoined them. He didn't hesitate to sit beside Raymond, taking his phone out of his pocket. 'I suggest we call him and Rita now.'

'Won't they be on the clock?' Raymond asked.

'I'm sure they can take some time.' Kingston was already dialling the number. He put it on speakerphone and set it on the coffee table.

Sydney shifted in her seat to be closer to the phone, listening as it rang. After several rings, Rita picked up.

'You're calling early, Kingston,' Rita said. 'Something wrong? Shall I call Jake up?'

'Please do,' Kingston said.

Rita put them on hold. Sydney noticed Raymond wince.

'You need better hold music,' he told Kingston.

'I don't exactly have much choice in what we have. It came with the phone plan.'

'It sounds like Centrelink's music.'

Kingston frowned and looked at him. 'Why have you been in contact with Centrelink?'

'Hey, I went to uni,' Raymond said. 'I received Youth Allowance.'

'How?' Kingston asked.

'My grandparents didn't "gift" me any of their money until after I graduated,' Raymond said. 'Before that, we were living off my mother's income.'

'Didn't they buy her that apartment?' Kingston asked.

'Yes, but it wasn't in her name,' Raymond said.

Sydney tried to put two and two together, realising what was being implied. 'Did your family game the system?'

'I was just thinking that,' Kingston said.

'No!' Raymond defended. He hesitated. 'Not really.'

Kingston gave him a look and Raymond squirmed. Sydney had to admit she was slightly disappointed. It was clear the Barry family had money, and there would have been no need for them to receive government payments. It sounded like they had taken advantage of loopholes.

The conversation ended as the hold music cut out and Rita came back on the line.

'We're both here,' she said. 'Be aware I have a meeting in thirty minutes.'

'And I can't really leave the security office for too long,' Jake added.

'You make that sound like something happened,' Kingston said. 'Did it?'

There was a moment's pause. Sydney could almost see Rita and Jake exchanging a look. 'You know that guy we've been having trouble with?' Jake said.

'The drunk?' Raymond asked.

'The same,' Jake said. 'He came back again.'

'Some people just don't know when to quit.' Raymond frowned.

'I thought the authorities had taken care of him,' Kingston said.

'They did. But every time they let him out, he comes back,' Jake said. Another pause. 'This time, though, he went straight downstairs.'

'Jake,' Kingston said.

'He went for the portal,' Jake continued. 'And not by accident. He made a direct beeline for it.'

'What?' Sydney exclaimed. 'How?'

'My theory is he used to work for Marcus,' Rita said. 'And is trying to extract some form of revenge.'

'That is a sound theory,' Kingston said. 'I doubt we will be able to test it.'

'Did he get into the portal room?' Raymond asked.

'No, it was locked,' Jake answered. 'Trust me, I make sure that door stays locked. I keep the card on me at all times.'

'Including the spare card?' Kingston asked.

'Including the spare card,' Jake confirmed. 'No one is getting in there without me knowing.'

'That makes for a change,' Raymond muttered.

'I heard that!'

'What happened to the gentleman?' Kingston asked.

'You mean after I tackled him?' Jake asked. 'Police. Criminal trespass. If he tries to return again, he won't be in for a good time.'

'Are we sure he's connected to Marcus?' Sydney asked. 'It's been over six months. It's odd that he's only showing up now.'

'That is true,' Kingston said. 'Unless Marcus had some sort of dead man's switch.'

'That went off at the six-month mark?' Raymond said.

Kingston nodded.

'That's possible,' Jake said. 'He showed up basically six months to the day.'

'Who else do you think he's connected to, Sydney?' Rita asked.

'John Smith,' she said.

'You're still having issues with him?' Jake asked.

'He made another appearance, yes,' Kingston said. 'And his questions are rather interesting.'

'We also had a guy try to break into our room today,' Raymond said. 'While we were out.'

'The receptionist caught him and he ran,' Sydney added.

'That's not good,' Rita said. 'That sounds like escalation.'

'They didn't get in,' Raymond said. 'And Kingston has the keys locked up and hidden.'

'Safely?'

'I cannot think of a more safe place for them,' Kingston said.

'I won't ask where in case the phones are tapped,' Jake said.

Sydney's heart rate increased at that. She stared at the phone, worried that someone might listen in. Kingston and Raymond didn't look concerned. At least, that was how they appeared. They had those blank expressions on their face again, exchanging sideways looks she couldn't quite read. She wished she could decipher their wordless conversation.

'So, what's the plan?' Jake asked.

'We don't really have one,' Kingston said. 'To simply continue as we are doing.'

'We've hit all the locations for the keys,' Raymond said. 'The next couple of days were really to take time to ourselves. See a few sights.'

'Isn't that what you've been doing all week?' Rita said.

'We've been working, Miss Taylor,' Kingston reminded her. 'Seeing the sights was secondary.'

'So, where you off to tomorrow?' Jake asked.

'Sovereign Hill,' Sydney answered. 'We want to see what life was like back in the 1850s. Get a picture of what things were like when Kingston came here.'

'Need I remind you I came here in 1880,' Kingston said. 'There was a lot of innovation at that time.'

'Still no cars, though,' Jake said. 'Wish I could go with you. I'd love to check out a theme park.'

'You know there are no thrill rides, right?' Raymond said.

'Hey, I like laid-back parks too,' Jake said. 'Just anything that's different. Take a break from the real world for a while.'

'You say that like a man who needs a holiday,' Kingston observed.

They heard Jake sigh. 'It's been a long week.'

'And *you* didn't have to do all the paperwork,' Rita said.

'I did enough of it,' he replied.

'Bet you're glad you're not there,' Raymond said to Kingston.

Sydney was. She would have been the one arms deep in the paperwork. She felt bad for her temporary replacement and was a little guilty that she was so far away. Sydney knew that there was nothing she could have done even if she had been there, but it didn't stop the feelings.

'I'd still leave the paperwork to Rita,' Kingston said with a smile.

'Lazy ass,' Raymond teased.

'I'll have you know my arse works very hard.'

'I'd still have the paperwork,' Rita said. 'You always find ways for me to end up with it.'

'You have a gift,' Kingston said. 'I'm prone to making mistakes.'

'Only because you get distracted.'

Sydney wondered what distracted him, and then her eyes shifted to Raymond. That was probably distraction enough right there. Given the look Raymond gave Kingston, he agreed with her assessment of the situation. He looked half concerned, half amused. Sydney looked back at the phone on the table, feeling bad for Rita. She was glad she wasn't the one who had to keep Kingston in line.

'So, you're back in three days?' Jake asked.

'Yes,' Kingston confirmed. 'Provided there's no major catastrophe on the highway, we should be back around lunchtime.'

'We should have a meeting when you return,' Rita said.

'That is the idea,' Kingston said. Raymond rolled his eyes, staring out the window. Not a fan of meetings. Sydney enjoyed them. 'We will also need to test the keys to see if they work.'

'Money on the fact they all lead back to where you found them,' Jake said.

'That does seem to be the pattern.'

Sydney nodded, thinking about the keys they had found in the past. All the working ones had indeed led back to the building where they had been found. It was a little disappointing. She'd hoped for keys to other planets. Kingston had already assured her that wouldn't be the case, as the only planet a key ever led to was Lierdan, and Kian had that key. She knew from the incident with Marcus that it no longer worked.

Still, Sydney could only hope that one of these new keys led somewhere wonderful. Maybe one would be a portal in Ireland. She'd never been to that country. She wondered how'd she'd explain herself if she ended up there via a portal. None of them had used the portals for travel yet, not including the portal between Melbourne and Adelaide. Heck, how would she explain the trip to Ballarat without having taken a plane or train?

'We really need to get back to work,' Rita said. 'Not all of us have the luxury of being on holiday.'

'We're working,' Raymond reminded her.

'It's hardly working.'

'Tell that to our legs.'

'So, you're unfit. I thought you looked a little round after your trip to Europe.'

Kingston raised a hand to cut off Raymond's retort; Rita was getting under Raymond's skin. She wondered what their deal was. They liked to pick on each other and always made needling jabs at each other. It was almost a sibling rivalry that they both partook in. They were clearly fond of each other, yet they fought so much.

'We'll let you go,' Kingston said, looking over at Sydney. She could see the question – did she have anything to add?

'We think John Smith is from Ballarat,' she added, realising that no one had mentioned it yet. 'Is that any help, Jake?'

'It narrows it down a little, but there's still probably a lot of John Smiths there,' Jake said. 'I really need a photo or some more details.'

'If we see him again, we'll try to find something for you,' Kingston said. 'Have a good rest of the day.'

Rita and Jake bid their farewells, Kingston hanging up. He slid the phone back into his pocket, looking between them. 'I think we should spend the rest of the afternoon to ourselves. Rest before we go out again tomorrow.'

'Sounds good to me,' Raymond said, stretching. 'I could do with putting my feet up.'

'TV?' Sydney asked.

'I think I'll go over Redmond's journal again,' Raymond said. 'In case I missed anything.'

She nodded, if a little stung. She had enjoyed their time together so far. Sydney was getting to know him better. She had also got to know Kingston a little better, although he was still quite reserved. He had his secrets. She wondered if Raymond knew them.

'Is that what you intend to do, Miss Madinah?' Kingston asked. 'Watch television?'

She nodded. 'It appears they play classical movies during the day. I wouldn't mind watching another one.'

'I wonder if I have seen it,' Kingston said.

She lit up. 'You want to watch with me?'

'I have found it unwise to distract Raymond when he is working,' Kingston said, looking at the man in question.

The look on Raymond's face was unreadable, but she could tell he agreed with what Kingston had said. There was history there. She had a feeling that history included some fighting. Raymond and Kingston had an interesting relationship. She'd seen how protective Kingston could get and how much Raymond hated it. Sydney didn't want to see what would happen if Kingston interrupted Raymond. She made a note to avoid doing it herself.

'I better get to it,' Raymond said, pushing himself off the couch. 'Enjoy your film.'

Kingston shuffled over on the couch and gestured for Sydney to join him. She couldn't see the television from where she was sitting, so she shifted to the spot Raymond had just vacated. Kingston switched on the television and found the channel Sydney was talking about. It was an old war film. World War Two, if she had to hazard a guess.

'Not a pleasant period,' Kingston said. 'The films romanticise it so much.'

'The war?' she asked.

He nodded. 'It was a lot of death and destruction.'

She had to remind herself he'd lived through the era. 'What was worse? World War One or World War Two?'

'Both.'

'Did you serve?'

He shook his head. 'I made myself disappear. It is also hard to be drafted if you don't have a birth certificate.'

'Did you spend the period in Ireland?'

'Moving around,' he said. 'I travelled Australia, primarily to the south of the nation. It was safer here.'

She could understand that. Europe was being bombed. 'Did you ever go to America?'

'Once,' he said. 'But only for a short period, and only to California. I was curious about Hollywood.'

California was on her bucket list. She looked back at the television. All the actors were good-looking, and everything was clean. There was no blood, and everyone in the movie seemed happy to be there. She knew that was far from reality. She felt terrible for all the people who lost their lives in the war.

She settled in to watch the film but could only think of Kingston living through it. It would be interesting to see what Sovereign Hill brought.

CHAPTER 20

RAYMOND drove them across Ballarat to the theme park an hour after opening time, parking at the back of the lot. It surprised Sydney just how many cars were already there. She counted several tourist buses as well. She felt the park would be crazy busy and wondered if they might have come earlier.

They found the main gates and paid to enter. The prices weren't too bad, and the person at the ticket booth directed them to the left and through a building. There were displays there that gave the history of the goldfields. It felt like a museum as they walked through the area. Sydney took her time to read everything and learn about the history of Ballarat and the goldfields.

Sydney couldn't help but gasp as they stepped out into the park. The yellow sand of the road crunched underfoot. Old-style buildings with verandahs lined the main street that went up a slight hill, and the smell of gravel and manure hit her. A stagecoach rolled past them, pulled by a team of beautiful Clydesdale horses. Sydney wanted to see everything at once, and she stared at the brochure in her hand, trying to figure out what to do first.

'I say we just walk the main street,' Raymond said, noting what she was doing. 'Take it from there.'

'That would be an excellent plan of action,' Kingston agreed.

They crossed the street and stepped onto the wooden walkway. She felt out of place in her garb. She looked around and saw several park employees dressed in period clothing.

'Think you could pull off that dress?' Raymond asked.

Sydney eyed the hoop dress that the nearby woman was wearing. 'How do you even move around in that thing? I'd be scared I'd knock someone over.'

'They were the fashion,' Kingston said. 'Everyone over a certain age wore them.'

'Mm-hm,' Raymond said, a half smile on his face. 'You'd know.'

Kingston side-eyed him. 'Is that a jest about my age?'

'Wasn't this what Australia was like when you arrived?'

'More or less,' Kingston agreed. 'I arrived in 1880. Things had progressed.'

'But there were still horses and carriages, right?' Sydney asked.

'There were.'

'It must have been a culture shock,' Raymond said as they watched a group of other tourists walking up the main street led by a tour guide. 'Coming from a futuristic world to this.'

'Very much so.' Kingston eyed them. 'How do you feel? Coming from your own world to this?'

'We still have our phones on us,' Sydney reminded him. 'And the internet.'

'And I had nothing.' Kingston sighed. 'You could say things have come a long way since 1880. Especially in hygiene.'

'How did they bathe?' Sydney asked. 'Back then.'

'Bucket of water warmed on the stove,' Kingston explained. 'You mostly bathed with a sponge and soap. Soap was a lot cruder back then. If you were lucky and wealthy enough, you could afford to have someone draw a bath for you. It was toileting that was the most interesting.'

'Bedpan, right?' Raymond said.

Kingston nodded. 'Chamber pot. A man would come once a week with his horse and carriage to empty thunderboxes, as they were called. Most sewage was just poured into open drains.'

'Oh god,' Sydney said. She didn't want to imagine the smell. 'How did you survive?'

'It took some getting used to, but I managed.' Kingston smiled. 'I was very happy for the day they brought flushable toilets to Australia. Even more so when they became a standard issue, not just a luxury for the wealthy.'

'What was communication like?' Raymond asked.

'Mail and messenger boys,' Kingston explained. 'There were telegraph machines that linked several of the major cities. Adelaide and Melbourne among them. Usually, however, you simply went and found the person to speak to them.'

'Do you remember when phones came in?' Sydney asked.

Kingston nodded. 'They were a novelty at first. Eventually, they also became standard.'

'And then mobiles came along,' Raymond said. 'And you weren't tethered to the wall anymore.'

'Communication has come a long way very quickly,' Kingston said. 'Progress has a way of doing that.'

Sydney nodded, turning back to the park. Where should they go first? The wooden walkway led past several buildings – shops. 'Should we go in and look?'

'That's what we're here for,' Raymond said, gesturing for her to go ahead.

They made their way up the street, weaving in and out of the shops. The merchandise was themed to the park, and she also found that some shops were workshops. The woodturner and metalworker were exhibiting their crafts while their wares were available to buy. She saw many things she wanted but could already feel her bank account crying.

'Well, look at that.'

Sydney frowned at Kingston's comment as they stood in one store. She followed his gaze and realised he was looking at the walking sticks. She studied them as she heard Raymond make a noise of realisation. It took her a moment before she realised what had caught their eye. The canes were like the ones that John Smith used.

'Do you think this is where he got them?' Raymond asked.

'It is quite likely,' Kingston said. 'At least some of them.'

'We've only seen him use two,' Sydney noted.

'And one of them is identical to the one sold here,' Kingston said.

'Adds to the argument that he's living in Ballarat,' Raymond added.

'Yes, it does.'

Sydney moved over to the canes, looking through them. She frowned as she saw a note written on the side of the case, and unscrewing the top of the cane, she found a hidden compartment. She showed it to Kingston and Raymond.

'Oh, now I'd love to check out his cane,' Raymond said. 'You realise he probably hid the town hall key in it.'

'That would depend on if he found it,' Kingston said.

'Someone did,' Raymond said. 'The compartment was empty, and I doubt Redmond had it.'

'There is a chance Redmond never put the key inside,' Kingston said.

Sydney nodded her agreement.

'The journal said he did,' Raymond said flatly. He wasn't about to argue. His mind was made up that John Smith had taken the key. She looked at Kingston and saw a weary expression on his face. He would not argue with Raymond either. Instead, Kingston found the hat rack.

'Ever have one?' Raymond asked.

'I had several,' Kingston said. 'I was never fond of them.'

Sydney admired the women's hats on display. Some were wide brimmed, and some were simply fascinators. They were adorned with ribbons and feathers of various colours. She'd never wear one, although she knew they would fit in at the Melbourne Cup. Instead, they moved on to the next store, slowly making their way up the street until they reached the top. There, they found a bowling alley. They challenged each other, using the heavy wooden balls to try to knock over the crude wooden pins. Kingston proved to be good at it.

They made their way back down the other side of the street. They found a candlemaker creating candles, and a bakery with ovens in the back. None of them had purchased anything. Sydney did not want to carry anything with her until it was time for them to leave. They watched a live show on the main street, surrounded by the crowd. Once the show was over, they explored the back roads.

They came across a house set up to demonstrate what life was like; it surprised Sydney how similar it was to what they had now. There was no electricity, of course, and she noted the chamber pot under the bed. She couldn't imagine using a woodfired oven for heating and cooking, and she wondered how they kept food cold without a refrigerator.

She put herself in Kingston's shoes. It sounded like the world he came from was more advanced than what they had right now, and he'd come through to the world being presented to her in the theme park. It would have been a massive shock to the system. Did he have to learn how to live this way? Then she thought of Marcus and realised he'd gone through the same thing, and against his will, no less.

'Something's on your mind,' Kingston observed, surveying her as they left the house.

'I was just thinking about Marcus,' she said. 'How he didn't choose to live this way.'

'Hm.' Kingston nodded. 'It took a while to adapt to the new life. No amount of preparation really conveyed what it was like.'

'Wait, how do you prepare?' Raymond asked.

'They had lessons for those who were chosen to go through,' Kingston said. 'Language was just one of them. We also had to learn the culture and etiquette.'

'There's a difference in etiquette?' Sydney asked.

'When you come from a life where you can demand anything and have it handed to you, learning manners takes a lot of work,' Kingston said. 'Especially for some.'

'Like Marcus,' Sydney guessed.

'From how Kian has described him, it does appear that way.'

Sydney felt pity for Marcus. She pushed it down. The man had been intent on killing all her friends and forcing her to him. Instead, she looked over at Kingston. He was an example of someone who had adapted. Kian was another one. Neither of them knew how many had come through the portal. How many had adapted, and how many had resisted the change?

'We should find something to eat,' Raymond said, pulling out his park map to study it. 'Looks like we have three options.'

'Can we go to that bakery we saw on Main Street?' Sydney asked. 'The food there smelled delicious.'

'I second that sentiment,' Kingston said.

'Main Street it is then,' Raymond said. 'And it looks like there is a lake near it. Maybe we can find a spot there to sit and eat.'

After lunch, they found the mine and joined in on a tour. The park had gotten busier since they arrived, but when they got down to the mine, they found it wasn't too bad. There were pre-arranged tour groups making their way through, but there were also designated times for spontaneous groups. They joined the next one.

It wasn't until they were well underground that Sydney felt a little claustrophobic. It was so silent this far underground. The air damp and heavy. It was also cold. She pulled her jacket tighter and stuck close to Kingston and Raymond. Part of her wanted to reach out and grab one of their arms so she wouldn't lose them. Something told her Kingston wouldn't mind. She wasn't sure about Raymond. He'd probably think her weird.

The tour guide went over the history of mining in Ballarat, including how dangerous it was for miners. It was a fascinating history, and a side of Australia Sydney had never seen. Australia was built on gold mining. She was in awe at how the miners had worked, and it didn't surprise her to learn how many had gotten sick. It also disturbed her to learn the ages of the boys who worked in the mines. She was glad she lived in the now.

Sydney soon stood next to the water pump, listening to the water dripping its way around as it thumped above her. She'd heard it from above ground, but they hadn't gone to see it yet. Panic rose in Sydney as she thought about it breaking down and being unable to pump water, causing them all to drown.

'You okay?' Raymond asked her. He was watching her in the dim light.

'I'm fine,' she lied. She looked at the narrow elevator cage beside the pump. 'Imagine having to crowd onto that to get down here.'

'I'll pass,' he said, shaking his head. 'I never would have survived as a miner.'

'Nor would have I,' Kingston agreed. 'I'm glad my father chose a much more refined occupation.'

Raymond eyed him. 'That sounds like classism.'

Kingston seemed to consider his words. 'I meant nothing by it.'

'Right,' Raymond said. 'You sure some of that elitism from your home isn't still in your DNA?'

'I said I meant nothing by it,' Kingston reiterated. 'Miners were hardworking people. But my father's occupation was equally important. As was Redmond's.'

Sydney looked at Raymond and saw that he was still giving Kingston the side eye. She couldn't help but agree with him. Kingston's comment sounded a little classist. She was pleased with the distraction, as it let her nerves calm down. The tour guide moved them on and went further through the mine. The tour guide explained how the miners found gold and the process of getting it out.

Sydney sucked in a deep breath of the fresh air as they reached the end of the tour. She blinked at the brightness, and it took a moment for her eyes to readjust to the light. Looking at her watch, she saw they hadn't been underground for that long. To think the miners would spend hours underground.

Next was a fascinating gold pouring since they had just seen where it came from. Sydney was sure she'd accidentally spill the molten gold if she ever had to do something like that. They then went to look at how the water pump worked from above ground. It was loud. Sydney realised that the people working at the time wouldn't have had the safety gear they had now and would have damaged their hearing. Just more evidence of the progress society had made.

They finished their tour of the park and even took a shot at some gold panning. A man was there giving demonstrations about how it worked, but Sydney was sure she was doing it wrong. She looked over at Kingston and Raymond and noted they looked equally perplexed by everything. Raymond thought he had found some gold, and the three crowded around the pan. He eventually decided he'd found a particularly shiny grain of sand.

By the time they finished going around the park, Sydney was exhausted. She decided they'd walked more that day than in a week. She needed one of those step trackers. They made one last circle of the park to buy souvenirs. Sydney found something for

Rita and Jake. They'd both wanted to come but had been unable, so she couldn't leave them out.

They headed back to the main gate. Sydney made a note to study the history of South Australia, as it might come in handy at the hotel. It was almost time for the park to close. It had been a long day.

CHAPTER 21

RAYMOND'S feet and legs were aching badly. He longed to climb into a bath with bath salts and relax for an hour. That would have to wait until they got home. He knew if he brought up using the spa again, the other two would argue for their turn.

Climbing into the car and getting the weight off his aching limbs felt good. He was half tempted to make Kingston drive, but Raymond didn't like anyone else driving the car except him. He was a little protective of his Nissan. Even his mother only drove it on rare occasions because she knew how much he didn't like it.

He waited until everyone was settled before turning over the engine, grinning as it roared to life. He'd never get over that sound. Raymond carefully manoeuvred the car out of the car park. Crowds gathered around the buses – it was the end of the day, and the park would soon be closing.

The park offered an evening show, but they'd decided beforehand not to go. It wasn't until late in the evening and would cost extra. They called it a sound and light show, re-enacting the Eureka Stockade. It was tempting to watch it, but now that they'd finished their day, he just wanted to return to the hotel and kick back.

As he drove, he realised a car was following them closely. He frowned, turning off onto a side street to get the tailgater off his tail. The car followed. It could just be a coincidence, so he took another turn and watched as the car continued to follow. He set his jaw, realising that it was no accident.

'What's wrong?' Kingston asked, looking at him.

'Not to alarm anyone, but we've got a follower,' Raymond said.

Both Kingston and Sydney turned to look out the back. Raymond had to fight to keep from rolling his eyes. Subtlety evaded them. Getting an idea, Raymond prodded Kingston on the side of the arm.

'GPS,' he said. 'Police station.'

Kingston nodded, pulling out his phone. After a moment, the voice came to life, barking out directions. Raymond followed them, letting the GPS guide them to the Ballarat police station. It was on the way to their hotel, which made things easier.

'How long have they been following?' Kingston asked.

'Since we left the park,' Raymond said. 'They appear to be trying to get into the back seat.'

'They are close,' Sydney agreed, looking out the back again. 'I think it's the guy who was watching the hotel.'

Raymond couldn't tell. Sydney had the best view of the car. He noted the car's make and model so they could give it to Jake. He glanced back at Sydney.

'Snap a photo,' he said. 'We can send it to Jake.'

He watched as Sydney scrambled to get her phone out. Raymond returned his attention to driving, and soon the GPS announced they were nearing their destination. He spotted the building up ahead and had to admit it was ugly. He couldn't tell what era they had built it, but it was a cube made up of blue and white panels with an overhanging roof.

'Not the prettiest building,' Kingston said as Raymond swung them into an empty park.

He watched as the car following them continued to drive, not even slowing down as he headed along the street. He looked back and saw Sydney typing something on her phone and realised she'd probably sent the picture to Jake already.

'How long should we wait?' Kingston asked.

'Give it a minute,' Raymond said.

They sat in the car, Raymond switching off the engine to avoid wasting fuel. They kept an eye out to see if he came back.

'But why would he follow us?' Sydney asked. 'He knows where we're going.'

'Intimidation,' Raymond answered.

'But why?'

'He's trying to scare us,' Kingston agreed, looking out the back window. He reached out and rested a hand on Raymond's arm. His grip was tight.

'I don't think he's coming back,' Raymond eventually said. 'I say we leave while he's gone.'

'Agreed,' Kingston said. Sydney nodded from the back.

Raymond switched the car back on and pulled them out of the park.

They made it back to the hotel without further incident. The receptionist said nothing to them except a greeting, which Raymond took as a good sign. He didn't relax until they were in their room and the door was locked behind them. Straight away, Kingston said he was going to call Jake. Raymond expected him to pull his phone out and make the call in the living area as usual, but Kingston made his way to their room. Raymond made to follow, but Kingston pulled him up short.

'Calm Sydney down,' Kingston said softly, pressing a hand into Raymond's shoulder.

Raymond nodded, turning and heading back into the living room to find Sydney sitting on the couch with her head in her hands. As he got closer, he could see that she was shaking. He hadn't realised how badly the ordeal had affected her. He sat beside her, reaching out and resting a hand on her shoulder.

'You okay?'

There was a moment's pause before she sighed heavily, lifting her head to look at him. 'How do you do it?'

'Do what?'

'Remain so calm?'

He considered his answer. 'Because I have to.'

She frowned at that before turning to look at the dark screen of the television. 'You know, after they followed us in Melbourne, it took me a week to calm down. I still think I'm being followed sometimes. Marcus made me very aware of security cameras being everywhere.'

He hadn't thought about security cameras. Sydney had told him that Marcus worked in security. At the time, he'd found that interesting, given Kian also worked in the field. Like father, like son. He guessed he could see where she was coming from. There were security cameras everywhere, always watching. The problem was, *who* was doing the watching?

'Security cameras can also be a benefit,' he said. 'They're there for our protection. If something happens to one of us, Jake can use them to track us down.'

'But he couldn't with you,' Sydney said. 'He tried, but he couldn't. We thought you were going to die.'

To be fair, Raymond had also thought he was going to die. He doubted that would be of any comfort though. Raymond squeezed her shoulder and gave her a tight smile. 'I'm not that easy to get rid of.'

She smiled back then looked down at her hands. 'I don't understand why he was following us. He knew where we were going. It seemed pointless.'

'As I said – intimidation,' Raymond said. 'He's trying to send a message.'

'What message?'

'That he knows everything that we're doing,' Raymond said. 'He was trying to show us he knew we were at Sovereign Hill and that he has his eye on us.'

'Do you think he was in the park as well?'

'Hard to say.' Raymond shrugged. 'I certainly didn't see him. I didn't get that feeling when we're being watched.'

She looked up at him. 'You get a feeling?'

'I do.' He thought about how to phrase it. 'It's hard to describe. I have a sixth sense for these things. It's how I always know when someone is watching me in the office's doorway.'

'You always know who it is, too,' she observed. 'How do you even do that?'

'Just a gut feeling,' he said. 'That, and I always know when Kingston is watching me.'

She smiled, looking up at him. He met her eye and returned the smile.

'Thank you,' she said.

'For what?'

'For being here,' she said. 'I needed someone to talk to. I feel like we've really gotten to know each other over this past week.'

'It was long overdue,' he said. 'We'd barely met when everything went down, and then I went to Europe for a while afterwards. We needed to spend some time together, you and I.'

'Yes, we did,' she agreed. She chuckled. 'I still can't believe you were in a threesome.'

'Sometimes, neither can I,' Raymond admitted. 'I pinch myself. I used to pinch myself back then, too.'

'You just have that sort of personality.'

He frowned. 'What do you mean?'

'Likeable.'

He snorted. 'I wouldn't go that far. I've been accused of being distant and aloof at work.'

It was her turn to frown. 'Really?'

'Getting close to people means they start asking questions,' he said. 'So I try to keep people at arm's length.'

Realisation sparked in her eye. 'Everyone you know knows about the portals.'

He nodded. 'Everyone I consider a friend or family, yes. Everyone else is just an acquaintance.'

She watched him, as if she was sizing him up. Raymond shifted uncomfortably.

'You know you don't have to tell people about the portals.'

'I just avoid people,' he admitted. 'Not to mention, the people I work with can be rather nosey. You should meet Jennifer.'

'Jennifer?'

'She's an older lady at the same level as my mother,' Raymond said. 'She's dead set on setting me up with her daughter. Jokes on her – we both know about it and have no interest in each other and use each other as an excuse to prevent her from setting her up with anyone else.'

'So Jennifer is like your mother,' Sydney said.

Raymond considered that. 'She is a bit. That's probably why they clash so often.'

'They're not friends?'

'They claim to be, but I think they're more frenemies.' Raymond shrugged. 'With friends like Jennifer, you certainly don't need enemies.'

Sydney chuckled. 'I knew someone like that in high school. She was always trying to compete with me but still wanted to hang out all the time.'

'I've avoided people like that for most of my life,' Raymond said. 'Andrew, Tanya, and I compete a little, but it's all in good fun.'

Sydney looked up at him, and she seemed so open to him right now. 'Am I your friend?'

'Of course,' he said. 'We've definitely moved beyond the acquaintance stage, don't you think?'

'I do,' she said. He frowned at the look she was giving him. Then her eyes dropped to his lips. He could almost see what she was thinking. She leaned in a little. On instinct, Raymond pulled back. She was trying to kiss him!

'I suggest we have an early night,' Raymond said, avoiding eye contact. 'It's been a long day.'

She was silent for a moment. 'True. Shall we make dinner?'

'I'll help,' he agreed.

Dinner was a casual affair of sandwiches with pre-sliced meat. None of them were really up to cooking and just wanted to relax. It also meant there were fewer dishes to be done, and Kingston even commented they should have gone to the restaurant that night. The other two agreed.

Once everything was cleaned up, they turned in early for the night. They bid each other good night, Kingston heading to bed first. Raymond did one last lap of the apartment to ensure they locked everything up, noting that Sydney was watching him. He assured her everything was fine, and she disappeared into her bedroom. Soon enough, Raymond headed for his room.

'You know, I think you're right,' Raymond said as he closed the door to the bedroom.

Kingston was already stretched out on the bed, his phone in his hand, scrolling.

'About what?' Kingston asked.

'Sydney,' Raymond said. He sat on the edge of the bed. 'I think she has a crush on me.'

Kingston smiled but didn't look up from his phone. 'What makes you think that?'

'I swear she was just thinking about kissing me.'

Kingston's head snapped up. 'Really?'

Raymond nodded, settling onto the bed and resting his head on his arm. He looked at Kingston, noting the concern in his eye at the news. 'Trust me, I wouldn't do it.'

'Are you sure?' Kingston asked, putting his phone on the bedside table. 'You've been in a threesome before.'

'Would you want to be in a threesome with Sydney?'

'No.' Kingston shook his head, shifting down on the bed to lie beside Raymond and face him. 'There's only one person I'm interested in being with.'

'So you don't swing that way?'

'I didn't think I swung any way until I met you,' Kingston admitted. 'You could say I'm Raysexual.'

Raymond pulled a face. 'Never say that again.'

Kingston laughed, caressing Raymond's face. 'It is the truth. No one was before you, and no one will be after you.'

'Don't say that.' Raymond didn't like what those words did to him. They made him feel ill. 'You're over a hundred years old. You're going to outlive me. There will be plenty of people after me.'

'I don't like to think about that.' Kingston frowned. 'The outliving part.'

'It's going to happen,' Raymond reminded him. 'Especially given I am the Keeper. We don't exactly have long life spans.'

'You will,' Kingston said. 'You'll live to retire just like your grandfather did.'

'Maybe.' He wasn't so sure about that. Not with the way they kept being followed. He'd already had several attempts on his life, and with this latest follower, it was likely to happen again. It was one downside of having broken the code to find the keys.

'There's no "maybe",' Kingston said. 'I will make sure of it.'

'You can't always be with me,' Raymond reminded him. 'And we can't predict the future.'

'I am the Protector,' Kingston said. 'I will protect you at all costs.'

'Just don't get yourself killed,' Raymond said. He didn't want anyone dying because of him, especially Kingston.

'I don't intend to,' Kingston said. 'I've already failed the Barry family once. I won't do it again.'

Raymond knew he was talking about his great-grandfather. 'That wasn't your fault.'

'Yes, it was,' Kingston said. 'Going to Werribee was my suggestion.'

'The key was there. You would have gone anyway,' Raymond reminded him. 'Anyway, how'd did you work out which door was the portal on Werribee's end?'

'We tried several doors,' Kingston admitted. 'Near where the key was located.'

'Ah. So we can unlock the portal from the other end with the key.'

'It appears so.'

'That's concerning.'

'Why?'

'Because that means anyone can use a key to access the main portal and the door between Adelaide and Melbourne.'

Realisation crossed Kingston's face. 'Oh.'

Not something Kingston had previously considered then. Raymond sighed, envisioning the issue this could cause in the future. Maybe they should add a motion sensor to the little room where the portals were. That way, if there were any unauthorised movement, it would alert Jake. It was an idea they'd have to explore once back home.

Raymond pushed the thoughts to the back of his mind. He looked at Kingston, lost in his thoughts. Kingston's hand was still on Raymond's face where he had been caressing it. Raymond narrowed his eyes, wondering just how thin the walls were in this hotel. Sydney hadn't commented about being able to hear their television, so they must be thick enough.

He smirked, planting a hand on Kingston's chest and pushing

him over onto his back. Kingston frowned, only for it to disappear as Raymond moved with him, swinging a leg over his waist to straddle his hips. He positioned himself above Kingston, hands on either side of Kingston's head.

'Enough thinking for today, Edward,' Raymond said, smiling at him. 'I say we find other ways to preoccupy ourselves.'

Kingston's hands came to rest on his hips. 'What do you have in mind?'

Raymond smirked, leaning down and kissing him. Kingston opened himself up to him, one hand sliding into Raymond's hair and holding him close. They held the kiss. Raymond knew he was probably smudging his glasses, but he didn't like taking them off. He wanted to see.

Kingston's hands moved again to pull at Raymond's shirt, fingers finding the buttons and undoing them. Raymond returned the favour, breaking the kiss to mouth at Kingston's neck as the older man tilted his head back to grant him better access. Kingston was already panting; Raymond smirked. He nipped at the skin, wondering if he should work a mark onto his collarbone.

They both jumped as the phone rang. Raymond groaned, the mood killed, as he glared over at Kingston's phone.

'I swear if that's Rita,' he growled.

Kingston picked up his phone, the screen reflecting off his face. He raised a brow with a half-amused smile as he pressed the button to accept the call. 'Miss Taylor.'

Raymond groaned again, rolling off Kingston to drop onto the bed beside him. Rita was getting into a bad habit of calling just when things were getting heavy. It had happened a few times when they were in Europe and then when they had returned to Melbourne. It was as if she had a 'mood kill' detector.

'I see,' Kingston said, a frown on his face. 'When was this?'

Raymond frowned, noting Kingston's tone. He shuffled closer so that he could hear Rita.

'Just this evening,' Rita was saying. 'They said they couldn't hold him.'

'Have you told Jake?' Kingston asked.

'I let him know first,' Rita said. 'He intends to spend the night at the hotel, just in case.'

'What's going on?' Raymond whispered.

'They let that man out,' Kingston whispered back.

The man that had tried to break into the portals. If he was out, he might try again. 'Maybe Jake can stay in the bunker,' Raymond suggested.

'Did you hear that?' Kingston asked Rita.

'I did,' she said. 'I take it Ray-Ray's listening in on our calls.'

Raymond bristled at the name. 'Hard not to, Margarita.'

'You have a habit of being nosey,' she said.

'Look who's talking.'

'Enough,' Kingston said gently. He returned his attention to the phone. 'I take it you've had a restraining order organised?'

'Waiting for it to be finalised, but we can trespass him.'

'Good. Call us if anything happens.'

'We will.'

They bid their farewells. Kingston sighed heavily as he set his phone on the side table. 'This man is proving himself to be a nuisance.'

'Shame we can't just sic Jake on him and be done with it,' Raymond said. 'If the guy disappears, he wouldn't be a problem anymore.'

'We can't solve everything by killing people.' Kingston looked at Raymond, a hint of concern in his eye. 'What happened to you? There was a time when killing caused you to have a panic attack.'

'Life,' Raymond said. 'The job.'

'It shouldn't have happened.'

'I was naïve back then,' Raymond said. 'I didn't realise what I was getting into. Now I know. I deal with it.'

'I wish you didn't have to.'

Raymond shrugged it off. It was just part of the job, and he'd long come to terms with it. He was still embarrassed by how he'd reacted that first time he'd been forced into the situation of killing someone. That didn't mean he enjoyed doing it. The number he'd killed, he could still count on one hand.

'Anyway, let's not dwell on that now,' Kingston said, turning to face Raymond fully and raising his hand to caress his cheek. 'Where were we?'

Raymond chuckled, their lips meeting.

CHAPTER 22

SYDNEY awoke to find her body still aching from all the walking. Particularly her calves and feet. She was glad that they didn't have to go anywhere that day. They would pack up and leave tomorrow, so today would be a day to rest and recuperate. She got out of bed and found that the two men weren't up yet, so she headed for the shower.

It wasn't until she was making breakfast that she heard movement and the shower going. Most likely Kingston. Raymond was not a morning person, at least not until he had a cup of coffee. She flicked the kettle on and settled at the table to eat. She was almost done when Kingston emerged into the living area.

'Good morning, Miss Madinah,' he greeted.

'Morning,' she said cheerfully. She paused. 'Why do you always call everyone by their titles and last names?'

'Because it is polite to do so,' Kingston said. She figured it was some relic from the past.

'You know you could just call me Sydney.'

'I do at times,' Kingston reminded her. 'I simply prefer the old way.'

She nodded, sipping from her coffee. She could hear the shower again and knew it had to be Raymond. Sydney glanced at her watch and saw it was later than they had been getting up. They'd all slept in.

'What will we do with the food we don't eat?' Sydney asked.

'Take it with us,' Kingston said. 'We can use it when we get home. Split it amongst ourselves. However, I think we planned quite well, so there isn't going to be much left.'

She'd noted that. They didn't seem to have enough even for dinner that night. They'd need to go out and dine somewhere again. She'd raise it with the two men when they were both out.

Raymond emerged when Kingston was halfway through his breakfast. Raymond looked exhausted, his hair mussed and damp. Sydney had to admit he looked cute like that. She turned her eyes away and found Kingston watching her. Feeling like she'd been caught, she averted her eyes back to her coffee.

'What's the plan?' Raymond asked as he made his breakfast.

'I thought we didn't have one for today,' Sydney said.

'I don't believe we do,' Kingston agreed. 'Today should be a rest day.'

'Well, we need it,' Raymond said. He rubbed his leg. 'Remind me not to let Rita know I'm feeling it.'

'She was simply jesting with you,' Kingston said. 'If she were here, she would be in the same situation.'

Sydney nodded emphatically. Raymond came to join them at the table, Sydney trying to keep her eyes off him. The top few buttons of his shirt were undone, and her eyes kept wanting to be drawn to it. She could feel Kingston studying her, so she was on her best behaviour.

'I think I'll go over the journal one last time,' Raymond said. 'Just in case I missed anything. That way, we can go out this afternoon if necessary.'

'I thought you'd been over it already,' Sydney said.

'Better safe than sorry,' Raymond said. 'I don't want to return to Melbourne and realise I missed a key.'

'I believe you were thorough,' Kingston said. 'As you often are.'

Raymond narrowed his eyes at him.

'There are times you're not,' Kingston said. 'You have a tendency to become distracted.'

'Usually your fault,' Raymond accused.

Kingston shrugged and sipped from his coffee.

Sydney wondered what that was about but didn't dare ask. It was something private. She wished she could dig into their lives more, find out the meaning of their private jokes. Jake and Rita had them, too. Sydney was still the new girl on the block and had a lot to learn about the group. This trip helped a lot, but she had a long way to go.

They finished their breakfast and cleaned up, Raymond retreating to the bedroom for some privacy while he went through the journal. Sydney wished she dared to ask him if she could look at it. She wanted to read them. Not to find the code but to see into the world of Redmond Barry. She was sure the journals were fascinating to read in their own right.

Sydney could feel Kingston's eyes on her as she sat on the couch and switched on the television. As she hoped, an old movie was screening. It looked like it was about halfway through. She sensed Kingston moving over to join her, sitting down on the couch beside her.

'I'm curious,' he said, breaking the silence.

'About what?' she asked.

'About why you'd think about kissing Raymond.'

Her body stiffened, a rock forming in the pit of her stomach. It had been a moment yesterday. She'd seriously considered leaning in and kissing him and had almost done it, but he'd pulled away. Something had sparked inside her to make her do it. Did she regret it? Maybe. She wasn't sure. She wished he hadn't pulled away – she wanted to know just how soft his lips were. They were soft in her dreams.

Of course he'd noticed, and of course he'd told Kingston. Kingston was his boyfriend. Sydney swallowed, knowing that Kingston was technically her boss. It was unwise of her to make a move on his partner.

'Um...' was all she could get out.

'You're very aware of our relationship,' Kingston continued. 'And yet you still considered it.'

'I'm, uh... sorry?' She didn't know how to phrase it. How do you explain something like that? She was sure it would make things awkward between them.

'So you admit to it.'

She stared through the television.

'I can see the appeal,' Kingston said. 'Raymond has very kissable lips.'

There was no argument from her in that regard. She'd thought about kissing them many times. But he was off limits, so she'd kept it in her fantasies. She'd pushed things a little too far yesterday.

'You have had a crush on him for some time,' Kingston observed.

What did he want her to say, exactly? Yes? Deny it?

'Hm.' He rested his head on his hand as he faced her, his elbow on the back of the couch. She could feel him studying her. She risked a glance and saw that he wasn't angry. In fact, he looked amused. Like he was trying not to laugh.

'You're... not mad?' Sydney asked.

'As I said, I can see the appeal,' Kingston said. 'You know, he comes with a lot of baggage.'

She nodded. She didn't know all of it, but she knew enough. Sydney wanted to help him with some of the weight of it.

'But he's not a man in need of saving,' Kingston continued. 'He's more than capable of taking care of himself.'

'I know that,' Sydney said.

'But do you?' Kingston raised a brow, scrutinising her. 'He doesn't share his load with anyone. Not even me. He's a very private man.'

She frowned. 'Why are you telling me this?'

'In case you want to play white knight,' Kingston said. 'In case you view him as a broken man who needs rescuing. Someone to "fix".'

'No, I don't view him like that,' she admitted. She had a little, but she'd overcome those thoughts. If anyone could take care of himself, it was Raymond. However, Sydney had harboured thoughts of nursing him back to health after Marcus tortured him. Kingston and Rita had done most of the work, but she'd tried to help.

'Good,' Kingston said. 'You also should know he's incredibly loyal.'

There it was. The faint threat in his voice. He was warning her off. Raymond was his, and Raymond wouldn't cheat on him. Sydney nodded. She'd had a feeling that was the case. Raymond may have been in a threesome before, but all parties had consented. In this case, she wasn't invited. Kingston was slamming that door closed.

'I understand that.'

'Don't make this awkward, Miss Madinah.'

'I don't intend to.'

He nodded, turning to face the television. The conversation was over. He'd gotten his message across. She was to back off. She knew she'd tested the boundary yesterday, and this resulted from it. Sydney wondered why Raymond had said nothing. Maybe he was too polite. Did he even know Kingston was saying this to her? She had a feeling he didn't.

She tried to focus on the movie but was lost because she had not seen the start. She didn't know which characters she was supposed to side with or their motivations. Sydney wondered if Kingston had ever given Jake 'the talk' about Rita. Workplace relationships were never a good idea. Raymond was outside of the workplace, so he was 'safe'.

After a while, she fidgeted, too aware of Kingston's presence. She couldn't take it anymore and stood, moving over to look out the window and see if their follower was standing in his spot across the road. He wasn't. She retreated to her room. There was no television, so she made do with her phone. Things really were awkward now with Kingston – she needed a break from him.

She decided she needed to check in back home, so she sent Rita a message asking how things were going with the hotel. Being out of the loop was strange when so much was happening. She worried about that man coming back and causing issues. Sydney couldn't have physically confronted him – that was Jake's job. Jake was an excellent head of security, and his bouncer experience was handy for problem guests.

It was almost ten minutes before Rita sent back a detailed reply. The man hadn't come back. The police had told them he could be trespassed if he did, and they were organising a restraining order to prevent him from coming near the business. Rita never complained about her job, but Sydney could imagine how much paperwork came with it.

Sydney let herself become distracted by her phone, searching for a place for them to eat for the evening. Sydney scanned a guide about Ballarat and found something that piqued her interest. She made a note of it, deciding to suggest it later. She lost track of time while lying on the bed as she browsed through her phone.

Sydney looked up at the knock on the door.

'Sydney?' Raymond called. 'Kingston's got Jake and Rita on the phone.'

Sydney pushed herself off the bed, made her way to the door, and opened it to find Raymond already on his way down the hall to the living area. She followed him and saw him drop onto the couch beside Kingston, the phone on the coffee table. As she set herself in the chair, she wondered who had rung who.

'We're all here,' Kingston said out loud, barely glancing in her direction. 'What did you find?'

'Not much, I'm afraid.' Jake sounded exhausted. 'There are a lot of John Smiths around. None of them match the description you sent to me.'

Raymond must have forwarded their notes. Sydney looked up at the two men. Kingston had a frown on his face, while Raymond looked like he had expected the news. Sydney had half expected it herself but had hoped that Jake would have been able to find something. There couldn't be too many John Smiths in Ballarat with a cane.

'Whoever this guy is, he picked a common name,' Jake said.

'Obviously,' Raymond muttered.

'I need more to go with,' Jake said. 'Did you ever get a photo?'

'We haven't seen him for a couple of days,' Raymond replied. 'He wasn't at Sovereign Hill, and we've spent today indoors.'

'How about your stalker?' Jake asked. 'He back?'

'He wasn't when I looked earlier,' Sydney said.

Raymond moved over to peer out the window. He paused for a moment before returning. 'Still not there,' he said.

Sydney was tempted to tell Jake about how the guy had disappeared into the tunnels under Ballarat but refrained. She eyed Kingston and Raymond. Kingston had his arm across the back of the seat behind Raymond's shoulders. Kingston's arm slid around them as he sat down again. Raymond didn't seem to notice or care, focusing entirely on the phone on the coffee table.

'John Smith must want to blend in,' Rita said. 'If I wanted to blend, I'd also pick a common name.'

'So, we remain where we started,' Kingston said. He didn't look happy. 'Until we get a picture.'

'Hopefully, we won't need to,' Raymond said, looking at him. 'We're leaving tomorrow.'

'Which means he is also running out of time,' Kingston said.

'What do you mean?' Sydney asked.

He finally looked at her. 'It means that if he intends to try something, it will need to be soon.'

'He doesn't know we're leaving,' Raymond pointed out.

'Heritage Week ended today,' Kingston reminded them.

'Actually, I think there's an event tomorrow,' Raymond said. 'But you're right about the buildings not being open. That ended today.'

'So he'd know we'd leave,' Sydney said. 'He knows we're tourists.'

'We assume he knows,' Raymond said.

'If he is indeed who we think he is, then he'd know where we're from,' Kingston said.

'You mean he'd know you're from Melbourne and Adelaide?' Jake said.

'That he would.'

'But what if he isn't connected to Lierdan?' Sydney asked. 'What if it turns out he's just a friendly local?'

'You mean like Marcus?' Kingston asked, eyeing her.

Sydney felt like she'd been slapped. That was a deliberate blow. Marcus had tricked her into thinking he was just a friendly local to get to her. And it had worked. He'd used the information he'd gathered from her to work out Kingston and Raymond's secrets to use against them.

'That wasn't her fault,' Raymond chastised Kingston.

'We got played,' Jake agreed. 'Remember, Kian played us as well.'

That was true. Kian had made himself known as the Overseer only after working out Marcus had been coming after them. Sydney was glad he had worked it out when he did because she was sure Kingston and Raymond would be dead if he hadn't. She gave Raymond a small smile in thanks for defending her and got a little one in return.

'It seems everyone has ulterior motives,' Kingston lamented. 'I wonder how many others are connected that we don't know about.'

'Trust me, after the Kian thing, I've been looking into everyone,' Jake said. 'Dot and Lizzie are in the clear. As is everyone on staff. No one has anything suspicious in the past as you do.'

Kingston frowned at the phone. 'Suspicious?'

'No birth certificate or record of you before you came a few years ago.'

'Ah.'

Sydney felt a little violated by the idea of Jake looking into her past. She could understand his caution. Her history was relatively dull. She didn't even have a parking ticket to her name. The most exciting thing for her was going to America, and even there, she'd kept mostly to herself.

'So right now, John Smith is the only suspicious person,' Raymond said.

'It seems that way,' Jake said. 'That and the guy that keeps hitting the hotel here.'

'How goes that?' Kingston asked. 'Any updates?'

'Not as yet,' Rita chimed in. 'We're waiting to hear back about the court order.'

'He hasn't shown his face again,' Jake said. 'Trust me, I'm monitoring things.'

'You're going to need a vacation when it's sorted,' Sydney said.

'Yes,' Raymond agreed. 'You're overdue for one.'

'Short-staffed, remember?' Jake said.

'When things sort themselves out, schedule some time off,' Kingston said.

'I'll try.'

'In the meantime, keep us updated if something happens,' Kingston said.

'You as well.'

Kingston picked up the phone, bidding farewell and getting two replies. Sydney didn't even have time to say goodbye before he hung up. Raymond remained quiet, rubbing his jaw with a thoughtful look.

'Something on your mind?' Kingston asked.

'Not really,' Raymond said. 'I'm just finding it odd that the Medina Grand gets hit at the same time we pick up a follower.'

'Now that you mention it, it is rather odd,' Kingston said.

'But that drunk guy showed up before you two got back from your vacation,' Sydney said. 'They wouldn't have known we were planning to go to Ballarat because even I didn't know.'

'Also true,' Kingston said.

'You're saying it's an actual coincidence,' Raymond said. 'I generally don't believe in those.'

'But they can happen,' Kingston said.

'I guess.'

They fell into silence, each lost in their thoughts. Sydney was thinking about how there could possibly be a connection between the guy at the Medina and John Smith. It made more sense to her to connect the guy at the Medina to Marcus, even though it had been six months since he had died. Maybe he really did have a kill switch that sent out correspondence in the event of his death.

'We really must figure out something for dinner,' Kingston said, breaking the silence.

'I have an idea,' Sydney said.

CHAPTER 23

SYDNEY'S idea turned out to be a good one. They made their way across town to Bakery Hill, pulling into the car park at Pizza Hut. Typically, Raymond wasn't that mad about pizza, but when Sydney had explained it was a dine-in buffet-style Pizza Hut, he'd jumped at the chance. He hadn't been to one since he was a child.

They made their way inside and were soon seated at a table. The smell of pizza made Raymond's mouth water. They took turns going to the buffet table and finding a selection of pizza, salad, and pasta. Raymond felt like he had been transported back to his childhood. He spotted the ice cream machine and promised he would return for it later.

'How did you find out about this place?' Raymond asked Sydney as they ate.

'I came across it while searching for places for dinner,' Sydney said. 'It was on a website about unique dining experiences.'

'I remember when this was relatively common,' Kingston said. 'Unfortunately, most of them shut down.'

'I don't know why,' Raymond said. 'I love the idea of all-you-can-eat, even if it is pizza.'

'You're not a pizza fan?' Sydney asked.

'I have it from time to time,' he admitted. 'But I wouldn't go out of my way to have it.'

'Food snob,' Kingston reminded her.

'I am not!'

Raymond noted that Kingston had put extra sauce on his food and rolled his eyes. The pizza had more than enough sauce. They ate their first round of food, going back for seconds. Raymond was surprised by how hungry he actually was. He put it down to all the walking he'd done that week. They also had little to eat the day before.

'I wouldn't want to frequent a place like this too often,' Sydney said, eating some of her salad. 'I think I'd put on too much weight.'

'I must agree,' Kingston said. 'The choice of food is surprisingly wide.'

'There aren't that many buffets around anymore,' Raymond lamented. He'd always liked a good buffet. He liked the idea of paying a flat fee and then eating as much as possible. Raymond knew Sydney was right. You'd put on a lot of weight if you went to one too many times. Better to save them for special occasions.

'Check out at ten a.m.?' Sydney asked.

Kingston nodded. 'As per the usual.'

'Probably better to make sure we're all packed up tonight,' Raymond said. He looked over at Sydney. 'Are you going to be okay riding in the back seat again?'

'I was fine on the way down,' she told him. 'It's a little tight, but it's not that bad.'

'Maybe we should have hired a car,' Raymond said. 'You would have had more room.'

'I love your car,' she said.

'Although it does make one think you're overcompensating,' Kingston teased.

Raymond scoffed, kicking Kingston lightly under the table. If anyone knew he wasn't overcompensating, it was Kingston. He saw the twinkle in Kingston's eye and knew he meant no malice by the comment. They ate a little more. They seemed to agree that two plates of food were enough before they hit the ice cream machine.

It was a pleasant surprise to find a range of toppings. Raymond sampled a bit of everything. By the time he'd finished loading it up, his bowl looked like a sweet monstrosity. He returned to the table and discovered that Kingston had gone with ice cream with chocolate sauce, while Sydney had done the same as Raymond.

'Why?' Kingston asked, looking at their bowls.

'Why not?' Sydney said with a smile.

Raymond nodded his agreement and tucked in. The amount of sugar was almost overwhelming, but boy did it taste good. He was going to make the most of having unlimited access. He felt like a little boy again. His mother and father rarely took him out for dinner when he was small. They reserved it for special occasions, and more often than not, it was at a fancy restaurant. His father argued Raymond should enjoy the novelties of childhood, so that's how he'd been introduced to dine-in buffets. After his father had left, they'd stopped going to them.

'You're going to make yourselves sick,' Kingston commented when they went back for seconds.

'I say that every time you drown your meal in tomato sauce,' Raymond retorted. On his second helping, he'd gone for a simpler serving, which he noted Sydney had also done.

'We're not eating that much,' Sydney said.

'You won't even remember the trip tomorrow,' Kingston said. 'I'll drive while the two of you are in food comas.'

'It's not that bad,' Raymond said. 'We're enjoying ourselves and making the most of the fee. That's all.'

'This is my last helping,' Sydney assured Kingston.

'I remain to be seen,' Raymond said.

Kingston looked at Raymond with disapproval, but Raymond

shrugged it off. It was going to be his last helping, too. He'd loaded his plates up and was getting full. He really had gotten his money's worth. Sydney was eating a lot slower this round, so he knew she had to be getting full herself.

'You ever eat out at buffets much?' he asked her.

She shook her head. 'Special occasions.'

'Same.'

'They weren't the most hygienic of places,' Kingston said.

'What do you mean?'

'Fingers were used rather than tongs.'

Raymond shuddered at the thought. He couldn't imagine fingers all over the food someone else would eat. He polished off his ice cream, scraping the bowl clean. Sydney struggled to finish hers. He honestly had room for thirds but didn't want to push his luck.

'You're both going to come to regret that last bowl.' Kingston eyed their plates.

'I think I already am,' Sydney admitted.

Raymond chuckled, licking his spoon to tease Kingston a little. He got a half glare but spotted the twinkle of amusement. He also caught Sydney watching him and quickly put down the spoon. It was better not to stoke that fire. They finished their drinks, making one final toast to a successful trip. It was non-alcoholic, but that didn't matter to Raymond.

They cleared their table as best they could. Raymond noted that the table nearby had been left in a gigantic mess, with spilt drinks and pizza crusts everywhere. He didn't know how people did that. They had paid when they arrived, so they thanked the host behind the counter for their meal and received a smile and a good evening as they left.

The streetlights outside were on, casting shadows as they walked to the car. It smelled like it was going to rain again. Raymond pulled his jacket tighter around himself to ward off the biting chill of the wind.

'I don't think we're going to need breakfast after that,' Sydney observed.

Raymond chuckled in agreement. He wouldn't put it past his body to wake up hungry, anyway. They still had some bread left, so he could have toast. Toast and coffee for the drive home. They should be back by lunchtime. They could grab a bite to eat at the cafe at the Medina Grand. Simon would be happy to see them. He felt Dot and Liz would pry for details about their holiday.

Footsteps rushed up behind them, and before he could react, Raymond saw Kingston slump to the ground with a sickening thump.

'Kingston!' Sydney cried out.

Raymond spun, pushing Sydney behind him and finding himself face-to-face with the man who had been watching their hotel, wielding a crowbar.

'What do you want?' Raymond asked, keeping himself between the attacker and Sydney.

The man grunted, swinging the bar at Raymond. Raymond dodged. This man was going for the kill. Raymond pulled his switchblade out, flicking it open. The man saw the move but didn't look concerned. He had more reach with the crowbar than Raymond had with the knife.

Raymond saw the flinch the second before the crowbar moved again, dodging it for a second time. Sydney's panicked breathing came from behind him, and he silently urged her to run for the car, but she was fixed in place. Her fight or flight mode had gone into freeze. Not good.

The man made a few more swings at Raymond, and Raymond quickly worked out his tells. On the next swing, Raymond grabbed the crowbar with one hand and tried to wrestle it away from the man. They fought, but the man had a strength advantage. He shoved Raymond hard. Raymond lost his footing and fell to the ground.

Raymond quickly scrambled to his feet as the man attacked

again, the bar striking him in the upper arm. Pain blazed through the spot, his arm going dead. Raymond grunted, hoping he hadn't broken it.

The man aimed the next blow at his knees, and he jumped back out of the way. The last thing he needed was a broken kneecap. It confused him that the man was silent, made no demands. All other attackers in the past had wanted something from them.

'C'mon, buddy,' Raymond said, trying to move the fingers of his left hand. He couldn't feel them at all. 'What do you want?'

The man attacked again. Raymond wanted desperately to dance around him but had to keep himself between the attacker and Sydney. His eyes glanced down at Kingston and noted he hadn't moved yet. What he wouldn't give to have the extra body helping him. Kingston had improved in fighting since the first time they had met. They'd been attacked then, too, and Kingston had been rusty. Raymond had been working with him to improve his fighting skills.

The man was wearing a hoodie, obscuring his face. The bulk of it made it harder to read his tells. Given how he was fighting, this wasn't the guy's first rodeo. That made him dangerous. Had someone ordered a hit on them?

Raymond yelped as the next swing caught him on the hip. Collapsing to the ground, his leg reverberated from the strike. He scrambled to get his footing, his leg not wanting to cooperate with him. He put his arm up to wield off the next blow, dropping his knife as the crowbar hit his arm with a crack, pushing Raymond back onto his haunches.

'Raymond!' Sydney called out.

The man turned towards her, stopping to pick up Raymond's switchblade. Raymond struggled to get to his feet as the man stalked towards Sydney. He could see that the guy was leading with the knife. Raymond finally pulled himself to his feet, seeing Sydney was still a deer in headlights.

He threw himself across the space as the man brought the crowbar towards Sydney. Raymond grabbed it with his right hand, the blow jarring his wrist. They struggled, Raymond fighting to keep him away.

'Sydney, run!' he yelled.

That finally brought her out of her daze. Sydney sprinted back to the car. Raymond was finally getting some feeling back in his left arm, so he brought it into play, trying to wrestle the crowbar away from the man. He was gaining ground, cursing the man for being so strong. Raymond might have had the height advantage, but the man definitely had the weight advantage. He must be all muscle under his baggy clothes.

He saw the man move the second before a burning pain blazed through Raymond's side. He gritted his teeth to ignore the pain, struggling with the man over the crowbar. Then the man yanked back, dragging Raymond forwards and sweeping his legs out from under him. Raymond went down hard, looking up and preparing for the next attack only to see the man sprinting away.

Raymond reached for his side, finding his blade buried deep inside him. He pulled it out, the pain blazing through him. He snapped the blade closed and pocketed it, looking up as a car peeled out of the car park. It must be the attacker. Raymond wondered what he had tried to accomplish. He could have killed them, but he hadn't.

Hearing running feet, Raymond looked up as two arms grabbed him. Sydney had returned. Her eyes were wide, and her skin pale.

'Oh my gosh, are you all right?' she asked.

'Check Kingston,' Raymond ordered, looking over to where Kingston still hadn't moved.

'I'm checking you,' she countered. Her eyes ran over him, widening as they spotted his side. Her hands pressed into the wound, and he had to grit his teeth to avoid making noise. 'Did he stab you?'

'I've had worse,' Raymond joked.

There was a shout. Raymond looked up – they had spectators. Someone was rushing back into the restaurant. He knew it was only a matter of time before the police and ambulance arrived. He began to formulate answers to the questions they would be asked.

'It was a random attack,' he told her.

'What?' she asked. 'No, it was–'

'It was a random attack,' he repeated. 'We don't know the guy. Attempted mugging.'

Realisation dawned on her face. 'He wanted my handbag, and you stopped him.'

'Exactly,' he said. 'He took out Kingston first.'

'They're going to want Kingston's name,' Sydney said.

'Just Kingston,' Raymond said. 'I'll handle the rest.'

People were approaching them, and Raymond saw someone check on Kingston. He could see that Kingston was breathing, so he knew he was alive. He was going to have one hell of a headache.

'When we get to the hospital, call Rita,' Raymond said. 'She and Jake will handle everything.'

Sydney nodded again. She was still pressing her hands down hard on his wound, trying to stop the bleeding. 'I'm sorry I froze.'

'You're fine,' he assured her. 'You ran when I told you.'

'I have pepper spray in my bag. I should have used it.'

'Next time.'

Someone from the restaurant soon joined them, and people trying to help swarmed them shortly after. It was the last time they got to talk for a while.

CHAPTER 24

SYDNEY was exhausted. The adrenaline had long worn off, and she just wanted to curl up in a corner and cry herself to sleep. All the ways she could have helped replayed in her mind. How she could have taken her mace out and sprayed the attacker in the face while he was facing off against Raymond.

The police kept her back for questioning while the paramedics loaded Kingston and Raymond into the ambulance. Raymond passed his car keys to her through one of the officers. She stuck with Raymond's story about how it was a freak attack. How they didn't know their attacker. She didn't know if a camera was facing the car park, so she tried to meld the story into what had really happened.

The moon was well and truly high in the sky by the time the police finished their questioning. One offered her a ride, but she told her she had a car. They found out which hospital they had taken Raymond and Kingston to and gave her directions on how to get there. She drove to the hospital, finding a park nearby.

Before she went in, she took out her phone and called Rita, updating her about everything that had happened. It was like something switched on in the other woman. She turned strictly professional and to the point, Sydney providing what details she could. When she hung up the phone, she felt they had put something into motion, and she didn't know what.

Entering the hospital emergency area, she gave her name and how she travelled with Kingston and Raymond. At first, they were reluctant to provide her with any information as she was not kin, but they soon updated her on what was happening. Kingston was receiving scans to check for head injuries, and Raymond was in surgery to repair the damage from the stabbing.

An hour later, she was sitting in the waiting room, unsure what was happening. There hadn't been an update in a while. The chairs were far from comfortable. Others were in the room, many just waiting to be seen. One had a broken arm, and another was so pale she was sure he was a ghost.

She started as her phone rang. Sydney quickly grabbed it from her pocket, seeing it was Jake's number. She answered.

'Jake!' she said.

'Are you okay?' he asked straight away.

'I'm fine,' she said. 'Just shaken up.'

'How are the other two?'

'I'm still waiting to hear anything,' she said. 'They were taking Kingston for scans, and Raymond was going in for surgery.'

'How long ago was that?'

'About an hour ago,' she said.

'So, hopefully, you should hear back soon,' he said. 'Rita has been on the phone nonstop since you called. She's making arrangements with the hotel you're staying at to give you a few more days to recover.'

Sydney hadn't even considered that. They were supposed to be leaving in the morning, and it had completely gone out of her mind after everything that had happened.

'She's also been talking to the hospital,' Jake continued. 'She's cleared it with them for you to get all the information on the guys.'

That explained why they had opened up to her. 'How did she do that?'

'Didn't ask.' Jake made an exasperated sound. 'I should have come with you.'

'You couldn't,' Sydney said. 'Understaffed.'

'I know. But I should have organised someone to come in so I could go.'

'It's not your fault.' He was starting to play the blame game. She had to be careful not to do it herself. 'It's no one's fault. It came completely out of nowhere.'

'Was it the guy who has been watching you?'

'Yes,' she confirmed. She glanced around, not wanting to say anything over the phone in case someone was listening. 'We'll give you all the details when we get back to the hotel.'

'That probably won't be tonight,' Jake said. 'They'll keep the two guys in overnight.'

'It looks like I might be here all night just waiting.'

'Don't stay unless you have to,' he said. 'They might kick you out, anyway.'

'Can Rita see to it that I'm not?'

'I'm not sure how much pull she actually has, but we can try,' Jake said. 'Anyway, I've got to go. I'm trying to access the security footage of the attack.'

'Good luck.'

Sydney hung up the phone, glad to have had the distraction. As people came and went from the emergency room, she went back to waiting. She had never been fond of hospitals. Sydney didn't know anyone who was. She'd had to go once to the hospital in America with a friend from college, and she had to admit she preferred the Australian emergency room to the American one. Back then, it had been for a simple broken arm. She couldn't even imagine what a stabbing would cost in America.

The whole event made her realise how dangerous it had been

for her to follow the man through Ballarat. He was willing to hurt them, and he could have killed her. It had looked like he intended to when he'd been coming at her. Raymond had saved her. She was in debt to him.

She looked up as a nurse approached her.

'We've moved Mr Kingston up to a ward,' he said. 'For observation. He was cleared for any fractures or damage but has a concussion. You're free to go up and see him.'

'Is he awake?' Sydney asked.

'Yes but rather confused,' the nurse said. 'Which is expected, given what he's been through.'

Sydney thanked him and took the slip of paper with his room number. The nurse gave her directions and an update on Raymond. Or rather, that there wasn't an update. He was still in surgery. He was in stable condition, which brought some relief to Sydney. She thanked the nurse and went looking for Kingston.

They had moved Kingston to the second floor of the hospital, to a semiprivate room. As she arrived, she saw a police officer leaving. The same officer had spoken to her, so Sydney smiled at her.

Sydney stepped into the room and found Kingston lying back on the bed with his eyes closed. His green eyes snapped open when she knocked. He seemed relieved to see her.

'Miss Madinah,' he said with a smile. 'I'm pleased to see you're okay.'

'He didn't even touch me,' Sydney assured him. She pulled up a chair next to the bed. Kingston hadn't been changed out of his clothes. 'How's your head?'

'I think this is the worst headache I have ever had,' he admitted, one hand coming up to massage his temple as he closed his eyes again. He frowned. 'Any word on Raymond? They haven't told me a thing.'

'Do you know he was stabbed?' Sydney asked.

Kingston's eyes flew open to stare at her in alarm. 'He was what?'

That was a no. Sydney bit her lip, trying to think of how to phrase things. 'He's fine. He's in surgery so that they can repair any damage, but they say he's in a stable condition.'

'Good. Good.' Worry creased Kingston's face. Sydney couldn't blame him. It would not satisfy her that Raymond was okay until she saw him. 'Who did this? The police mentioned a mugging, but I'm guessing that's a cover story.'

'Raymond came up with it,' Sydney confirmed. 'It was the guy who was watching our hotel.'

'I thought as much.' Kingston sighed. 'What was he trying to achieve? Was his intent to kill us?'

'I don't know,' Sydney said. 'He only had a knife because he picked up Raymond's. He seemed just to want to beat you.'

'How did Raymond fare?'

'He did well, considering.' She swallowed hard. 'I… froze. I'm sorry.'

'Not your fault,' Kingston assured her. 'Most of us freeze the first time.'

That sounded like he was talking from experience. 'Did you?'

'I did,' Kingston said. 'Long ago. Back when I first came to Adelaide. My father and I were accosted. He took care of it while I stood there, useless.'

That was how she felt. She had run through all the scenarios in her head about what she could do if she were ever in the situation again. She was still kicking herself for not having brought out her mace. 'Did Raymond freeze? Do you know?'

'No, he handled himself perfectly,' Kingston said. 'He was sick afterwards, though.'

'Because he killed someone.'

Kingston nodded. He looked at her with sympathetic eyes. 'Don't dwell on it. It will only make you feel worse. The good news is that you were unharmed.'

'But they hurt you and Raymond.'

'Maybe so, but we would rather it were us than you.'

She bit back her reply. She'd prefer it if they hurt none of them.

'What did you tell the police?' Kingston asked.

'The story,' she said. 'That it was an attempted mugging. For all we know, it was.'

'It is possible,' Kingston said. 'Perhaps they thought we had the keys on us.'

'I thought that too,' Sydney said. 'Given he came with a weapon, it must have been planned.'

'Most likely.' Kingston looked to the door. 'The police seemed disappointed that I couldn't give them any information. All I remember is walking out of the restaurant, a sudden pain, and then waking up here. They've treated me well, I will say.'

'I've been in contact with Jake and Rita,' Sydney said. 'Raymond told me to ring them as soon as possible.'

'That should always be the plan. If something goes wrong, call Rita.'

'How does she do it?' Sydney asked. 'She can't have connections here.'

'She is very persuasive when necessary,' Kingston said. 'And an excellent negotiator. She's invaluable.'

Sydney was realising that. She'd known Rita was good at her job, but she'd never realised just how good. Her level of respect for the woman was ever-increasing. She didn't even want to know what things Rita could do.

'Jake is trying to get a copy of the security footage,' Sydney said. 'I don't know how much luck he'll have.'

'That may be difficult,' Kingston said. 'He doesn't have the connections here.'

'No, he doesn't.' Sydney worried her lip. 'I'm not sure how much good it will do. The guy was wearing a hoodie, and I couldn't make out his face very well.'

'Something tells me the police will put an alert out,' Kingston said, eyes flicking back to the door. 'They can't have a violent attacker roaming the streets. Who knows where and when he might attack again.'

If that were the case, Jake could get a picture. 'Did they say when you can go home?'

'Not until the morning, and provided I don't have any severe complications,' Kingston said.

'Severe complications?'

'Vomiting, brain swelling, sudden loss of consciousness,' Kingston said. 'The usual.'

Sydney didn't know what the usual was. None of those things sounded good. It also meant he was being monitored so the nurses would come and go. 'Did they say anything about your scan results?'

'No sign of active trauma and no bleeding on the brain,' he said. 'They warned I might suffer some memory loss from prior to the incident, but I seem to recall everything leading up to it.'

They both looked up as the door opened. Sydney half stood as a bed was rolled in. She spotted a groggy Raymond lying on it. He was attached to an IV and looked like he'd just woken up. Kingston pushed himself up to look at him, and the nurses told him to please lie back down. He relented, the two of them watching as they set Raymond up in the room and then left them.

'Well, that was fun,' Raymond said after they had gone.

'You're awake?' Sydney asked.

'Barely.' Raymond rubbed a hand over his eyes. 'Before you ask, nothing was seriously damaged. It was more about checking and stitching things back together.'

'How are you?' Kingston asked.

'I should be asking you that,' Raymond said, looking across at him. 'How's the head?'

'A splitting headache,' Kingston said. 'You?'

'A fractured arm, a dozen stitches on both the inside and out, and quite a bit of bruising,' Raymond answered. 'But whatever they gave me makes me feel great.'

'How long until it wears off?' Sydney asked.

'About an hour.' Raymond eyed the IV. 'They said it could have been worse, but the blade was small enough that it didn't do much damage. I really hope they give it back. It was a gift from my grandfather.'

'They took your blade?' Kingston asked.

'Evidence,' Raymond said. 'I think they're trying to get fingerprints.'

Sydney thought about their attack. In the haze of everything, she came to a realisation. 'Wasn't he wearing gloves?'

'I wasn't paying that much attention,' Raymond admitted. 'I was more concerned about the crowbar.'

'Is that what he hit me with?' Kingston said.

'Yeap.'

'Did they say how long you'll be in for?' Sydney asked.

'Overnight,' Raymond said. 'So long as I can prove I'm fine. Not allowed to do any serious lifting for a while.'

'That will cramp your exercise routine,' Kingston observed.

'I'll find ways around it.'

Sydney wondered why Kingston had brought that up. She hadn't noticed either of them working out much during their stay in Ballarat. The walking was a form of working out, sure, but she hadn't seen any lifting or the like. Of course, she didn't know what they did in their bedroom. They could have been doing push-ups and chin-ups there, and she wouldn't be any wiser.

'Have the police talked to you yet?' Kingston asked.

'No,' Raymond said. 'I'm expecting them to. I'm guessing they'll be here in the morning after the anaesthesia has worn off.'

When he was more lucid. He seemed lucid enough right now. It tempted Sydney to ask if he was seeing anything out of the ordinary in the room. She'd heard that some medications made you hallucinate.

'Thank you,' she said to Raymond. 'For protecting me.'

He shrugged it off. 'Had to be done.'

'I'm sorry I froze.'

'Sydney, it's fine,' he said. 'Don't worry about it.'

'I can't help it.' She stared at a spot on the floor. 'I had mace in my bag. I should have helped.'

'Dwelling on things does no one any good,' he told her.

'Raymond's right,' Kingston said. 'Don't question the past. Live for the moment.'

'That sounds like a bad motivation poster,' Raymond teased.

'I think that's where I got it from.'

Sydney couldn't help but laugh. It wasn't even that funny. Her emotions were a mess. She wrapped her arms around herself and rocked a little. Her mind was still playing catch up with what had happened. How had it gone from a night of them relaxing at a buffet to two of them in hospital beds? They should be back at the hotel packing to go home.

'You're dwelling on it,' Kingston accused her.

She knew she was. Her mind kept looping back around. She tried to picture the attacker in her mind, but she'd never gotten a good visual of him. She sighed, knowing that it was futile. Their best bet was that one of the security cameras had gotten some view. Given the hoodie, she didn't know how much good that would do.

'I need to sleep,' Raymond said, closing his eyes. 'I think the meds are doing a number on me.'

'Better to sleep now while you're not in as much pain,' Kingston assured him. 'I, on the other hand, have been told to stay awake.'

Given his concussion, that made sense. Sydney leaned forwards. 'Want me to help you?'

'That would be ideal,' Kingston said. 'Perhaps you can tell me about your time in America. I have never been to New York. What's it like?'

Sydney was glad about the topic. She filled him in, watching

Raymond fall asleep in the other bed. Kingston focused on her words entirely, asking the appropriate questions. It was going to be a long night.

CHAPTER 25

SYDNEY stayed the entire night. She awoke to the sun coming up and Raymond and Kingston talking. Raymond was filling Kingston in on everything that had happened, downplaying his role. She wanted to correct him but was too tired.

The hospital cleared both Kingston and Raymond to go home. The police came to visit before they were released. Kingston and Sydney waited for Raymond to finish with the police, and Sydney hoped their stories aligned. She didn't enjoy lying to the police, but how exactly could she explain the guy was after keys to a teleportation portal?

'How are you feeling?' Kingston asked her as they waited.

'Tired,' she admitted. 'You?'

'I still have a headache.' He smiled tightly. 'I'm looking forward to returning home.'

'Will Rita fuss over you?' Sydney asked.

'She'll throw a bottle of painkillers at me and tell me to suck it up,' he said.

Sydney chuckled. She could imagine Rita doing just that. She remembered how Rita had called Raymond a baby for flinching while she cleaned up his wounds after he was tortured. It seemed like Raymond always got the worst of it.

'You know, Jake told me you two were a magnet for trouble,' Sydney said.

Kingston huffed. 'We don't seek it out.'

'But it does find you.'

He paused, his head cocked to one side. 'It does.'

They fell back into silence. Sydney wished Jake had come with them on this trip. If there had been four of them, then the man might never have gotten the jump on them. He must have picked Sydney as the easy target and Kingston as the threat. She shuddered to think of what would have happened if Raymond hadn't had his knife.

As if her thoughts had conjured him, Raymond appeared. Sydney noted his sallow skin despite the sleep he'd gotten the night before.

'All done?' Kingston asked.

'For now,' Raymond said. 'They mentioned they might have further questions in the future.'

'But we won't be here,' Sydney said. She didn't know how many extra days Rita had organised for them; it would all depend on hotel bookings.

'I mentioned that,' Raymond said. 'She wanted my number so she could call.'

'Are you ready to go?' Kingston asked Raymond.

'Yeah. But I'm not sure I'm up to driving yet,' he said. 'And you probably shouldn't if you still have a headache.'

'Which I do,' Kingston confirmed. He looked at Sydney. 'That doesn't bother you, does it, Miss Madinah?'

They wanted her to drive. She tried to work out how they would fit in the car. They'd have to figure something out. 'That's fine,' she said. They could sort it out once they got to the car. 'I'm not parked far away.'

'Then let us go,' Kingston said, pushing himself up.

Sydney scrambled to her feet, leading the way out of the hospital, glad to be putting it behind her. Sydney slowed her pace when she noticed the other two ambling behind her.

When they arrived at the car, Sydney was relieved that it was fine. She had worried the attacker might come back overnight and do something to it. Raymond chose to sit in the back seat. He didn't complain when climbing over, even though his stitches were surely sensitive.

They drove back to the hotel, Sydney frowning as they rounded the corner and found a police car sitting outside.

'That's concerning,' Raymond said.

'Maybe they're asking questions about us,' Kingston said.

'I don't see why,' Raymond said. 'They mentioned nothing to me about going to the hotel.'

Sydney pulled them around the back and into their designated car park. As Raymond pulled himself out of the car, he winced. Kingston saw it.

'Perhaps I should have gone in the back,' Kingston said.

'I'm shorter,' Raymond said.

'But you are also injured,' Kingston said.

'I'm fine,' Raymond said. He must have seen something on Sydney's face as he looked at her. 'Seriously, I am. I've had worse.'

Sydney knew that, but that didn't stop her from worrying. She still felt partially responsible for his injuries. He'd argue with her if she mentioned that. They locked the car and walked into the hotel; the receptionist looked up as they entered and rushed around the counter.

'Your room was broken into overnight,' she said in a hushed tone. 'I think it might have been the same man as before.'

That explained the police car. Sydney saw worry overcome Kingston's and Raymond's faces.

'The police are there looking things over right now. You might want to see if anything was taken,' the receptionist continued.

They nodded and headed up to their room, Sydney's stomach doing flips. Kingston couldn't look for the keys while the police were there. She also knew there would be more questions, given their involvement in last night's attack. They couldn't pass it off as random anymore, given that they had been targeted twice.

Kingston led the way to the room, finding the hotel manager with two police officers. Sydney recognised one from the night before. His face hinted he remembered them too.

'I am so sorry about this,' the manager said, approaching them. 'We've never had a break-in before.'

'Interesting that it's you three,' the police officer said. 'I would think this is connected to the attack last night.'

'We have no idea,' Raymond said, looking around the room. Everything had been overturned, as if the thief had been searching for something. They couldn't tell the manager or the police what. 'We thought it was random.'

'It looks like it was targeted,' the police officer said. 'Do you have any idea what they could have been after?'

'Depends what they took,' Kingston said. Sydney was more than happy to let the two men do the talking. 'Do you mind if we have a look to see if anything is missing?'

'Go right ahead,' the police officer said. 'Let us know if you find anything.'

They split up and went to their rooms. Sydney's heart sank as she saw the state of her room. The thief had even moved the mattress off the bed to look under it. She searched through her things, mentally checking everything off as she put them into order. Everything was still there.

She returned to the living area to find the manager straightening things up in the kitchen unit. All the drawers had been pulled out, so the manager slid them back in. The police must have already taken photos and collected their evidence. How long ago had the break-in been?

'How did you go?' the officer asked.

'All my things are there,' she said. 'Nothing was taken from my room.'

'No valuables?'

'I didn't really bring anything of value with me,' she admitted. 'I mostly only packed clothes, and they're all there.'

The police officer made a note on his tablet. Sydney went over to the kitchen to help with the cleanup. The manager insisted she had it, but Sydney wouldn't have a bar of it. She felt guilty about the state of the room and knew what a break-in would do to the hotel's reputation.

Kingston and Raymond came out of their room. She couldn't tell from their expressions if anything was taken. Had Kingston hidden the keys in their room? Sydney hoped it wasn't under the mattress.

'My computer is still there,' Raymond said to the officer. 'That's the only thing of value that I brought, apart from my wallet and phone, which I had on me.'

'So nothing was taken?' the officer asked.

Kingston shook his head. 'Not that we can see.'

'Do you know what the thief was looking for?'

'No clue,' Raymond said. 'Maybe they thought we had money stashed or something.'

The police officer didn't look convinced. Sydney knew what he had to be thinking – drugs.

'Do you mind if we bring one of our dogs to search this unit?' the officer asked the manager, confirming Sydney's suspicion.

'If it helps,' the manager said.

'Are you willing to allow us to look through your car?' the officer asked them.

'Go right ahead,' Raymond said. 'It's in the parking lot.'

Sydney knew their morning would be a long one as the officer radioed in his request.

It was several hours before the police finished reviewing everything alongside their canine unit. Sydney had worried that a previous tenant might have done something, but the dog seemed to clear the place. Raymond let them check his car. The police had complimented him on his choice of vehicle before searching it.

They had all been pulled aside for further questioning. The police were now looking at their attack the night before as targeted. Sydney wished she could tell them the truth, knowing it would help them find their person. It could only be the same man. She hoped they had gotten some form of security footage from the cameras.

The hotel manager and a maid helped them return the suite to order. Sydney hated how the manager kept apologising for the inconvenience. She was the one who wanted to apologise as they had brought trouble to the hotel. Sydney was more than exhausted when everyone finally left them alone, Kingston closing the door behind their retreating backs.

'Well,' Kingston said, turning to face them. 'This has been quite the excursion.'

'Pain in the arse,' Raymond grumbled, dropping to sit on the couch. 'You going to go check?'

'I will now.'

Kingston walked down the hall. For the first time, she noted he didn't go to the bedroom, but to the bathroom. The thief had also been through that room, and Sydney couldn't think of any hiding places there. She tried to remember if there was a vent in there.

After a moment, Kingston returned with the little lockbox, opening it up. He pulled out the small collection of keys. 'Safe and sound.'

'Wherever you hid them, you did a good job,' Raymond said.

Kingston smirked. 'Toilet.'

Sydney felt her brain stop for a moment. 'What?'

'They were in the toilet,' Kingston said.

'Come again?' Raymond said. Sydney could see he was in as much disbelief as she was.

'I hid them in the cistern,' Kingston said. 'The box is watertight. I thought it to be the last place a thief would look.'

'Well, you weren't wrong,' Raymond said. 'Because we still have them.'

Sydney nodded. She hadn't even considered the toilet a hiding place, but now that she did, she remembered how she'd read about a drug dealer hiding his stash in the same place. No one wanted to fish in the toilet for something, and it was the very last place someone would look if they were pulling an apartment to pieces.

'You don't keep all the keys in a toilet, do you?' Sydney asked.

'Of course not,' Kingston said. 'It's a temporary hiding place. The rest of the keys are safely hidden. It would take much work to get to them.'

She looked at Raymond. 'Do you know where they are?'

'I do,' he confirmed. 'It took a lot to get it out of him, though.'

'The fewer people that know, the safer they are,' Kingston said. 'And I am going to go put these back.'

They watched as Kingston headed back up the hallway to the bathroom. Sydney was glad he was fishing in the toilet, not her. The water was clean in the cistern, but that still didn't chase away the ickiness of it in her mind. Sydney retreated to the armchair of the apartment, glad to be sitting down again.

'We need to find out how many extra days Rita arranged for us,' Raymond commented.

Sydney nodded, pulling out her phone and sending Rita a text message. Kingston and Raymond needed a chance to get over everything that had happened. Sydney herself just wanted to go home. It had tainted the trip for her. She was missing her bed and wanted to return to work to take her mind off things.

'Are you okay?' Raymond asked gently.

She looked up. 'I'm fine. I'm not the one who was hurt.'

'You were still there,' Raymond reminded her. 'He went after you too.'

'And you stopped him,' Sydney said. 'You wouldn't have been stabbed if I'd just run to begin with. Or if I'd taken out my pepper spray.'

'Don't dwell on what ifs,' Raymond said. 'It will get you nowhere.'

She knew that, but that didn't stop her from doing it. She was sure that Raymond and Kingston would continue to remind her that nothing had been her fault. However, it didn't chase away the guilt she was feeling. She felt useless on this trip. Even following the guy had turned up nothing. She wished she had been forced to stay behind and Jake had been the one to come in her place.

'You're doing it again,' Raymond said.

She'd been caught. She worried her lip. 'Just thinking it would have been better if Jake had come too.'

'It would have been,' he agreed. 'But we can't change that. Jake wanted to come, but circumstances prevented it.'

And Rita had wanted to come. Sydney was sure Rita would have handled the situation better than she had. Rita had experience with this world. Sydney's phone chirped. She frowned.

'What is it?' Raymond asked.

'She only got one day,' Sydney said, looking back up. 'It was the most she could manage.'

'What who could manage?' Kingston asked as he rejoined them.

'Rita,' Sydney said. 'She could only get one more day for us here.'

'Ah.' Kingston sat on the couch beside Raymond, a frown on his face. He looked concerned but not surprised. 'The room must have been booked.'

Sydney nodded. They were lucky enough to have one extra day at such short notice. The entire trip had been lucky. Sydney didn't know how Rita had organised things so fast for them – she was a miracle worker. If Rita were the hotel manager, everything would run smoothly.

'One day is better than nothing,' Raymond said. 'It gives us a day to rest.'

'It does pose a slight problem,' Kingston said. 'We're not allowed to drive.'

'I guess I'm in the back seat,' Raymond said.

'No, I insist I be the one,' Kingston said. 'You are less likely to injure yourself if you sit in the front.'

'You're taller,' Raymond countered. 'You need more legroom.'

'Draw straws?' Sydney asked, knowing that they would not reach an agreement. Both men were stubborn.

Raymond narrowed his eyes and reached into his pocket, pulling out his wallet. He took out a coin, looking directly at Kingston. 'Call it.'

'Heads.' Kingston didn't miss a beat.

Raymond flipped the coin. Something in the way they were doing it told Sydney that this wasn't the first time they had used this to settle an argument. Raymond caught the coin and slapped it onto the back of his hand, revealing it. 'Shit.'

'I'm in the back,' Kingston said, almost smugly.

'Fine,' Raymond grumbled. 'Anyway, I need a shower and a change of clothes.'

'An excellent suggestion,' Kingston said. 'The blood is bothering me.'

Sydney avoided looking at the blood on Raymond's clothes. His jacket and shirt were more than ruined. She kicked herself for not returning to the hotel to retrieve a change of clothing for him.

Raymond pushed himself up and disappeared down the hallway, leaving Kingston and Sydney alone in the living room.

'What are we going to do about dinner?' They didn't have enough food in the apartment for a meal.

'Takeaway it is,' Kingston said with a smile. 'I'm certain I recall seeing something in the information booklet about takeaway possibilities.'

Now that he mentioned it, Sydney remembered seeing them, too. She found the book, joined Kingston on the couch, and flipped through it.

'A nice selection,' Kingston commented. 'These will do.'

CHAPTER 26

RAYMOND felt a lot better after the shower even if everything was still aching. He'd unwrapped the bandage on his arm to shower and saw that it would be an impressive bruise. Luckily, he had broken nothing, as he didn't like the idea of wearing a cast. It would make working difficult.

He checked his luggage's hidden pocket to ensure the journal was still there. Despite having turned out his things, the thief hadn't found it, much to his relief. It wasn't in a regular place for there to be a hidden pocket, which was why he'd purchased this bag. The pocket was designed to keep a passport, but the journal fit just as well.

Once dressed and freshened up, he returned to the living room to find Sydney and Kingston watching the news. It was a political story about Melbourne. Raymond had never bothered much with politics. He voted and kept up with what was happening, but he didn't invest heavily.

'We're doing takeaway for dinner,' Kingston said, picking up the book and handing it to him once Raymond joined them. 'Take your pick.'

Raymond dropped into the armchair and studied his options. He had never been big on fast food. He only ever had it when he was out with Tanya and Andrew, who seemed to love the stuff. They always went to the Melbourne Central food court when they came into the city. Raymond found it too crowded, but he dealt with it. That was the thing about city living – everywhere was crowded.

'I wouldn't mind some Chinese,' he said, looking up from the book. 'What are you two having?'

They exchanged a look of amusement, and Raymond knew they had chosen the Chinese. The food was good, he hoped. He'd never had a terrible experience with takeaway, but that could be his luck. He pulled out his phone to look up the menu online.

Soon, they all had their orders worked out, and Kingston made the call. That fact amused Raymond. Kingston deferred all his phone calls to Rita when they were back in Adelaide. He preferred to meet in person, and even that was a stretch for him. Kingston was, really, a recluse. He only interacted when he had to. Raymond had coaxed him out of his shell a little since they had met, but if Kingston had the choice of interacting or staying home, he'd choose to stay home.

As they waited, they went to their rooms to pack their things. Raymond had thrown all his clothes into a pile. The thief had mixed his and Kingston's clothes, so Raymond had tried to separate them as best he could. He carefully folded his shirts. Kingston had taught him a more efficient and space-saving way of doing things during their European trip, and he couldn't think of returning to the old way.

'How's the side?' Kingston asked as they packed.

'Fine,' Raymond said, stretching a little and feeling the stitches pull. 'Sore. It feels like it's burning.'

'I'm sorry I was no help to you,' Kingston said. 'It seems to be a common occurrence.'

'Edward, you were knocked out cold,' Raymond reminded him.

'He probably went for you first because he thought you were the bigger threat.' He paused. 'How's the head, by the way?'

'I feel like I have a migraine,' Kingston said, massaging his temples. 'I have an impressive bump where he hit me.'

'You should see my bruises,' Raymond agreed. 'Crowbars aren't fun.'

'They're not supposed to be.' Kingston looked to the door. 'Apparently, the others view us as magnets for trouble.'

'We are a bit,' Raymond said. 'Comes with the job.'

'Sadly, yes.' Kingston sighed, sitting on the edge of the bed. 'I am starting to think it is dangerous to go out.'

'Oh no, don't you dare,' Raymond said, knowing exactly where this was leading. 'Do not even suggest locking us down.'

'For the remainder of this trip, we should, yes,' Kingston said. 'It's only for one night.'

Raymond had no intention of leaving the hotel until the morning anyway. All he wanted to do was sleep. He knew it was his body wanting to heal. He still had some pain medications that made him drowsy – another reason he couldn't drive tomorrow. He still wished he'd be the one in the back seat.

'You're not going to argue?' Kingston asked.

'I've got no plans to go anywhere,' Raymond admitted, putting another shirt in his suitcase. 'But when we get to Melbourne, I will argue if you even think about restricting us. I have to go back to work. I doubt I could get any more time off.'

'Your mother is your supervisor. I'm sure she could arrange it.'

'You know she hates locking down just as much as I do.'

'Yes. Indeed.' Kingston smiled tightly. He looked at his watch. 'The food should be here soon. We will finish packing later.'

Raymond nodded his agreement, still suspicious that Kingston was thinking of locking him and his mother down. That hadn't gone well the last time Kingston had tried. Unable to get Raymond, Marcus targeted Olivia. Raymond didn't know how Marcus had even found out about her. It would have taken a lot of digging. Even Jake hadn't worked that out, and he ran everyone's backgrounds.

They left the bedroom and entered the living room, Raymond dropping onto the couch. He heard Kingston in the kitchen area getting plates. He thought momentarily about helping him, but his side was hurting. After a short while, Sydney joined them, undoubtedly having heard them come out.

A knock on the door sounded and Sydney received their dinner. It looked good and smelled even better. They ate, Raymond glad to be eating something substantial.

They were finishing up when another knock came on the door. They exchanged a look.

'Did we order twice?' Raymond asked.

'No,' Sydney said. 'I'm sure we only ordered once.'

'I'll go see who it is,' Kingston said, using his napkin to tidy himself up before making his way to the door.

Curiosity got the better of Raymond. He slid out of his seat and followed Kingston down the short hallway. He arrived just as Kingston opened the door. Instantly Raymond went on guard. John Smith stood in the hallway.

'Good evening,' John said, smiling amiably at them. 'I hope I'm not disturbing you.'

'I'm surprised to see you,' Kingston said, an edge to his voice. It was barely there, but it was enough to know Kingston had gone into fight mode.

'I heard about the attack on the news,' John said. 'I thought I'd come to see how you were.'

'How did you know we were here?' Kingston asked.

John paused. 'I believe you mentioned you were staying here.'

'No, I don't believe we did.'

'Ah. I must have seen it on the news as well,' John said, covering himself. 'They mentioned that a robbery in this hotel was connected to the incident outside Pizza Hut.'

'How did you know it was us?' Raymond asked.

'The description of the victims,' John said. 'Three out-of-towners here for Heritage Week. Two men and a woman. It could only have been you three.'

It was a stretch, but it made sense. That didn't mean that Raymond believed him. John's appearance just added to his suspicion that he was connected. He set his jaw, willing John to go away.

'How are you?' John asked. 'I believe the news said one of you had been stabbed.'

'Yes,' Kingston said. 'We're fine.'

'Pleased to hear it,' John said. 'A most unfortunate incident. It should not have happened.'

That piqued Raymond's interest. If John was behind the attack, then had he not ordered the attacker to kill them? He hadn't said that the attack itself was unfortunate, just the stabbing. Raymond's mind was in overdrive. John spoke in riddles, and it took Raymond a lot to read between the lines.

'How is Miss Sydney?' John asked. 'Is she well?'

'She's fine,' Kingston said. 'She wasn't harmed.'

'Excellent.' John nodded. So, Sydney hadn't been a target. 'Was anything taken in the robbery? It makes it seem like the events were linked.'

'No, nothing was taken,' Raymond said. John should have known that if he had been involved.

'Strange,' John said. 'One would have thought something would have been taken after so much effort. Are you sure?'

'We're certain,' Kingston said. 'All our things are here.'

John nodded, a tightness around his eyes. Maybe his subordinate hadn't checked in yet, so this was John's first hearing about the robbery's results.

'Thank you for your concern.' Kingston's voice was laced with dismissal.

'I am happy to hear you are all okay,' John said. 'No lasting damage?'

'None,' Kingston confirmed.

'Perhaps it would be wise to be more careful when you're going out. You never know when someone might come after you. It sounds like you are a target.'

Was that a threat? Raymond glanced at Kingston, knowing that if Kingston picked up on it, he might insist they lock down once they got back home. He saw the tightness of Kingston's shoulders. He'd noticed.

'Anyhow, I should leave you to your evening,' John said. 'When are you returning home?'

'Soon,' Kingston answered. 'We will be leaving soon.'

'Then I wish you a safe trip,' John said. 'I'm sorry that Ballarat has treated you so poorly. It's a wonderful town. Things like what happened rarely happen. Perhaps you were followed from your home.'

Did that imply that John wasn't from Ballarat? They would need to decipher what he said.

'Have a good evening,' Kingston said.

'You as well. Give my regards to Miss Sydney,' John said.

Kingston closed the door as John turned to walk away, his cane tapping on the floor as he went. Raymond turned, almost running into Sydney. He hadn't even realised she was standing behind him. Her eyes were wide and concern was etched into her face. Raymond ushered her gently back down the hallway. They returned to the table.

'That was interesting,' Kingston said, taking out his phone. 'And concerning.'

'I don't remember ever mentioning where we were staying,' Sydney said.

'No, we didn't,' Raymond agreed. 'Which adds to the fact he's watching us.'

'I suggest we contact Jake,' Kingston said. That explained why he had taken his phone out. He pressed the speed dial number, and after a few short rings, Jake answered.

'What's wrong, boss?' Jake asked. 'Everything okay?'

'We just had a visit from John Smith,' Kingston said.

'What?' Jake sounded alarmed. 'How did he know where you were?'

'That is the problem,' Kingston said. 'None of us ever mentioned where we were staying or what room we were staying in.'

'He might have gotten the room from reception,' Sydney said. 'But I'm pretty sure we told them not to let anyone in.'

'Which makes me think he knew what room,' Raymond agreed. 'And there is only one way to know that.'

'Sounds like he's your guy then,' Jake said. 'Did you get a picture of him?'

'Regrettably, no,' Kingston said. 'It would have been suspicious had we done so.'

'I should have tried,' Sydney said. 'I had my phone on me.'

'Could you even see him?' Raymond asked. 'You were behind me, and he couldn't see you.'

'I was trying to stay out of sight,' Sydney admitted. 'He creeps me out.'

'Any reason why?' Jake asked.

'Just… something about him,' Sydney said. 'Some people have a bad feeling about them. He comes across as pleasant enough, but… there's something.'

'Did Marcus have that feeling?' Kingston asked.

Sydney shook her head. 'No. I got nothing off him at all. It wasn't until he revealed himself that he changed. Before that, he was pleasant.'

'So your feelings aren't always reliable,' Kingston concluded.

Raymond gave him a look. That was rude. Kingston returned the gaze with one equally serious one. Sydney didn't look offended, at least. Instead, she seemed to be confused and a little guilty. Raymond knew she still felt responsible for everything that had happened with Marcus. She'd apologised enough, and Kingston didn't need to keep reminding her.

'Well, we're still at square one with him,' Jake said. 'Although it sounds like he's connected.'

'Are you sure you can't get anything on him?' Kingston asked.

'Not with that name. I need more details. It's a small needle in a very large haystack.'

'At least we're leaving tomorrow,' Sydney said. 'We might never see him again.'

'I wouldn't be so sure,' Raymond said. 'His comment about being followed made me wonder if he's even from here.'

'Notice that too, did you,' Kingston said.

'You think he followed you to Ballarat?' Jake asked.

'Hard to say,' Kingston said. 'It is entirely possible.'

'Well, that widens the field,' Jake said. 'I need something concrete to work with. Can you get the surveillance from the hotel?'

'That would be more Rita and your specialty,' Kingston said. 'I doubt they will just hand the footage over to guests.'

'I'll talk to Rita about it, then,' Jake said. 'Anyway, I've got to go. I'm about to clock out for the night.'

'Make sure you speak to Rita first,' Kingston said.

'Sure thing, boss.'

Kingston hung up the phone.

'John coming by is a bad thing, isn't it,' Sydney said. It wasn't a question.

'It is concerning,' Kingston confirmed.

'Maybe we should have followed him out,' Raymond said. 'We might have been able to see which car he got into and got the plates.'

'Too late now,' Kingston said. 'The odds are he would have noticed.'

'True.'

Kingston sighed heavily, leaning back in his seat. 'I think that's enough excitement for the week. I might finish packing my bags and retire to bed early.'

'Sounds good to me,' Raymond agreed.

'Me too,' Sydney said. 'It's been a long week. I think it's going to be another week before my legs and feet stop hurting.'

Raymond had forgotten about his legs and feet. Now that she had mentioned it, he became aware that he was still hurting. The medication had numbed the pain, and the stab wound overshadowed the ache. His arm hurt more than his legs. He looked at Kingston, tried to gauge what he was thinking, and saw that he agreed with Sydney. His head mustn't be too bad, then.

They both bid a good evening to Sydney and retreated to their room. Raymond instantly went back to where he had left off with packing. He frowned at how crumpled his clothing had become because of the thief, smoothing the wrinkles out as he folded things.

'That's bothering you, isn't it?' Kingston said, an amused sparkle in his eye.

'Like it's not bothering you,' Raymond countered. Kingston liked things to be immaculate. His home at the Medina Grand was a testament to that – it was impeccable. He knew Rita was more of a neat freak than they were, so how much was Kingston and how much was Rita in the main part of Kingston's suite was debatable.

'Not as much as it does you, it seems,' Kingston said, slipping another piece of clothing into his bag. 'Clothing can be ironed.'

True. Still, Raymond didn't want to scrunch his clothing up and put it in the bag. It would fit better if it were folded tightly and neatly. He tried his best to smooth out his clothing as he went through them, putting everything in its place. He packed as much as possible, leaving one outfit out for the next day.

'I'm finished,' Kingston said, looking over at him.

'Yeah, me too,' Raymond said. He turned to him. 'I feel like we're leaving behind unfinished business when we leave tomorrow.'

'How so?'

'We don't know exactly who is behind the attack,' Raymond said. 'And exactly what they wanted.'

'I think, given they didn't take anything, that it is obvious,' Kingston said.

'But what if it was the journal they were after?' Raymond said.

'Or it was both.' Kingston's lips formed a thin line. It bothered him more than he was letting on. 'Let's not worry about it now. Everything is locked tight. Nobody is getting in tonight. And if they do, they will have to contend with us.'

Well, that would not help Raymond sleep. He glared at Kingston for even suggesting that someone could break in overnight. Raymond slipped between the sheets and winced as his stitches pulled. He rubbed his hand over the bandage, feeling the bumps of the stitches underneath.

'Did you take your painkillers?' Kingston asked.

'Just before dinner,' Raymond assured him. 'I'm not due for any more for a few hours.'

Kingston nodded, switching off the light and plunging the room into darkness. 'Try to sleep, Raymond. We have an early start in the morning.'

Easier said than done.

CHAPTER 27

SYDNEY'S alarm dragged her out of a dreamless sleep. She was exhausted. It had taken her a while to fall asleep, her mind raced and worry played through her the night before. She'd worried that the thief would try to break back in or John Smith would come through her window. Eventually, she'd just passed out from sheer exhaustion. She had barely slept the night before, and it was catching up with her.

She dragged herself out of bed. She'd set her alarm a little earlier to have first dibs in the shower before the two men got up. Sydney went to the bathroom, grabbed a clean towel, and quickly showered. When she was done, she returned to her room to pack away the last of her clothing and things then put her suitcase by the door.

She heard movement in the suite as she finished, followed by the shower coming to life, and knew Kingston was up. Given Raymond had showered the night before, he likely wouldn't shower that morning, especially given he'd have to reapply his bandages afterwards.

She headed into the kitchen and dug out the last of their bread, just enough for one more day. She made herself some toast and warmed the water for the coffee. Kingston joined her, dropping his bread into the toaster. He'd had a relatively brief shower.

'Raymond awake?' Sydney asked.

'For once, yes,' Kingston said. 'He's just redoing the bandage on his arm.'

'He doesn't need help?'

'I offered, but he insisted he could do it himself.'

He was a stubborn man. Sydney imagined him lost in a tangle of bandages. She resisted the urge to check on him. She took her food to the table to eat. Kingston looked as tired as she felt. She had a feeling he didn't sleep well, either.

'How is your head today?' she asked.

'Better.' He gingerly touched the back of his head. She imagined he had a large lump. 'I still have a mild headache.'

She nodded. He'd probably have a headache for a while. 'Do you still need pain medication?'

'I don't believe so,' he said, making himself his cup of coffee. He made it a little darker and a little stronger than he usually did. She didn't miss that. 'Are you still able to drive today?'

'I can,' she confirmed. 'Are you sure you want to stay in the back seat?'

'Raymond and I already had that discussion this morning,' Kingston said. 'I am certain.'

She took a long drink from her coffee. If only they had hired a car with more legroom in the back seat. They hadn't planned that out well. Then again, they hadn't intended to end the trip with Kingston and Raymond injured. Sydney worried her lip, again feeling guilty that she had frozen. She knew they would tell her off if she mentioned it again, but she couldn't help it.

Raymond walked in and tried to steal Kingston's toast. Kingston slapped his fingers and shooed him away. Sydney couldn't help but chuckle at the move, Raymond pouting but giving up. He made his coffee and waited for the toaster.

Sydney took her time eating, and the two men eventually joined her at the small table.

'Are we leaving at check-out time or before?' Sydney asked.

'If we leave too early, we will get stuck in peak-hour traffic,' Raymond said.

Sydney hadn't even thought about that. Better to leave closer to the checkout time. She sipped her coffee, wishing she'd followed Kingston's lead by making her drink a little stronger. They were silent as they ate. Sydney wanted to quiz them more about how they were feeling. She felt the urge to fall into the caretaker role but felt they would reject it if she tried. Raymond had been so reluctant to let Rita treat him after he'd come back from being tortured.

When she was done eating, she washed her things and packed the last of their food into a bag they had left from when they bought it. There wasn't that much food left. She cleared out the fridge and cupboards of their food, ensuring everything else was clean and put in its appropriate place. When a guest left, she knew how much the staff appreciated a clean and organised hotel room.

She paused as she finished. 'Should I strip the bed?'

'Huh?' Raymond looked up. 'Why?'

'To save the workers time,' Sydney said.

'Probably best not to,' Kingston said. 'They might have a routine.'

That was true.

'Should I steal the last of the samples?' Raymond asked.

'We've been over this,' Kingston said, looking at him. 'What is the point? You will end up with a collection that you will eventually throw in the garbage.'

Sydney could imagine them having this conversation during their trip to Europe. Raymond was the sort to take the samples. Many guests did. But it was pointless. As Kingston said, what was the point of taking something you would not use? Hotels expected the samples to be taken, so they always stocked up. It was rare for guests *not* to take them.

She headed back to her room, dragged her suitcase out to the main living area, and then went back to make one last pass to ensure she'd picked everything up. Satisfied, she returned to the living area and found Kingston washing his plate while Raymond finished his coffee.

'You're all ready to go?' Raymond asked.

'I am,' she confirmed.

'I just need to finish packing,' Raymond said. 'Just a couple of things.'

'I am the same,' Kingston said. 'You are rather well organised, Miss Madinah.'

She wanted to comment that she had to be in her line of work. She let it go, just nodding and watching as they disappeared into their bedroom. Sydney gave the suite a pass to make sure everything was in order.

She turned on the television to pass the time. The news report detailed that the roads were busy, but there were no accidents along their route. She expected a smooth ride home. Sydney waited for the two men to join her. She contemplated telling them about her following their stalker but decided against it. It didn't matter anymore. After a while, the two men returned to the living area with their suitcases.

'Anything exciting on the news?' Raymond asked her.

'No accidents on the highway home,' she said.

'That makes for a change.'

She didn't know whether to agree. She rarely took in Melbourne traffic reports. Adelaide traffic was another matter; it would tell her if a guest might be stuck in traffic if they didn't check in at the right time. She saw that the weather would be mixed on the ride home. She hoped Raymond had good tyres on his car.

'You still okay to drive?' Raymond asked.

Why did they keep asking her that? 'Of course.'

'Remember, you're in the front,' Kingston said.

Raymond grumbled, crossing his arms over his chest, yet he didn't argue. Perhaps the bet had been enough to end the argument. They watched the news until it was time to leave. Sydney did a last pass to quiet the nagging voice in her mind that they might forget something. Kingston settled their account at the front desk, and the receptionist wished them a pleasant journey, apologising once again for the break-in.

When they got out to the car, they packed everything in, and Kingston climbed into the back seat. He sat behind Sydney, opting for what little extra legroom he could get.

Soon enough, they were on the road, cruising along the Western Highway to Melbourne. There was moderate traffic, most seeming to have cleared after the morning rush. Sydney had to admire how well the car drove. She had paid little attention to it the last time she drove, but now she had the chance, she wished she had a car like this.

'You know, Kingston, I'm surprised you don't have a car,' Raymond said. 'You could get out of the city more often if you did.'

'Insurance, registration, parking,' Kingston listed off.

'Freedom,' Raymond countered.

'Necessity,' Kingston replied.

Sydney had to agree with Kingston. When you lived in the city with everything within walking distance, you didn't need a car. Raymond had his because he often drove to Geelong to visit his friends and daughter. Sydney hadn't needed a car in New York. They'd let her use the company car whenever the hotel needed her to drive.

'What about you, Miss Madinah?' Kingston asked. 'Does your apartment come with an allocated parking space?'

'Mine doesn't, no,' Sydney said. 'You can get one, but it costs extra.'

'Most places do,' Raymond agreed. 'Our La Trobe Street apartment has the same policy. It's actually cheaper to rent a space where I keep the car.'

'Do you ever worry about it being broken into?' Sydney asked. 'I'd be scared to leave a car overnight in the city.'

'The garage has excellent security,' Raymond said. 'I think that's one reason it hasn't been targeted yet.'

'You think it will be?'

'It's possible.' Raymond stretched a little, his face impassive, before he glanced back at Kingston. 'You grabbed the keys, right?'

'Of course,' Kingston said. 'I packed them first thing this morning.'

'Good,' Raymond said. 'It would be awkward to go back and explain that we left something in the toilet.'

That *would* be awkward. The staff would probably think it was drugs and not let them back into the apartment. Sydney felt terrible that she hadn't even thought of the keys. She was glad she hadn't been the one responsible for bringing them. Sydney couldn't wait to try them out. At least one of them had to work.

'When do you go back to work?' she asked Raymond.

'Three days,' Raymond answered. 'Believe me, Mother is looking forward to having me back under her thumb.'

'Isn't that a conflict of interest?'

'What? Her being my supervisor?' Raymond shrugged. 'She works me harder than anyone else would. And I get away with less with her.'

'Your mother is a perfectionist,' Kingston said. 'As are you.'

'Not to the degree she is,' Raymond said. 'When I started working, they considered putting me under the supervision of a woman named Jennifer, but my mother insisted I work under her. She had seniority, so they listened to her. She had to promise that she wouldn't go easy on me.'

Sydney couldn't even imagine what it must be like working for Lucille. She was a hard woman. Although she seemed pleasant enough, Sydney had also seen the dark side of her. 'Does it cause conflicts?'

'All the time,' Raymond said. 'She's my mother. She knows what to expect from me and then expects better.'

Sydney negotiated around a slow car on the highway, thinking about what it would be like to work for her parents. She couldn't imagine it. Frankly, the idea scared her. As much as she loved them, she also loved the distance from them. It made her feel like she could be her own person and not worry about heavy expectations.

'When do you start back?' Raymond asked her.

'Same. Three days,' Sydney said. 'I'm actually looking forward to going back to work.'

'Really? How come?'

'After everything, I'm just looking forward to some normality,' she admitted.

'Fair enough.'

'What about you, Kingston?' Sydney asked, glancing at him in the rearview mirror. He looked cramped in the back seat, but he wasn't complaining.

'Rita will no doubt have a pile of documents ready for me when I return,' he said.

'But will you go through them or sit on them to spite her?' Raymond asked.

'Have you tried spiting Rita?' Kingston asked. 'It's not a battle that you will win.'

Sydney chuckled at that. She didn't want to get on Rita's bad side. Rita would be more than capable of making her life a living hell.

'But you're her boss,' Raymond pointed out.

'Sometimes I wonder,' Kingston said.

Sydney smiled, returning her full attention to the road. She saw Raymond watching out the window while Kingston was doing something on his phone. She had a feeling he was messaging Rita. No doubt letting her know where they were and their ETA. After everything, Sydney didn't blame him.

She kept one eye on the rearview mirror, noting the surrounding traffic. She was worried that someone might try to follow them from Ballarat. So far, no car stood out to her. Every other car seemed to move normally in the traffic as they drove towards Melbourne. They pulled off at a service station at Ballan to pick up some food for an early lunch and refuel the car.

Before Sydney even knew it, they were in city traffic. Roadwork on one of the major roads slowed them down. Sydney was patient as they idled in the traffic. She saw many people gawking at the car as they moved. She felt very self-conscious about it. One person snapped a photo. Raymond spotted it.

'It's just a car,' Raymond said.

'A nice car,' Kingston pointed out. 'You don't see many of them on the road.'

Raymond shrugged.

'At least it's not someone following us,' Sydney said.

'I was wondering why you kept checking the mirrors,' Raymond said. 'No one suspicious back there?'

'No,' she said. 'Nothing that stands out.'

'I doubt they would need to follow us,' Kingston said. 'They will know where we are going.'

'That hasn't stopped them before,' Raymond pointed out. 'The intimidation thing, remember?'

'A drive through town is one thing. A drive to the city is another matter entirely.'

'True.'

Sydney had thought they would have been worried about someone following them. It seemed like she was the only paranoid person in the car. It also surprised her that they hadn't slept. They were both wide awake and alert, Kingston on his phone and Raymond car watching. Kingston looked troubled. She wanted to ask him what was wrong but kept her focus on the road.

She navigated their way into the CBD, Raymond telling her

which way to go. Relief washed over her as she eased into the allocated parking space and turned the car off. She hadn't damaged the car. It had been worrying her that she would side-swipe something simply because of the car's price.

They unloaded their bags. Sydney could tell Kingston was hurting from being crammed into the back seat. Raymond double-checked that the car was locked and led them into the library.

Stepping into the library felt like coming home. They made their way through the corridors and down to the lower levels. Raymond unlocked the door to the apartment, the three of them easing their way carefully down the stairs, their luggage bags clunking their way down.

'There you are!'

Sydney winced at the sternness of Lucille's voice. She spotted her making her way down the hallway. Instantly, she grabbed Raymond, looked him over, and lifted his shirt. He swatted her down.

'Mother!' he protested.

'I need to see you're in one piece,' Lucille said. 'Rita told me all about what happened. Why didn't you call me yourself?'

'I didn't want to worry you,' Raymond said.

'You spent a night in the hospital and didn't bother to call your own mother?'

Sydney grimaced. It probably should have been her that called Lucille. She didn't have Lucille's number, but Rita or Jake could have given it to her. Sydney wanted to apologise, but Kingston touched her arm, shaking his head. She nodded. She understood.

'Now,' Lucille said. 'What are your requirements? Any special orders?'

'Just to not pull the stitches,' Raymond assured her. 'And no heavy lifting.'

'You don't need to lift anything in your job, anyhow,' Lucille said. She brushed a hand through her short hair, her blue eyes scrutinising her son. 'Will this affect your ability to work?'

'Not at all,' he told her. 'I can still sit and do my job.'

'Excellent. What about pain medication?'

'Enough for a week, and then I'm onto normal painkillers if I'm still hurting.'

Sydney would expect these questions from her own mother if she were in this situation. Raymond cared little for his mother, but Lucille clearly worried about her son. She hoped it was more to do with the fact that he was her son and not that he was the Keeper.

'Don't worry, Mother.' Raymond's voice was gentle. 'I'm fine, and I can work normally.'

That didn't seem to ease her stress. Sydney could see that her eyes were tight.

'Now, how about some coffee?' Raymond said. 'While we wait for Rita and Jake to come join us.'

'It would be nearing their lunch break,' Kingston said, looking at his watch.

'And where were you?' Lucille snapped, glaring at him. 'When Raymond was being stabbed?'

'Unconscious on the ground,' Kingston said simply.

'Oh.'

Lucille didn't expect that, which told Sydney that Jake and Rita hadn't given her all the specifics. Sydney hoped Lucille didn't turn her attention her way next. She didn't know how to answer that question.

'Mother, the coffee,' Raymond urged.

Lucille nodded and disappeared down the hall.

CHAPTER 28

RAYMOND'S posture softened when Lucille disappeared to fetch the coffee. Kingston's hand pressed into the small of his back, so it must have been noticeable.

'I'll help her,' Sydney said, pulling her luggage to the kitchen and dining area.

Raymond grabbed the handle of his luggage and rolled it towards his room. He opened the door, noting that it felt a little musty. The door must have been closed the entire time he was away. Being deep underground made it impossible for him to open the windows to let in air.

Raymond parked his luggage by his bed, frowning as he heard the door close. Kingston had followed him in. If the door was closed, then Kingston wanted privacy. Raymond turned towards him and saw an unreadable expression on his face. That was never a good sign. Raymond hoped it didn't mean that Kingston was reconsidering locking him and his mother up because of the attack in Ballarat.

'What is it?' Raymond asked.

'It's just something Rita said to me while I was messaging in the car,' Kingston said, stepping forwards. 'She said that it sounded like you were fortunate.'

'What do you mean?' Raymond asked.

'That more damage wasn't done,' Kingston said. 'That you didn't hit a major artery or organ.'

Ah. Raymond could see where he was coming from. He had gotten lucky in terms of the stabbing. His knife had been small and didn't penetrate far, but it could still do a lot of damage. He kept it sharp. He'd really hoped he could have retrieved it before they'd left Ballarat, but with the ongoing investigation, that had been impossible. It might be another month before he saw it again.

He had a spare switchblade that he could use in the meantime, but the one he'd left with the police had been a gift from his grandfather on the day he had officially become Keeper. It had the Barry family crest on it. Raymond didn't know where his grandfather had gotten it, but it was special to him.

'I could have lost you again,' Kingston said.

Again? Oh, he meant when Marcus had kidnapped him. Raymond shrugged it off. He always felt a little uncomfortable when Kingston got emotional. Kingston had been super clingy after the ordeal with Marcus. Raymond had eventually talked him down in an effort to get things back to normal. Raymond was never one who enjoyed being fussed over.

'I'm fine,' Raymond assured him. 'It's really just a scratch.'

'You have several stitches, including internal ones,' Kingston countered.

'But that's all. It won't take me long to heal.'

Kingston didn't look assured by that. Raymond wished there was some way he could put Kingston's mind at ease. What was it precisely that Rita had said? He'd have to steal Kingston's phone later to look at the chat messages. If he knew exactly what she said, countering the arguments would be easier. Rita wouldn't have intentionally worried Kingston. She would have just been stating facts.

'Seriously, I'm fine,' he said again. 'I didn't even break a bone. You know I'm strong.'

'Yes, but you're not invincible,' Kingston said. 'Even though you like to pretend that you are.'

He didn't, did he? Raymond brushed the comment off. He *had* to put on a strong front. It was part of being the Keeper, just as it was part of Kingston being the Protector. Weakness just gave the enemy a way of getting in. That was why Raymond had kept Olivia hidden. She was a weakness, and Marcus had found her and used her to get to him.

'I know I'm not invincible,' he told Kingston. 'I'm a Keeper. We die young.'

Kingston's face dropped with horror. 'Do not even say that. You are not going to die.'

'It's going to happen,' Raymond said. 'Bar my grandfather, every single Keeper before me died young. Even Redmond was young for being one of your kind.'

'I will not allow it to happen,' Kingston said matter-of-factly. 'You will surpass your grandfather in age and retire.'

Doubtful, but Raymond didn't want to cause Kingston any more distress by saying that. He'd broken the code, which painted a target on his back. Word was out now, and people would be coming after him. The trick would be staying one step ahead of them, and so far, they weren't doing an excellent job of that.

'I watch my back, you know that,' he assured Kingston. 'It's not like I'm trying to die.'

'Sometimes I wonder.' He sighed, looking deflated. 'There are times I wish we had never become Protector and Keeper. We would be safer.'

'We also would never have met,' Raymond pointed out. 'We only met because I became Keeper, and you're the Protector.'

'That is true.' Kingston's lip formed a thin line. There was sadness in his eyes. 'Fate is an interesting mistress. It both gives and takes away.'

'It has taken nothing yet.'

'Your safety.' Kingston shook his head. 'I have considered with great seriousness simply locking you away.'

Raymond shot him a glare. 'Try that, and it's not the bad guys you'll have to worry about.'

'I am aware.' Kingston shrugged it off, stepping across the room and embracing Raymond tightly. 'I just don't want to lose you.'

'I'm right here,' Raymond reminded him, returning the hug. 'I'm fine.'

He felt Kingston nod. 'I love you.'

Raymond's eyes widened at those words, his whole body stiffening. He swallowed hard, questioning if he'd heard it correctly. Instantly, his mind went into denial. He must have misheard. But there was something about how Kingston held him, as if he were the most precious thing in the world, and that told Raymond he had understood what he said.

A knock on the door pulled them apart, Raymond glad for losing contact. His mind was racing at a thousand kilometres a second. He opened the door to find his mother.

'Well, where are you?' she asked. 'We're all waiting.'

'Coming,' Raymond said, not looking back at Kingston. He feared what he would find if he looked at him.

They followed Lucille to the dining room to find Sydney, Jake, and Rita all waiting for them. It was as if Jake hadn't slept in a few days. He spotted his mug with coffee already sitting at the table in the usual spot to the right-hand side where Kingston would sit at the table head.

Slipping into his chair, Raymond looked over at Jake. 'Are you okay?'

'I should be asking you that,' Jake said. 'You're the one who was stabbed.'

'I've slept, at least.'

'Jake's been staying at the hotel in case that problem guest comes back,' Rita said.

'Did he?' Kingston took his seat.

'Not after that last time,' Jake said. 'We were able to get the trespass order sorted. If they come within a hundred metres of the hotel, we can have them removed.'

'That is good news,' Kingston said. 'It sounds as if they were causing a lot of trouble.'

'It would be nice if we knew what triggered them,' Rita said. 'And if we should expect more of them.'

'You think there could be more?' Sydney asked, alarmed.

'There is always a chance,' Kingston said. 'Although it is curious what caused them to arrive now.'

'I still say Marcus had a dead man's switch,' Jake said. 'Six months after he died, he sent out a message.'

'That is logical but still curious,' Kingston said. 'And concerning. Who might he have sent messages to?'

'That's one thing keeping me up at night,' Jake admitted. 'Especially when you all started being followed.'

'Who was this man?' Lucille asked.

'The one who attacked us, or John Smith?' Raymond asked.

'Both.'

'We have little information on either,' Kingston said. 'It is likely you have more information on your problem guest than we do on either man.'

'Well, that's helpful,' Lucille said sarcastically.

'John Smith is an extremely common name, Mother,' Raymond reminded her. 'And we don't have any details about our attacker. He's just a faceless man.'

'You don't even know what he looks like?'

'He's slightly shorter than Raymond, works out, and appears to know how to pick locks,' Kingston said. 'He always wore a hooded jacket, meaning we could not see his face.'

'The police are looking into him, anyway,' Raymond said. 'If they find anything, we'll know.'

'But what if he leaves Ballarat?' Lucille asked. 'And follows you here?'

'No one followed us when we were driving,' Sydney said.

'And how do you know?'

'Because I was looking,' Sydney said.

'Sydney drove,' Raymond said.

'Seriously?' Jake looked surprised. 'You let someone drive your car?'

Raymond shrugged it off. He knew what Jake was getting at. Jake had begged for a turn to drive since he'd first seen the car. 'I'm on strong pain medication, and Kingston suffered a head injury. Sydney was the only one out of the three of us safe to drive.'

'Fair enough, I guess,' Jake said, disappointed. Raymond couldn't blame him. Maybe Raymond should organise for a day on a weekend when he and Jake went down to Great Ocean Road, and he'd let Jake have a go. He didn't know what sort of driver Jake was. But then, he hadn't known what sort Sydney was before he'd let her behind the wheel.

'That doesn't mean they didn't follow you,' Rita said. 'Chances are they already know where you are, so they didn't need to follow closely.'

'We discussed that,' Kingston said. 'It is possible. What is also true is they followed us to intimidate us in Ballarat.'

'Which means we need to be wary,' Jake said. 'Keep our wits about us for the next few weeks to see if anyone shows up at the library or the hotel.'

'Yes.' Kingston nodded emphatically. 'It would not surprise me if we encountered a new watcher.'

'Oh, yay,' Sydney said, eyes cast down.

'We've handled it before,' Raymond assured her. 'We can do it again.'

'Need I remind you that "handling it before" involved the Overseer needing to step in and Marcus killing himself,' Lucille said. 'I still don't think we cleaned all the debris up.'

'It's fine,' Raymond said. His mother could always see phantom dirt in places.

'It is not fine,' Lucille said. 'It could attract flies.'

'This far underground?'

'Flies are motivated.'

'We will do another cleaning pass if you desire it,' Kingston assured her. Raymond wished Kingston didn't always try to please Lucille about things like this. It just added to her validation. 'We were thorough the first time.'

'So right now, we don't know where any of our latest problems are,' Rita said. 'They might have followed you from Ballarat, or they may not have. They could still be in Adelaide, or they might have left.'

'It is a bothersome situation,' Kingston agreed. 'But I will enjoy the peace while it lasts.'

'There is still the matter of this John Smith,' Lucille said. 'Do you know if he was behind what happened or not?'

'It was strange of him to appear at our hotel,' Kingston said. 'He should not have known where we were staying, and we left instructions with the receptionist that we were not expecting visitors.'

'Which means he shouldn't have had your room number,' Rita said.

Kingston and Raymond nodded.

'I think he's in on it,' Jake said. 'Gut instinct.'

'Time will tell,' Kingston said. 'I'm sorry we could not obtain more information on him.'

'I think that's the point,' Jake said. 'If he chose that name, he wants to disappear.'

'I will need to sit down with Kian and have a discussion,' Kingston said. 'Perhaps the description will jog Kian's memory.'

'Add that to your to-do list,' Raymond noted, failing to maintain eye contact after what Kingston had said in the bedroom. He couldn't ignore him forever, but Raymond needed some time alone to let his mind catch up.

'So right now we just go back to normal,' Sydney said. It wasn't a question.

'As we always do,' Kingston confirmed.

'Easier said than done,' Jake grumbled. 'I have my people on high alert after the recent attacks. We're all tired. We can't take things down a notch until we're certain he's not coming back.'

'I have to agree with Jake,' Rita said. 'Until we're sure that man is gone, we can't rest on our laurels.'

'Understandable,' Kingston said. 'I imagine the entire event was upsetting.'

'We've all been through it, haven't we,' Sydney said. Again, not a question. Raymond noted the grey bags under her eyes. She looked like she needed a vacation after her "vacation". Some normality would be good for them all.

'That just raises the question of the keys,' Lucille said, eyes firmly on Kingston. 'You remembered to bring them back with you, yes?'

Kingston slid out of his chair and went to the hallway where his bag was. Raymond took a moment to look down at the table at his mother. There were new worry lines on her face. He narrowed his eyes at that. She rarely showed any emotion other than anger when dealing with him. Worry was just not something she would convey.

Kingston returned with the small lockbox, sitting back down and setting the box in front of him. He opened it, taking the keys out individually and putting them on the table. Raymond eyed the bent key, still bothered by it. How had it managed to be bent so severely? The only conclusion was that they had jammed it when it was put into its hiding place.

'What on earth happened to that one?' Jake gestured to the key in question.

'No clue,' Kingston said.

'I was hoping my grandfather might repair it,' Raymond said, glancing at Lucille.

'He might,' Lucille said. 'We will need to ask him.'

'Should we try some of these keys?' Rita asked. 'I've been curious to find out if they work or if we wasted our time retrieving them.'

'Odds are one at least works,' Jake said.

They gathered at the portal door. Kingston stepped through first and into the small room, standing beside the second portal door. He took the first key and turned it in the lock. No change in air pressure told Raymond that it was a dud. Sure enough, Kingston opened the door to show the storage room.

'No good,' Jake said. 'The portal on the other end is gone.'

'It does appear that way,' Kingston agreed.

He closed the door and removed the key, putting the next one in the lock. He turned it, and this time there was a shift in the air. Raymond's heartbeat quickened as light illuminated under the door. Kingston carefully opened the door to reveal a room on the other side that was not the storeroom. It was familiar. Raymond instantly placed it.

'The Mechanics' Institute,' he said.

'Definitely,' Sydney agreed. 'It even has the smell of the books.'

'Agreed,' Kingston said, closing the door. 'Likely, this is the key we retrieved from that building.'

'Another key that leads back to the building it was found in,' Jake observed. 'Seems to be a frequent thing.'

'It appears that way,' Kingston agreed.

He closed the door, removing the key. The light under the door faded and went dark. Kingston put the third key in the lock and turned it. Again, there was a shift in the air and a light under the door. Another key had worked. Raymond had to bite his lip to keep from telling Kingston to hurry and open the door.

Kingston carefully opened it, revealing a room that Raymond couldn't place. The smell was also unfamiliar, and the light on the other side wasn't natural but the glow of a building. He searched his mind to place any of the buildings in Ballarat or Melbourne but couldn't think of any.

'Where is that?' Sydney asked.

Kingston shook his head. 'It does not look familiar.'

Jake pushed them aside, stepping through the doorway before they could stop him. He walked into the corridor and then moved along it, disappearing from view. Raymond felt the urge to join him but knew waiting would be better. It was easier to run away when solo.

They all held their breath, staring after Jake and waiting for him to return. After a few minutes, he came hurrying back, quickly closing the door behind him and pulling the key out of the lock to close the portal.

'Were you being chased?' Rita asked.

'I don't think they saw me, but I couldn't be sure,' Jake said.

'They?'

Jake turned towards them, his eyes wide and face pale.

'What is it?' Raymond asked.

'That place,' Jake said, swallowing hard. 'It's the White House.'

ACKNOWLEDGEMENTS

Thank you to my darling husband Chris, for all your support. Thank you for reading my work and listening to my updates, and for designing my website from scratch. Thank you to my daughter for being her beautiful self. Thank you to my parents for nurturing my love of writing from a young age. To my sister Kristine for reading my writing experiments, and for her amazing job with the covers of this series. To my in-laws for their support. Also to Nikki and Sarah who were there when I first conceived the idea for *Portal* that has blossomed into this series.

AUTHOR BIO

Katrina was born and raised in Ballarat. She attended local schools in the east of the city. She wrote her first book in primary school, which was submitted to Penguin by a teacher and rejected. During high school, she wrote pieces for local newspaper *The Courier* in its youth section, and several were published. She attended Federation University and completed a Diploma/Bachelor of Arts (Professional Writing & Editing), and a Post Graduate Degree in Education (English/Media) at the University of Melbourne. She spent a year in Nhill as an English and literature teacher before moving to Melbourne, where she worked three more years as an English/literacy/journalism teacher. She currently lives in the western suburbs of Melbourne with her husband and daughter, writing in her free time.

CREDITS

EDITOR

Anna Bilbrough of Coven Press

COVER CREATION

Cover designed by Kristine Slater

INTERNAL FORMATTING

Alana Lambert of Coven Press
Body: Adobe Caslon Pro/11.5pt/16pt Spacing
Embellishments: Good Times

www.ingramcontent.com/pod-product-compliance
Lightning Source LLC
LaVergne TN
LVHW091717070526
838199LV00050B/2433